MAN FROM ATLANTIS

A NOVEL BY

PATRICK DUFFY

A PERMUTED PRESS BOOK

ISBN: 978-1-61868-639-8
ISBN (eBook): 978-1-61868-638-1

MAN FROM ATLANTIS
© 2016 by Patrick Duffy
All Rights Reserved

Cover art by Christian Bentulan

PERMUTED
PRESS

Permuted Press, LLC
275 Madison Avenue, 14th Floor
New York, NY 10016
permutedpress.com

Silence.
Darkness thickens
As the inside races out.
Complete blackness.
Absence of black
But why the silence?
No voice to these thoughts that
Fall into the dark.
The beginning.
Of time.
Perhaps
Another beginning.

CHAPTER ONE

A Mediterranean-style house stood alone on a small indentation off the California coast, protected by the ocean to the west and acres of wild countryside to the north, south, and east. On this day, the light and heat of the midday sun had passed, blue sky shimmered with the remaining warmth, and soft rhythmic waves sounded from the beach. In the pool on this property lay a body, face down and motionless. Every so often, a sand fly would hover above the dark strands of drying hair on the exposed head before buzzing off into the gentle breeze. Other than that, the ripples in the water had long since flattened out, and the surface was glassy smooth.

A lone seagull had been circling above the house by the ocean for almost thirty minutes, its orbit getting ever lower. The only movement now was that of a number of papers and folders, once stacked neatly by the lounge chair, which were now being lifted gently by the breeze to move along the deck. Some lodged against the legs of chairs while others limply soaked in the water at the pool's edge. A few were lifted and turned as if being read by some invisible person. Soon the large white gull was dipping with each tightening circle, despite the rustling papers, to just above the water and the true object of its attention, the plate of food on the table by the pool. When at last the genetic alarm system in the big bird shut off and feelings of potential danger were erased, he cupped his wings, dropped his webbed feet from under his belly, gracefully halted in the air, and dropped the foot or so to the edge of the glass-topped table. For a moment, he stood adjusting his wings repeatedly until the starched rustle of feathers grew quiet and were tightly wrapped to his body. Now satisfied, the smooth head turned, the intense eyes made their last surveillance scan, and the bird stepped to the plate. By this time, the breeze had started to push the body slowly toward the far side of the pool. The bird ignored the movement and darted its beak to the closest piece of food and, with a toss of its head, the crust of bread disappeared down its throat. Another quick look around, and the bright yellow beak, with its orange tip, took aim and procured another found treasure. Then, in a split second, its systems activated and, with a squawk, the big wings were beating furiously. The dry clapping of feathers lifted the large bird quickly off the table and, with a steep banking turn, the gull—in an instant—was thirty feet above the deck and turning out to the protective sea for safety.

The movement that caused this complete retreat had been a flash of light from the moving handle of the French door that led to the pool area. Being turned from the inside, the polished brass surface had bounced the sun's ray directly into the eye of the large bird. The sloping roof protected the southern exposure of the glass doors from the direct rays of the sun. At this time of the summer day, the porch edge cast a slanting shadow along the entire face of the house. Its angle sloped just above the curved brass handle of the French-style door before reaching the legs of the teakwood bench along the wall.

In its momentary spotlight, the elegant s-shaped door handle completed its turn and stood poised in its downward position. It seemed almost to be pointing to the pair of pale-green suede high heels and slender legs that rose into the skirt hem, hidden under the blue-black shadow just inside the door. The lower panes of beveled glass caught the dancing light and its reflection as the door slowly pushed open. Through it, past the shadows and out into the sunshine, stepped the woman.

She was in her mid-forties and moved with a calm determination. Definitely not dressed for relaxing by the pool, she undid the two buttons of the light green suit jacket she was wearing and opened it. A matching silk purse hung from her shoulder and swung a little towards her back as she stood squarely on her green high heels, legs a little apart, with her hands on her hips. The powder-blue blouse was tucked carefully into the waistband of her skirt, revealing a well-kept figure. Her strength and fitness were obvious in the formation of her calves and thighs and in the strong slope of her shoulders, visible above the deep neckline of the blouse. Her skin had the supple gold color of one who spends a good amount of time outdoors, but the softness indicated intelligent care. The makeup was carefully done. Almost not discernible—except for the soft shade of blue above the eyes and the careful lining and coloring of her lips, the bottom one of which she slowly drew into her teeth as she gazed carefully around. She looked at the body for a moment and then without emotion, ignoring him, she stepped to the chair and table by the pool, set the green bag by the plate, and methodically started to go through the remaining files and folders. Not able to find what she was looking for, she walked the short distance to the steps that led into the pool.

Several sheets of soggy paper clung to the first step, and she easily dropped into an almost sitting position at water's edge. Resting on her heels, with an effortless limber move, she reached down to the water and retrieved the scattered pages. The skirt now rode up to mid thigh and stretched tightly to her as she remained there with her elbows on her knees and let the drops fall from the pages back into the pool. With only a brief occasional glance to the man in the water, she quickly scanned the limp papers while constantly replacing the one strand of dark-blonde hair that always escaped from the small ponytail tied at the nape of her neck. Holding several pages away from her body, the muscles in her thighs tightened, and she rose easily and turned again to the table. She calmly sat on the edge of the chair and now stared at the man floating face down. Her eyes revealed nothing. No concern for a dead fellow human being. No indication that she should rescue and revive him. The look just lingered a moment, moved slowly from the top of the man's head, across his back, and down to his feet—she seemed, if anything, merely intrigued by the stillness of the body. The tan and muscled back was now dry and his strong arms were submerged and hung down and away from his torso.

Turning her head away, she reached for the clear glass pitcher. The ice rang a fragile melody on the crystal as she held it in both hands a moment. Leaving a perfect print of her right palm, she grabbed a slender tumbler and poured it full of ice and water. Putting the glass to her lips, she left it there briefly, letting the tiny floating bergs rest against her skin before she took a long slow drink. Running her tongue along her lower lip, she stood and looked at the man. Never taking her eyes off his long back, she dipped her fingers in the glass and grabbed a handful of ice. Holding the pieces in her hand, she seemed to enjoy the cold as the cubes started to melt. The water filled her palm and began to run through her fingers and drip to the deck. Each teardrop of water fell to form dark circles on the rough cement only to immediately soften and disappear in the afternoon heat.

For a moment, she was still, and then her fingers closed around the cubes and she suddenly threw them at the body in the water. Two hit the man—one just above his shoulder blades and another bounced off his yellow trunks. The third frozen missile overshot and plopped with a small water plume just past his dark hair.

"Mark! Mark! Wake up!"

As the noise and ice reached the man, the impossible happened. The large body rolled to one side, dropping the left shoulder under the water's surface, as the head lifted. His lids were already open, revealing brilliant green eyes. The wet face tilted ever so slightly and he smiled kindly at the woman who was now drying her hands on a napkin.

"Hello, Elizabeth," he said.

Without the slightest show of effort, he knifed over and, with one fluid undulation, propelled himself to the steps of the pool. He stepped out of the water and walked to the woman with the same easy motion. He was in his late forties, 195 pounds, very fit, and someone who constantly swam and worked out.

How long has it been? she thought as he approached. *Seventeen years? No, longer! And here I am, still getting that elevator feeling in my stomach. Get a hold of yourself, Elizabeth.*

She did get a hold of herself, but it took a moment. She was transfixed by his eyes and realized she was holding her breath. It was the slight tilt of Mark's head, which she had come to recognize as his habit when something was starting to puzzle him and he was about to "think inside it" as he said, that put her feet back on planet earth. She gasped, turned a little too quickly, and sat in one of the chairs by the table.

"Mark...I'm sorry to wake you, but I can't find your final results on the deep-sea probe salinity test we ran last month. I have to report something to the board in a little over an hour, and I thought that would keep them happy until we can let them in on the Torelli project."

"It's still in my files on the computer, Elizabeth." He took the two steps needed to circle around and stand in front of her. "I have not printed it out just yet, but I can tell you that the probe's outer casing was ionized by an electrical leak from the equipment inside. Niacin amide particles crystallized on the intake valves and that caused the higher than expected readouts. I could have told you the salt-chemical ratio does not significantly change in that part of the sea even at the six mile depth of the trench."

She realized the silliness of her next question even as the words left her lips. But it was one of the many times where her mouth moved a split second faster than her memory, and her words were followed almost immediately by Mark's small smile and reply.

"Because I have been there."

The smile and his body so close to her completely derailed her train of thought. Reaching just past his leg, she grabbed the large white terrycloth robe that was lying across the back of the next chaise. When she stood with it, Mark took it from her hand and draped it over his shoulders. Even as she tried to convince herself it was the kind and proper thing to do, she knew that once he put it on, the conversation between them would be much easier for her to focus on.

Why, she thought. *Why do these feelings come and go in waves like this?*

Weeks could go by and sometimes months, where she and Mark would work together, and all there would be was the work— late hours, sleeping on cots at the institute if it got late, hours in the pools, testing tanks or the ocean, and still it was only the work. Mark was a close friend, a unique and brilliant coworker, a comrade. But it was the work!

Once she had brought the subject of Mark up to her father using the familiar, "I have this friend" approach, which she was sure he immediately saw through. He had taken a great amount of time explaining the wonderful relationship he had with her mother.

"The passion that pulled us almost violently together," he had said, "after a while faded into some deep recess. It caused a bit of a panic when we thought it was over. We had seen couples we knew part, saying they had grown apart. And we were desperate not to be in their number."

Elizabeth could still remember the almost raunchy smile that came over her dad's lips when he sat back in the green leather chair in his dim study and thought for a moment before continuing.

"Then one afternoon I was reading some student papers on the patio and Roberta was in the garden weeding. The late afternoon sunlight was a deep yellow. You know the kind that makes all the colors deeper and richer." Elizabeth recalled him being completely caught up in the memory.

He went on. "I heard the hoe tink as it struck a rock and I looked up. She was there in a patch of dancing sunlight that bounced through the branches of that big acacia tree by the wall. I swear it almost took my breath away—her hair undone and her arms and neck glistening with perspiration and her body moving so beautifully under her long skirt and top. I just stared. After a moment, she stopped. She was completely motionless. It was as though somewhere from very deep my passion was calling to her because she slowly turned to me and smiled. 'Yes,' was all she said.

"I know children don't want to know certain things about their parent's love life so I will just tell you this. From that moment, I never worried when the affairs of love went into retreat and only the friendship was active. It was a wonderful comfort to know that either one was only occupying the *now* for awhile, and the other was waiting for its turn." He then shifted his focus back to his daughter who had curled her arms around her knees where she sat on the little green footstool. Peeping over the top of his reading glasses, he smiled warmly at his only child. "Tell this... *friend* of yours that sometimes the waiting is almost as enjoyable as the actual thing itself. Oh! And sometime I sure would like to meet this friend of yours."

From then on, she understood the waves of change that her feelings cycled through, but that didn't make them easy to mask in order for her to get on with the work.

She looked at Mark and came out of her reverie. The sun highlighted every muscle and contour. The poreless wet skin seemed to almost melt as the water glided off. Mark then pulled the robe around himself and tied a single knot in the sash. At least now she could lock her gaze on his face and not step into the pleasing trap of watching his body.

Elizabeth was constantly amazed that she could regress (at least she told herself it was regression) to that young oceanographer of over seventeen years ago and feel the same feelings she had when they first met.

Why, all of a sudden, do I see him so differently? But then it really wasn't so different. This rotation of friendship and desire had cycled in waves, starting from the very first time she had seen Mark in the emergency room all those years ago.

The call Doug Berkley had received when they were at the party caused them to race to the hospital. At first, when Elizabeth stepped into the emergency room and stood to the side, she could not see the young man. Doug and the ER doctor were looking down at the X-rays, and the staff was trying to revive him. As the ER conversation progressed, curiosity drew her in.

"Man seems to have forgotten how to breathe."

One step.

"We took some pictures and his lungs seem to be completely desiccated."

Another step.

"Even though we've had him on pure O from the moment he got here, I'd say from the color of his skin, he is severely oxygen starved."

From that moment, she was at the side of the gurney. She looked down at that face. Even with the almost blue-black color that was darkening his skin, she was taken aback by how handsome he was. After she told them she was navy and Doug introduced her as Doctor Elizabeth Merrill, she was allowed to assist with the examination. The dry raspy labor of his breathing was evident even from under the oxygen mask that covered his nose and mouth. Touching the gray smooth skin on his chest, she was shocked by how cold it was. The familiar texture also told her that the trunk of his body had no hair follicles. She had to race to keep ahead of the rolling input of information she was getting.

Then the ER doctor opened one of the young man's lids and shined his penlight on the eye for her to see. That was when—as she thought of it often over the years—*it* happened. There was something about that eye. Not the *something* they all saw, which were the brilliant yellow-green lines that glowingly radiated out from the pitch black iris. It was something else she saw. *It* was the life of this person. Without knowing one piece of his history (or one thing that could ground her feelings for him to her life), she knew his soul. In that brief moment, she remembered herself thinking, *I know you. I don't know of you, but I know who you are. And if I can I will help you live. Because I want you to know me too.*

It was then that she did what she almost never did. She completely took over a situation where she was not in charge. Thankfully, with Doug's support, she briefly bronched the man's lungs and, seeing what she intuitively knew was there, she disconnected him from the IVs and forced the entire ER team to get her, Doug, and the patient into the waiting ambulance. With the sheer force of her determination, the driver reacted as if it was normal to be told to drive a dying man back to the beach. The pain she felt with every tortured breath the young man took was almost unbearable.

With the back of the ambulance open, Doug and the driver carried the body to the shallow water's edge, and she floated the lifeless form out to where it was a little over waist high. She pushed him in small tight circles and let the water wash completely over her body. Even with the cool night air and the cold of the bay's saltwater, she could feel the skin under his arms warming.

"Breathe. Breathe. You can do it," she whispered the words to herself. She thought: *I can't lose you. I can't. You don't know me yet. I haven't had a chance.*

And then it happened. She had just released her hold on him to adjust her grip when his body moved slightly away from her on its own. She held him by the waist, and he began to roll to the left. He turned completely onto his back under the surface. She stared down through the water and into the electric-green eyes of her future. That same instant, she made a vow. She would let time dictate every part of her relationship with this person. Whoever he turned out to be, she would never let her personal desires lead him anywhere he did not want to go.

This will be my secret until you discover it for yourself, she whispered to her heart. The pain she felt stab at her life stood vigil from that moment on.

Even then she was her intellectual father's intellectual daughter and immediately told herself that *the feelings of love or pain are completely unprofessional and lengthen the road to discovery.* She was always curious how the famous Professor Barry Merrill, a Ph.D in four (count them four) disciplines— Oceanography, Ichthyology, Physics, and Ancient Cultures— could still employ phrases like, "Focus on one bird, not a flock," or "Lizzy, you talkin', gawkin', or thinkin'?" or his famous (and laughed at, behind his back, in all his classrooms): "All right, people! Let's bear down or reboot."

But focus and think and bear down she did.

"Mark," Elizabeth said as she walked around to the back of the chaise and came out of her recollections, "I'll access your files from the lab before I head on to the board meeting. I will give them enough to get their profit-margin mouths watering. With the salt thing solved, I can answer whatever they might want to know." She reached to the table, opened her purse, and removed the electronic planner. Both thumbs tapping her entries, she continued, "What are your plans for the day?"

"I have a few hour of work out there in the test gardens." Mark nodded in the direction of the surf.

She quickly finished her notes. "Have all the transplanted specimens survived?"

"The deep water ones are doing surprisingly well and the reef urchins are making interesting color changes in this warmer water. It makes a very unique sight with all of them from so many different places in the world in one spot."

"Someday I would love to dive out there with you and see what you've done. With all these meetings, I don't get in the water nearly as much as I would like to."

"Of course, Elizabeth, anytime you would like."

"Business first, of course."

This last statement came out almost as a groan. As much as it took a lot of time, she actually liked the board and its head Gasten Heycourt. She knew the drill and did it as well as anyone. Her reports were always complete and exciting, and her all-around knowledge was second to none in her field. It was during their grilling that she danced the dance. She answered all their questions. At least the parts she felt they needed to know. She delivered updates on key personnel and their projects (except Staci Torelli's, of course), and she had done so for years now. She would mention Mark Harris somewhere deep in the list as "a good bright worker who was helping in several areas."

Sometimes she almost enjoyed the idea of keeping Mark's real identity top secret—even from the people who were funding (his) their work. She learned her lesson with the military when Mark was first found, and he almost became a weapon instead of the treasured key to the future she always believed him to be. The big test came when, because of the funding available, she took Mark to the navy as a top secret experimental program. Everything worked well until a coworker, who had become a close friend, *leaked* to her the government's plan to find ways to replicate Mark, either through genetic cloning or through normal biological reproductive means. Their ultimate goal was to be able to use his extraordinary abilities as an *expendable* weapons system. It was then that she felt herself become that Jekyll/Hyde type person. She promised herself to protect Mark no matter what, even at the risk of her own life and, at the same time, to dedicate herself to discovering everything Mark knew. Even, as the years taught her, the things Mark didn't even know he knew.

With Gasten's money and her AORI (All Oceans Research Institute), these fifteen plus years had generated knowledge and created revenue that made it the foremost institute of its kind in the world. The more the institute accomplished the more her personal fame grew. It spread out from the scientific world and into mainstream America and beyond. With her second *Time Magazine* cover, she was bombarded with media attention. She soon realized that the more the world focused on her, the more she could cover Mark in anonymity. Elizabeth's ability to deliver results and capture literally every award and commendation that the scientific world had to offer had allowed her to run the institute with little or no interference.

"When the meeting is over and the board members are satisfied, their profits will continue and I will kindly turn Gasten down one more time for dinner or a weekend at his place in Mexico or the trip to wherever or...whatever, then I will meet you at the institute around four and we can continue with the Moline test." She had just slid the planner into the pocket of her purse when the silence made her look up at Mark. He stood there with a soft but questioning look on his face.

Those eyes held her weightless for a moment... "What?"

"Elizabeth, why do you not return Mr. Heycourt's affection? He must care for you very much or else why would he try so hard to win your heart?"

The simplicity of Mark's question and the lump in her throat, which stopped her from giving him a straight, honest answer, made her only choice to stand and prepare to go. She stood there, so close for a moment...

"Yes, I suppose...Gasten is actually very nice and I like him a lot, but there is a big difference between caring for someone and loving them. Sometimes winning someone's heart is impossible." *There, that's enough*, she thought. *As much as I want to open the door, I can't take advantage of the moment.*

After finding Mark almost two decades ago, she tried to resume the dating life of a young single woman. Many times, wonderful men had entered her life and she was genuinely attracted to them. No matter how far the relationships went—long romantic weekends were very enjoyable—there always came a time when her very professional mind would overpower her pleasures. Mark's face would haunt her, and she would find herself thinking of him while at dinner or even in more uncomfortable situations. Eventually, she stopped dating except when it was the right thing for a business or social evening and began to substitute work for a relationship of the heart.

As the last words left her lips, her eyes still couldn't leave his. On the outside, she appeared calm and detached. *Damn being my father's daughter.* Her mind pleaded with Mark to understand. *Please know and understand me. Know the things I can never tell you.*

There it is again, Lizzy, the rollercoaster. That stupid elevator bringing stupid water to my eyes!

Clicking the clasp closed on her favorite purse, which joined a glittering snake's head to the body that twisted down the front of the green silk, she was thankful to look away and have a moment to force the tide to ebb from her eyes.

"Someday you'll understand, I'm sure."

Knowing anyone else would have seen through her little false, parental-like statement—but glad Mark never doubted her sincerity—she ended her near-confession with a slight touch to his shoulder and turned to leave. "I'll see you at AORI around four, bye!"

A few steps from the door, she stopped and turned back to Mark. He still stood at the table watching her.

"If you get there before me, would..."

In mid sentence, her eyes snapped to something at the corner of the deck. The shadow she swore was there when she turned wasn't there now. It seemed to have split in half and dropped to become the dark line of flagstone and horizontal shadow just below the bougainvillea and now was gone completely. The interruption of the sentence and her expression, prompted Mark to look to the corner and then back at her.

"What is it, Elizabeth?"

She turned from him and looked back to the spot for a moment. Seeing nothing out of the ordinary, she gazed once again at Mark and smiled.

"Nothing, I guess. I thought I saw something at the edge of the wall." She tipped her head back a little so that she could see the light catch the white wings of several large gulls circling high against the clear deep blue. "A bird, maybe. A shadow from one of those gulls, I guess."

After another glance at the corner, she continued. "What I was going to say was, if you get there before me have Jason run yesterday's results through the computer so we know where we are."

She turned and walked through the door, closing it behind her.

Mark watched her go, and when the door clicked shut he waited until the dark form of her head evaporated into the black interior before turning and walking to the far corner of the deck, to the place that had caught her attention.

It was only eight or ten feet from the deck and its flagstone wall to the ground. Grass clumps were as thick as a planted lawn for the first few yards and then separated into gray-green islands in a sea of sand as they got closer to the water. From where the last couple of tiny clumps made their final stand, it was perhaps fifty yards to the surf. The beach was as it almost always was, deserted. The only activity being the small shore birds, chasing the retreating waves in order to pick up the exposed sand mites.

He stood there for awhile, comforted by his closeness to the water. As his gaze moved out along the horizon, he could see a few gulls gather over a school of herring that jumped out of the water, trying to escape the larger fish or seal or whatever had disturbed them.

CHAPTER TWO

Mark turned his car off the highway and onto the long lane that led to the institute. As he drove along the manicured driveway and away from the noise of the other cars on the highway, he was glad Elizabeth agreed to get him this Tesla 600. It wasn't only that the electric car was quiet and smooth in its operation that had won her over; it was that in the other cars he had test driven, Mark was able to accurately identify the chemicals and their air-to-solid ratios, released into the passenger area by the exhausts. The lab verified Mark's findings after follow-up tests.

Elizabeth had always enjoyed discovering some new ability of Mark's.

"It makes me wonder what you think of the perfume I wear," she once said.

As he stopped at the security gate, he smiled—remembering the way the color in her face had changed when he told her he preferred the smell of her *under* the perfume.

He reached into his jacket pocket for the plastic AORI pass and slid it quickly in and out of the slot at the gate. He looked to the left and into the small dark lens so the computer could match his photo and his face. It still felt strange to him that this much security was needed when most of the results for what they did at the institute became public knowledge soon after they discovered it. Elizabeth explained that the competition for patents on the type of work they were doing and the discoveries they made, made it necessary.

The lights under the monitor turned from red to green and the large iron gate slowly swung open as the sharp, curved metal points simultaneously retracted into the iron slots in the pavement that ran across the entrance. Mark drove through and into the large parking lot. As it was almost four o'clock, many of the 200 employees of AORI had already started to leave for the day.

Mark's Tesla slid silently past the main building, and he nodded a hello to the older man heading for the exit in the black SUV. At the end of the lot, he turned after coming to the large sign that read: STOP! RESTRICTED ACCESS TO CODED PERSONNEL ONLY, and into the small alley between it and the adjoining building. This narrow access road ended at a wall under a walkway. The entire alley, walls, overpass walkway, and large white gate in the wall were solid. No windows. No openings at all. He passed under the walkway, and when his car approached the gate it began to automatically open. As it closed behind him, he accelerated towards the imposing wall several hundred yards ahead. Above this wall, he could see the roofs of several buildings beyond.

His blue car came to a halt at a solid metal gate. The large sign read: STOP! BLUE PASS ONLY FROM THIS POINT. From this position, the twelve-foot high, stone wall completely blocked any view of the buildings, and now he could not even see the red tile roofs but only the razor wire looping menacingly along the top. At this point, Mark took out the blue card from his pocket and placed it into the tray that had just extended from the kiosk by his window. The smoked glass window slid open, revealing two compartments, one above the other. From the bottom compartment, a small section extended outward until it almost touched the side of his car, while the opening on the top revealed a round lens about two inches in diameter. Mark put his left hand into the opening in the bottom tray and rested it on the soft surface inside. At the same time, he looked directly into the lens as he had done at the main gate. He could feel the minute rise in temperature on the palm of his hand as the computer read his information: fingerprints, respiration, chemical composition, and other input that would match the sequence reading it took when he left work the day before.

He had no question as to the importance of the security measures. Elizabeth and he had gone to great lengths over the years to protect information about him from getting out. When they had severed ties with the navy program, they had been successful in demanding ownership of all their files. Some military scientists had mustered out of the service and gone immediately to work for Elizabeth, and the old admiral in charge of the program had since retired and was now dead.

The hardest blow that fate had helped them with was when the entire crew of research submersible *Cetacean* was lost in a collision with a Russian submarine under the polar icecap. Elizabeth formed AORI with Dr. Raggit and Dr. Lucca, and The Man from Atlantis no longer existed to the world. From the day of its completion, almost nineteen years ago, only a total of eleven people had ever passed through this gate and into Beachlab #1. Only those eleven, three of whom had since retired, had known Mark's true identity and history. At least as much of his history as he knew. Of the three who retired, only Dr. Raggit was still alive. He finally moved into an old house he had lovingly restored on the lake at Arrowhead. Over the last four years, each time Mark and Elizabeth visited him, the rows of newly-painted canvasses expanded and the folders of poetry grew.

"Mark," Dr. Raggit would say, wiping his hands with the turpentine soaked rag, "I have only two desires now. One is to create beauty." And with a chuckle he'd continue, "Even though with over twenty-five open art shows, no one has yet bought my beauty. And, two, I want to live quietly and read other's ideas of beauty." And with that Mark and Elizabeth knew they were in for at least two hours of Thomas reading the latest poems that had moved his soul.

The good doctor would discover a piece and read it over and over until, he said, it became a part of him. Then he would write it out completely with his beautiful penmanship from memory and add it to the neat piles that grew in his study. He would always hold poems as his voice gave substance to the scripted lives, but his eyes never looked at the pages. Mark remembered Dr. Raggit's response when Elizabeth had asked him why he wrote out the poems after he committed them to memory.

"It's like a big circle, Elizabeth, my dear. I keep the poems that touch me, but I don't know why they do. After I have pounded them into my head and heart, I feel they are a part of my creative soul. But then, just like I can see a painting of mine in my head, I have to also put it on the canvass. Sort of like saying, yes, there it is! See I was right. It is beautiful! Then a part of the real me finds a voice it never had before."

That was Mark's introduction to poetry, and from the moment he heard the first lines he understood their attraction. These words could expand the definition of their creator.

"Elizabeth." His voice had broken the silence they were both enjoying on the drive back to the coast after the first poetry session. "I would like to read more poetry."

"Of course, Mark, we can get whatever you want." She glanced briefly at him then continued to watch the road as she drove. "What would you like to find?"

"There are many parts of me that live in silence. I wish to find a way to give them a voice. A feeling kept silent can sadden the heart."

His response almost caused her to drive off the road.

The engine noise was all the sound for miles.

"Sometimes," she explained, "we want to have the world know our feelings but must make sure the knowledge of us will create good."

He turned to her. "Would not the knowing be the good?"

"Sometimes the beauty of the poems we read is the only way the poet can express his heart without revealing the knowledge of who he really is. He can create the most value from the safety of his secrets. Often the heart should only reveal small hints as to what is there and let the one who reads the words define the writer." She glanced at him quickly. "And sometimes we simply have to hope that people will know who and what we are without us telling them."

The other two scientists who had worked at AORI and had left for the quieter life were now dead. Dr. Tony Lucca had been the first to replicate, although in a very minor way, Mark's sonar-like silent communication. He dubbed it the nonaudible voice. The breakthrough came when he was able to dictate a constant frequency and a linear direction for sound waves in water. He had suffered a massive stroke only months after retiring and died, never having come out of his coma. Two years following that Mariyeh Sherwood, who had made incredible progress in accelerated cellular regeneration, was missing and presumed dead, having gotten lost in a snowstorm while on a skiing trip to Switzerland. Never heeding Elizabeth's constant encouragement to document all her experiments, unfortunately, her discoveries disappeared with her. The institute was never able to carry forward with her work. Both of these losses saddened everyone at the institute and made their devotion to the happiness and wellbeing of Dr. Raggit all the stronger.

Mark allowed the memories to fade as he passed through the gate and drove towards the parking structure ahead. Beyond the buildings in the distance, he could see the sandy beach and the blue of the ocean.

Only eight cars in the world had the microchip that opened the #2 white gate. Jason, Mark knew, was very proud of the fact that these seven other people, the best brains in the business, had never found the chip or even knew when he had installed it in their vehicles. The high point in his James Bond-like daring was when Professor Nagashima drove directly from the dealer in his new car and was shocked when every gate opened and Jason met him with a smile at the Beachlab door.

Mark pulled into the covered garage area and into his space. He knew Elizabeth had not arrived because the space next to his was still vacant.

"I'll get it for you, Mark. I was just leaving anyway." Jason was coming out of the lab before Mark could close his door. The young man dropped the large shoulder bag he was carrying, took the power cord from its hook, and plugged it into the Tesla. Jason always moved with the spring-like action of a dancer. He more or less jumped from a starting position and seemed to have a flourish of some sort to accentuate most things he did. His dark hair was cut short around the sides but rather long at the top, which added to the physical punctuation. He dressed in the fashion Mark had seen on the music channels of his TV and always had a pocket or bag that produced whatever was needed at any given moment.

After rechecking that the power plug was firmly in place, Jason reached into the backpack and pulled out a cap with a large capital D on the front. Spinning it from the bill on the end of his finger, he pulled it onto his head and started for his own car.

"You're cooking, Mark. Catch you tomorrow."

"Jason," Mark leaned on the roof of his Tesla, "Elizabeth would like you to run the results from yesterday's work for us before you go, but if you do not have the time, I can do it myself."

Jason beeped the alarm on the green VW Bug a second time and immediately started back toward the lab door. Putting the keys into a pocket on the front of his bag, he flipped his cap back into the top opening.

"Hey, no problem. It's probably a good thing 'cause Jessie's being a real twit lately. Besides, it'll save me from driving all the way to San Diego to loan my sister my camera for some music video she's doing, which isn't working right anyway!" Jason had already put his palm on the scanner before Mark could get to it.

"Why do you give all the equipment female names, Jason?"

"I dunno; maybe so when they work right I can pretend it's because they like me! They really like me!" Jason looked at Mark and laughed and gave the little wink he always gave when he thought he'd been clever. Mark placed his hand quickly on the scanner as Jason removed his and followed him into the ready room where the door silently opened. With the click of the closing lock on the outer door, Jason pushed one of several small buttons on the side of his wristwatch and stared intently at the silver face.

"Here," he said, never taking his eyes off the watch, "I'll show you what I mean."

"The room darkened a little and the reddish grid lines ran over the two while Mark cocked his head a little and smiled.

"See what I mean." Jason kept staring at his wrist. He tipped it up in an awkward lift, hand over his shoulder for Mark to see. "Check it out. It's been over ten seconds and she hasn't completed the scan, and I mean, Dude! Like it's us!"

Mark stood in the whirling red grid staring at the large silver watch with, what he considered, far too many hands and dials.

"Jason, thank you, but I can tell when there is a fluctuation in the system."

When Mark stopped talking, the grid halted, the lights brightened, and the slight pop signaled that the airtight door to the lab was about to open. The hiss of the airlock was covered by Mark's voice.

"This wait was four point two seconds shorter than the delay last Tuesday," Mark said. And with that he turned and walked into the lab leaving Jason standing there looking back and forth between him and his super-watch.

Lab #1 was referred to as the Beachlab by the few members of the team who were authorized to pass through the last gate and enter the security room. Over the years, the distinction was made between them and where they worked and the other hundred plus employees of AORI. The Beachlabs were three buildings behind the security wall that did most of the initial experimentation concerning Mark. The two beyond where Mark now stood, housed the aquatic studies facilities and the sub-dermal studies facilities. The aquatic studies building housed all the tanks and their necessary equipment. Hundreds of smaller aquariums contained thousands of species of aquatic life being studied, while several larger tanks could accommodate fish and mammals up to the size of full-grown orcas. Two of these larger tanks were connected to the ocean by long underground channels that ran under the sandy beach and opened under the water some two hundred yard away. They were part of the surf line.

The other site, Beachlab #3 was basically a state-of-the-art medical facility. Ongoing studies of Mark's physical and mental abilities were done there. Hallways, overhead bridges, and underground passages connected the entire three building complex. Everything in the institute, including the large main buildings outside this secured area, was connected by thousands of miles of optic fiber electronics to the building where he now stood. Beachlab #1

From where he was, Mark could see almost all of this main nerve center. Before him were eighteen computer desk cubicles. They were enclosed with desk-high walls and slightly higher file cabinets. Situated in an almost haphazard fashion in the center of the room, they constituted home base for the six men and women who worked for Elizabeth. Although each person had their personal area, depending on the projects they were involved in, a scientist would move from one station to the next, keeping ongoing studies up and active and available to comrades. The consoles belonging to the three original members of the team that were no longer here, however, were more or less retired. The work they had accomplished was still in the system, but the work areas were seldom occupied.

Beyond the workstations, lining the outer walls, were the offices of Elizabeth and Mark—hers on the left and his to the right, with the massive mainframe in the middle. These rooms were glassed in floor to ceiling.

There was only one person in the room when Mark entered, a young woman intently working at a station about midway into the room. Walking past shelves of flash drives, old discs, and manuals of reference materials, he approached the back of the woman's chair.

"Good afternoon, Staci."

The attractive young lady lifted her head from where she had been intently staring at the row of monitors lining the counter and pushed the wire-rimmed glasses back to the bridge of her nose. The many screens filled with all sorts of equations and data charts reflected various angles of her, and Mark could see the cloth elastic that held back her streaked blonde hair, the two earrings in each ear, and her profile from both sides.

"Oh, hi, Mr. Harris. I didn't hear you come in."

"Why?" Mark stopped at her chair and waited for her to respond.

His response to what was obviously a rhetorical statement caused her to think a second before continuing on. "Well, I guess it's because we...the...we... who aren't like you, haven't developed our brain's ability to devote equal, one hundred percent dedication to all of our senses...simultaneously...yet. Whether or not they are center of peripheral."

Mark only continued to look into her eyes. When a slight blush of color started to appear in her cheeks, Staci continued with a little smile. "To tell you the truth, I think for the time being I like it better to be able to tune out when I want to."

She sat there smiling at Mark, clearly pleased that she had been able to explain herself without being condescending. Then a rapid beeping from one of her monitors got her attention.

"Oops! Excuse me, Mr. Harris." And with a quick swivel of her chair, she grabbed her laptop and started to make notes.

He walked past her. As he did, once again, he kindly reminded her, "Staci, I wish you would feel comfortable enough here to call me Mark."

"Huh? Uh huh. Yes, sir."

Her words trailed off into a mutter and, with a smile, he went into the lab followed now by Jason who tossed off a, "hey, Stace," to the girl as he glanced off and on at his watch and counted to himself.

The glass door slid open as Mark approached, and the two of them stepped into Jessie's control center. About forty feet of the back wall was actually a floor to ceiling map of the world. The glass surface of the map was really just a protective covering over the six ultra-high definition screens that projected the scene being fed from Jessie. This one-dimensional world was, just like the real one, in constant motion. By commanding Jessie the screen could show ocean currents, weather patterns, and the positions of vessels on land or sea. With another command, the screens would fill with pinpoint locations of every satellite now in orbit. In front of the map was the command console. Looking a lot like a captain's bridge from a large ship, it formed a gentle arc and accommodated four large captain's chairs. In front of each chair was a keypad, phone, and bank of monitors. Considering its enormous capability, the command center for Jessie was quite uncluttered.

The room hummed with the sound of the cooling system and whirring and gentle clicking of the computer running all aspects of AORI. Mark stopped at the small console in front of the glass wall and door that divided Jessie from the rest of lab #1, just as Jason plopped into one of the captain chairs at the console station. Mark watched Jason talk, arrange papers, move his briefcase out of the way with his foot, and activate a program on Jessie. At the same time, he continued to look at his watch and push different buttons on it.

"Hey! Stace! Come on over here." He had touched the intercom button to the right of his keypad. "We're gonna punch up your yesterday stuff on the wet string thing. And we gotta book 'cause Dr. Merrill just came through number two."

This last remark brought Mark's attention to the top center of the screen on the big wall. That section was no longer showing northeast Asia and part of the polar ice cap but had divided into eight sections that rolled to eight others every four seconds and then on to another eight before repeating. Twenty-four security cameras that watched continuously the entire lab complex, and with more commands would display the over two hundred cameras of the institute. Mark saw Elizabeth's Mercedes as it passed through the gate. The next screen caught the car as it passed into the parking area and into her space next to his Tesla. The screen stayed on her instead of rolling to the next rotation as they were all programmed to be action sensitive. His head tipped a little to the side while he watched her pause as she passed his car and touched the driver's door handle. She left that screen, and he tracked her to the screening station at the entrance.

"Here, Mark. I'll show you what I mean about little Miss Jessie."

Mark turned back to Jason as his fingers flew across the keyboard inputting codes and symbols and finally coming to a rest as the main monitor started a readout of names.

"Here, before Dr. Merrill gets in, check this out." Jason pointed to the screen for Mark to follow. "This is me. Here's Dr. Merrill and Stace and you." His finger touched an area of the screen and Mark saw the entire right hand of the monitor fill with graphs and lines as Jason activated the touch screen. "You already know most of this stuff, but here look at this! It's like she gets the hiccups or palsy or something. And if she's tripping up on this easy stuff, I don't know what else... Here it is."

Mark watched Jason's finger move across the readouts until it stopped and followed one line in the middle of the screen. "Your basic heartbeat, oxy content, respiration, yadda, yadda. This is it. This one is the biotrack for the carbon dating. Most of the time it's like a rock. Steady as a preacher. For everybody except sometimes for you, that is."

Mark could see the line as it inched slowly to the right under the dateline at the top of the screen. Very steady and straight until, at uneven intervals, it rose in a small hump before straightening out once again.

"Crazy, huh? I mean it's really tiny. Maybe only a split second or two and not for every reading, but she is definitely giving you a stretch now and then. I'll recalibrate it again next week or maybe just take her out to dinner." Mark didn't see Jason's little smile and wink because his own head tilted and he started to *think inside it.*

Mark's ears heard the pop and opening door through the computer noise and the glass wall. He turned to see Elizabeth enter from the ready room and gather up Staci as she crossed the floor and stepped through the opening door.

"Sorry I'm late, everyone." She stopped at the small desk, dropped the armload of papers and her presentation on top, and started to remove her pale green suit jacket.

"Which country did you turn down today, Dr. Merrill?" Staci smiled as she asked and handed Elizabeth her white lab coat, with the hand not carrying a stack of folders.

"No country. Just cocktails."

As she was buttoning the coat, Jason's attention was suddenly focused on the monitor. After touching another part of the screen, he quietly asked, "Dr. Merrill, are you...?" But Mark didn't need to watch the readout to understand. He interrupted and touched Jason lightly on the shoulder, stepped up, and held one side of the white coat for her to slip her arms into.

"Elizabeth, what happened?"

Jason stopped tracking her elevated heart rate, salinity read, retinal read, and all other signs after he realized Mark had picked up on most of them without the aid of Jessie's new experimental Pentium XII chip.

"After the board meeting, Gasten wanted a word alone with me. He told me that he received a call when Dr. Raggit hadn't shown up today to speak at the museum's art and science luncheon. After calling his house and his mobile, he notified the police in Arrowhead. They went over and, as far they could tell, he hadn't been home for at least a week."

As he watched her stand in silence, Elizabeth absent-mindedly drew the small charm that hung from the fine gold chain inside the neck of her blouse. Turning it slowly in her fingers, she stared at it as small creases deepened on her forehead. Mark felt there was more and softly began to lead her into expressing her thoughts.

"That is not so different from his behavior when he was here... before he retired, Elizabeth. He was always packing off to some other experiment in an instant."

"Yes, Mark, but he was a fanatic about staying in communication. And the other thing is that he had been looking forward to giving his speech for months. It was on Tagore, one of his favorite poets."

Everyone at AORI knew that Dr. Raggit would call or Email or log into Jessie several times a day whether he was at the lab, at home or even on vacation. He carried that habit with him into retirement, and at no time could Mark remember him being completely out of touch.

Staci put her five-stack of CDs into the remote tower of the computer while she said, "Maybe he has just finally learned what it means to be retired, Dr. Merrill."

"Yes, Staci, I'm sure that's it. Anyway, Gasten said he would follow up with the people in Arrowhead and get back to me. Now," she gave a little clap of her hands and turned to the console, "where were we yesterday?"

Even with her show of concentrating on Staci's new work, Mark knew the situation with Thomas Raggit was still occupying Elizabeth, but he would think inside that later. For now, he joined the others. For the next several hours they reviewed Staci's cross-referencing of her test results and Jason, having decided against going to his sister's altogether, worked on Jessie's calibrations and fiddled with his camera.

The rest of the day went on as usual, and the lab was completely deserted except for the four of them.

It had been two hours since Dr. Nagashima had left when Mark came to the surface of the glass tank. He swam to the edge and draped his arms over the metal rim. "You put number four up three percent and the rate in number six fell off quickly. Either by shading or possibly by removal."

Seeing Elizabeth sitting in the console chair and smiling pleased him. She seemed to have forgotten her earlier angst over Dr. Raggit. She looked peaceful, tapping the end of a pencil she was holding against her lower lip. He always felt a great responsibility for her state of mind and would do whatever he could to make her happier.

"Amazing, absolutely amazing!" Staci's voice came from behind the rolling screens at the other end of the lab.

The tank that Mark stepped out of was part of a labyrinth of water tanks of various sizes all connected with clear plastic tubing. In addition to the water and tubes, there were freestanding plants and dry terrariums; some with and some without inhabitants. The entire village was wired into a web of literally thousands of interconnections, signal boosters, and relays, with the entire system ending in various remote ports of Jessie. All of this was being watched over very intently by Jason who responded with, "One hundred percent, Stace!"

Mark reached for the stack of towels by his robe when a clatter of metal was heard behind the screen. Staci emerged with several small tools in one hand and a clipboard in the other. "Don't worry, Dr. Merrill. I'll pick that stuff up before I go tonight. I totally knew he would do it! So far, he has been perfect on every blind test, and reciprocal readings are exactly the same. It's all interconnected!" Staci continued to pick her way around the tubes and wires to where they were standing, talking all the time. "Mr. Harris..."

"Mark, please."

By now Elizabeth, smiling broadly at her young scientist's enthusiasm, had risen from her chair and was standing next to Mark.

"Huh?" Staci was excitedly looking at the readout paper on the metal clipboard she was carrying. "Mr. Harris, your response on both triggers was simultaneous to the input. Simultaneous! Before the information could disperse through the water. And the drop in photosynthesis wasn't from shading but because I removed two kelp leaves!" By now she had almost reached him, all the while showing him the small scalpel used in the test. "Did you feel..." Staci's moment of excitement occupied some of the attention she should have been giving to her surroundings, and the last bundle of wires on the floor grabbed her foot and she shot straight into them.

With no show of effort or surprise, Mark dropped the towel, while at the same time lifting Elizabeth off her feet and out of the way of the collision. Almost at the same moment, with his right hand, he caught Staci in midair. The clipboard, paper, and tools she was holding crashed to the floor. With his arm around her waist, Mark held her against his body, her feet dangling.

"I'm sorry." She brushed hair away from her eyes and pushed her glasses back to the bridge of her nose as he set her gently to the ground. "Those darn wires are..."

No other words left her lips. With her vision twenty-twenty again, the first thing she saw was that not everything had fallen harmlessly to the floor. The scalpel had embedded itself in Mark's forearm. The pretty young scientist was frozen with shock and could only stare at the shining piece of metal, seemingly glued to Mark's body.

"Oh, my God!" The words were barely a whisper as Jason steadied her. "Oh God, I'm sorry."

"Mark, are you all right?" Elizabeth, by this time, had a hold of Mark's wrist and was carefully lifting his arm to assess the trouble.

After a moment of silence, he responded, "Yes, Elizabeth, I am fine. It has done no interior damage. It can be removed."

Jason, after easing Staci into the closest chair, took a quick look at the weapon and started for the cabinet next to Mark's tank. "I'll get the first aid kit!"

"No, Jason, it's not necessary." And with that Mark watched as Dr. Merrill gently grabbed the handle of the instrument and smoothly drew it from his arm.

"No of course not. Sorry I forgot." Jason was back at Staci's side as she weakly rose and stepped to Mark and Dr. Merrill.

"But, it was so deep. You'll need a..." Staci stared in disbelief as the blade was drawn from Mark's flesh and the red muscle tissue beneath his skin was visible.

Before the first drop of blood, which was rushing to the surface, could escape the opening, the edges at both ends of the wound started to draw together. In the space of less than three seconds, the entire two-inch opening had closed and the scar itself disappeared in the following five. In no more than fifteen seconds even the red discoloration was gone and no evidence remained of the previous trauma. Mark then extended the fingers of his left hand to their widest capability. As the fingers spread and the hand flexed, the webbing that normally lay retracted between them pushed forward. Repeating the motion several times, Elizabeth could see the skin extend to the first knuckle of each finger, indicating no tendon or ligament damage had been done.

Mark could only guess what was going on inside her mind, as Staci remained speechless. After Elizabeth handed her a glass of water from the desk, Staci looked from Mark's arm to his eyes. "How...why did the..." The chair was once again very inviting. Her knees were not steady, and she sat with a small thud.

"I am sorry, Staci, that you did not know." Mark sat on the edge of the desk and Elizabeth continued the explanation.

"We have all known about this ability of Mark's for so long I guess we just forgot to tell you when you came aboard. You see, for someone like Mark, who lives in the sea, it would be the most dangerous thing to let blood escape from open wounds. The almost instant signal that is sent to all predators would mean certain death from even the most minor accident. It seems somewhere, long ago in Mark's ancestry, they developed the genetic ability to close and heal all exterior lesions on their bodies. He must still be aware of damage that could occur under the skin, but his kind also have the ability to, more or less, get a reading on their own body and its functions, and that's why he knew it was all right for me to remove the scalpel."

"Please be assured, Staci. It was an accident and no damage was done." With that said, Mark lifted her to her still unsteady feet. "I think perhaps that is enough work for tonight. You should go home and rest. Jason?"

"Sure, Mark. I'll drive you home, Stace. Goodnight, Dr. Merrill!" With that, Jason grabbed his pack from the back of the chair where he had been sitting, threw it over his shoulder, and helped Staci remove her lab coat as he guided her to the door. "Hey, Staci, how 'bout I film you so you can see the color start to come back into your face?" With his little smile and wink to Mark and Elizabeth, they went out the door, down the long hallway that led to lab #1, and to the exit room.

"Mark, I'll notify security, and we should let it go for the night, too."

"Yes, of course, Elizabeth. It has been a long time since lunch. Would you like to have dinner before you go home?"

"Sure, that would be nice. Let's go to Somers-on-the-Pier. It's close."

"I will meet you there as soon as I change into my clothes."

Mark watched Elizabeth gather her papers into her briefcase and give that little finger wave that she seemed to use only for him. She exited through the door and headed to her office.

The large room comforted him. It was still but not quiet. There were the computers humming and water moving in and out of the tanks.

He walked to the largest of the indoor tanks. The cement oval occupied a full one third of lab #3. The wall was five feet up from the floor, but the water depth dropped another fifteen feet. Standing there, he leaned against the top rail and looked over the edge. At the bottom, he could see that the gate that led to the sea channel was open. For a moment, he considered slipping over the side and swimming out and into the bay, but then he was content just to stand there and watch the ceiling lights reflect off the surface. His hands touching the cool salt water, and he thought of the years he and Elizabeth had spent together. She was a good person but so confusing to him in many ways. He more than trusted her. It was almost as if he belonged nowhere else and to no one else. It deeply affected him when she was less than happy. He felt good when some gesture he made or things would happen that made her smile or laugh. Why should that be?

With his past so dark and impenetrable, he could consider nothing more than the present. But what about the future? What was the future? He could not, as hard as he tried, think of his life past AORI, the ocean, and Elizabeth. That must be what it was. His future would be those three things and that would be good.

Why then did he sometimes feel like he was starting to feel right now? Again he felt there was a question and no words to tell him the answer. All these years had told him so much about what he was. There were databases here full of more information than had ever been gathered about any one person in the history of the world. But there was more. More he did not know. The simplest things. It was the same old feeling of a hand on the shoulder that he knew was not really there, bidding him to turn around and see the life that was following him. He knew he would turn as he always did when he had that feeling. He also knew that, when he did turn, there would be nothing. He would be alone!

He must try harder to think inside this later, but now his heart lifted a little as he headed to his rooms to change and meet Elizabeth for dinner.

CHAPTER THREE

The night sky was clean and the moon was almost completely full. Its reflection on the ocean looked like the paintings in the book of American Realists that Elizabeth had given to Mark. Rough, horizontal dabs of golden-yellow made a path that always led them as they walked along the beach. The tradition had begun many years ago. In the early days, the work at the lab had been more frenetic. When the two of them would make the escape for a meal at their favorite restaurant, they would park in the empty lot at the old pier and use the quiet walk of half a mile or so to relax. Now they would use this stretch of sand as their place whether they walked it alone or together.

The dinner had been quiet, but Mark felt that her silence was not from being unhappy but rather she was thinking deeply. Taking their time at the table and sitting outside on the deck afterwards had pushed the moon high overhead by the time they decided to go. They walked in silence from the restaurant towards the dark outline of the boat pier in the distance. It looked to Mark like a slender arm and hand pointing elegantly to the lot where their two cars were parked.

"Mark?"

He knew when she was ready she would break the silence, and he was glad he had waited.

"Mark, I hope I haven't been bad company tonight."

He smiled a little, knowing she knew he did not think that at all. Being in her presence was always a comfort to him and conversation was never what he sought.

"Today has been such a strange one. I don't feel much better about Thomas Raggit being out of touch. After printing out his logins to the institute and giving them to the police, I agree he could be on another of his thinking retreats. It's as though little pieces of the last twenty-five years were sprinkled all through it. Finding you napping in the pool," a little smile between them, "then the accident at the lab." She paused another moment. "Other things. It made me go back through all the times since you and I first met until now and put a real value on all we've accomplished."

"We have done many great things, Elizabeth. You can be proud of your work at AORI and all it has accomplished."

"Yes, I know, but I also think about you, Mark. Almost everything AORI has done could not have been done without you. You have been the key to unlocking the wonderful things we have been able to give the world. But what have we given you?"

"I do not understand."

"At the end of every day, the staff, the doctors, Jason, and even young Staci...they all go home to their other lives. Their families, pets, loved ones, whatever. But where do you go, Mark?"

"To my house and out there...to the sea." For a brief moment, he thought how good it would feel to be swimming just under the surface, following the golden drops of light above him, westward.

"Yes, I understand that. And I think I can feel what the ocean does for you. How it comforts you. I worry though, Mark, that you need more. That you need what we can't give you."

By this time, they had reached the pier and Mark stopped by one of the large pillars sunk far into the sand. He felt the increased dampness of the surrounding old wood. He instantly recognized the different plant life netted by the pylons from the retreating tide and all the familiar types growing on the logs. The mussels and other varieties of shellfish all had voices to his senses, and he knew his place with them. The other things were there too. The creosote that covered the wood, the trace of fuel he could smell in the foam tips of each wave, even the perfume and lotion the people wore that day on the sand. These things and thousands of other voices spoked with him every moment. Always in his mind. "Elizabeth, are you worried that I'm unhappy?"

"Are you?" She turned to him, took his arms in her hands, and looked directly into his eyes.

"Are you? Are you really happy, Mark?"

All the other voices faded in his ears now. Looking at her upturned head, he followed the moon's reflected treasure deep into her hazel eyes. The perfume of her body silenced all others, and he tried to define what he felt from her touch and gaze. He could feel beyond the touch and behind the look to something deeper in her and in him too. It was more than kindness and care. It carried the feeling of no beginning and an endless future. It felt correct.

"Elizabeth, when I go out to the sea it is because that is where I belong. It is my home. When I return, it is because of you."

He felt the increase in her heartbeat as she gently pulled him towards her. The kiss was brief. He had seen people kiss before and many times had been kissed on the cheek or hand—by Elizabeth and others—but he had never kissed. How curious that this kiss, this taste of her skin and the touch of her body up against his, after all these years of being so close to her, should feel so different. Her body leaned against him, and he enjoyed the slight pressure as she pressed closer. He felt the fabric of her jacket touch his hands. His palms rested on the soft curve of her hips, and he pulled her to him. The smallest sound came from her. He wanted to hold and protect the gentle thing that made that sweet sound.

Elizabeth settled away from the kiss, but still held Mark's arms in her hands. Her eyes opened and she breathed deeply before starting to speak.

"Mark...I..."

What was it that signaled to him at times like these? What voice was the first warning? Often, in the sea, he would react to avoid danger before he was aware that any existed. So what was it now? Did he feel the air start to compress? Was there a sound of something moving in the air? Did the darkness of the night get the smallest bit darker for an instant? Or was it just a feeling? Whatever it was, his response was simultaneous. One second he was looking into her eyes, and the same second was shared by him sweeping her into his arms, around and under the safety of the pier. The footprints where they'd been standing were obliterated, and the beach shook when the huge block of cement crashed down from above.

Elizabeth's scream and the sound of the parking barrier landing did not block Mark's ability to hear footsteps fading out onto the pier.

"Are you all right?"

With her beginning to nod, Mark was off at a run. He covered the distance from under the pier up to the gate before she could say, yes. He paused briefly before exposing himself and, with the shadows cast by the moonlight to conceal him, he made his way as fast as possible along the length of the pier. As always happened when danger threatened, his senses intensified. The only sounds were the waves, the breeze as it passed through the railings, the traffic along the road by the beach, Elizabeth's breathing, and her footsteps as she slowly made her way up the sand to the gate.

Was that a different noise in the water? Not enough to tell. He could feel no motion on the walkway other than the waves as they struck each pylon. But there was a smell! It was different— not something he could place but definitely something that did not belong.

It did not belong but yet it *did* belong! This smell was familiar. As it faded into the on-shore breeze, he tried to concentrate and retrieve the memory of it. It was gone. The air was clean and the promise his memory had teased him with fell back into the darkness. He continued to the end of the wharf, past the closed food stand, and the big double doors that enclosed the weekend rental boats. On reaching the end, he stopped at the long benches where during the day people fished or sat and ate their lunches, and he knew he was alone. Except for Elizabeth who had come through the gate and was standing at the far end waiting for him to return.

"There is no one here, Elizabeth." The inside voices were quiet now, and he turned from the ocean's dark horizon and walked back to her.

"Mark, there's no one on the beach in any direction for hundreds of yards!"

"Perhaps it was an accident." Even as he spoke, everything was telling him it hadn't been. The smell! What was the smell? Even the memory gave him a strange feeling in the pit of his stomach. It had not only been familiar, but now he realized it had actually made him feel good. Almost comforted. He was now trying to think inside this. What could comfort but be beyond memory, beyond knowledge? He wanted to get deeper, but he had no logic to guide him.

"Mark, that block must weigh at least a ton. It didn't just fall. Look!"

She had walked to the edge of the railing where the walkway of the pier met the pavement of the parking lot and was pointing at the ground. He joined her to see the large, dark rectangle of asphalt that, moments ago, lay under the cement parking barrier. It was now down in the sand.

With his arm around her, which he knew comforted her, he followed the impossible route of the cement block from its beginning in the parking lot, onto the pier, over the railing (without a scratch), and onto the beach. Below them, it stuck out of the sand in the very spot they had been standing. With one hand on the rough wooden railing and the other around her shoulders, he could feel that her breathing was still rapid and her heart was beating much faster than normal. They remained in the moonlight for awhile longer.

The smell! Where does that smell belong?

The next morning, Dr. Merrill pulled into her parking space while. Dr. Yoshio Nagashima was retrieving his cases and lunch sack from the trunk of his car. Since Yoshio came to work here twelve years ago, Elizabeth could not remember one day that his wife Kyoko had not sent his very traditional lunch along with him.

"What have I got today, Yosh?"

"Pretty much the same as yesterday, except perhaps some ono, which we should put in the refrigerator right away."

Elizabeth switched her briefcase to under her left arm as she took the paper bag from Dr. Nagashima and slid her right hand into the scanner.

"Dr. Merrill, has Jason spoken to you about the Junite Exatron System?"

"Jessie? He mentioned some random fluctuations in some of the readouts. Do you think it's a problem, Yosh?"

Dr. Nagashima slipped his hand into the scanner as she removed hers and walked to the opening door.

"No, doctor. It does not appear to be a problem. All data functions are cross-checked hourly and seem to be exact."

The pop of the inside door, with the lights coming up, started them into the lab, with Elizabeth going towards the lounge's refrigerator, but she stopped when Dr. Nagashima continued.

"But it also does not appear to be random."

Elizabeth had learned to understand Yosh's methods. When he was on to something in his work or had made some tangential discovery, he never gave information that might bias his findings to another scientist.

"Anything more you can tell me, Yosh?"

"I ran tests on the complete system yesterday and can only tell you the anomalies in the readouts are factual and must be taken at face value. I have not included anything more until I spoke to you."

"I'll take it from here. Thank you."

For Dr. Nagashima not to let his curiosity led him in this, meant only one thing. The road he suspected was there concerned Mark. Without her ever having to say it to the staff or make specific regulations concerning him, everyone in Beachlab section of the AORI knew that Mark and all information and discoveries about him were to be handled by her and her alone. When Staci started to formulate her wet string theory, because Mark was the only way she could gather empirical evidence to prove it, she brought it to Elizabeth for the go ahead. This problem that was not a problem with Jessie puzzled her, however. These were merely readouts from the security mode of the computer, not any work that was being done in which Mark was involved.

Jessie took all the vital signs along with a lot of the scientific data of each of the nine people in Beachlab as they entered and left the lab daily. It was a system devised to insure absolute security. In essence, each person leaving for the day left a new human password unique to that moment in time. It contained what they had for breakfast and lunch, what cologne or perfume they wore, and what residue lingered on them from the work they were involved in that day, among thousands of other data bits. It broke everything down into its elemental particles weighed it, logged it. The next day the reading was done on them with Jessie computing almost to the single atom the changes that could possibly occur within that finite amount of time. And only the same person, a few hours older, could reenter.

A minute later in her office, Elizabeth finished the last piece of octopus as she waited for Jason to come in with all his data. That flavor, this early in the morning, always reminded her of the Imperial Hotel in Tokyo long ago. Each morning for a week she and Dr Yoshioka Nagashima, the brilliant young phenom of the Nagao Oceanographic Institute, would sit and have breakfast, (she, the traditional Japanese and he, pancakes swimming in maple syrup) while she tried everything to convince him to come to the US and work with her.

He was newly married and his wife was right out of an Utamaro print. Alabaster skin, hair (Elizabeth had never seen it down, but it had to fall well below her waist) in dark clouds held with wooden pins and always the traditional kimono and obi. Her family's history went unbroken for over nine centuries and for all that time not one member had ever left the country. He said she was so set on not leaving Japan that he could never accept the new position being offered. So for six days Elizabeth would slide an envelope across the polished cherry-wood table next to his plate. He would not seem to notice the action or the large white hotel stationary. She would then excuse herself to go freshen up. Upon her quick return, the logo-encrusted envelope would be gone. She knew never to talk directly about the money being offered. This way he could look at the figures while she was gone. Each time she returned, he would launch into a discussion about some scientific thing or another, and she would know she had failed again. For six mornings she waited three minutes in the ladies' room, the envelope disappeared, and her knowledge about his work increased. He didn't know just how much Elizabeth wanted him and his inductive genius at AORI.

At a farewell dinner on her last night in Tokyo with Yosh and his beautiful bride, in a private tatami room of a grand old restaurant, she happened to slip in a toast, that it was too bad they could not come to America, because she was looking forward to building a beautiful traditional Japanese country house for them. At the click of the porcelain sake cups, she took note of the quick look of "Why didn't you tell me?" Kyoko gave her husband.

Elizabeth's message light was blinking by the bed when she returned to the hotel, and three weeks later she was at the LA airport welcoming her new coworker and his wife to California.

The sound on the window as he entered and "Knock! Knock!" brought Elizabeth back to the present as Jason slid into the chair at the end of the long conference table. The eleven other plush leather chairs were neatly arranged around it. Each one in front of the recessed monitor screen and the mahogany insert that, when pushed, would rotate to reveal a keyboard. Elizabeth rose from her desk, circled around it, and came to the chair next to Jason's pile of CDs.

"Here is everything for the last ten years, Doc. I put it in two separate files. One from before and one from after the installation of the new Pentium XII but readings are pretty much the same."

She knew when she asked him, upon arriving, to retrieve this information he would be fast and thorough.

"Thank you, Jason. Explain to me quickly what you found, okay?"

"Sure." Jason picked up one of the CDs from the stack and inserted it into the receiver as a large monitor rose from the table. "Just as an example, here is the last one from yesterday when I came back into the lab with Mark before four o'clock."

Elizabeth got up, came around her desk, and joined him at the large conference table. His finger traced one of the many lines as it fed out along the monitor from left to right. He continued, "You know, between the palm sweep and ready room, we get a ton of info. Everything from body temp to respiration rates and from chemical reads to plain ol' body weight."

"Yes, I know and a few of us think maybe the body weight thing is going a step too far."

"Oh, come on, Doc. You look great. You're in really good shape for a... I mean your body...I'd sure... You don't look..." Elizabeth decided to let him off the hook before he had a complete meltdown.

"Don't worry, Jason. I'll take that as a compliment and you still have your job. The readout?"

"Sure." His voice was a little higher in pitch than when he came in "Well, here I am, up here. See how the line goes straight across? Right from the night before when I left...to here where I came in with Mark."

"Yes?"

"Well here is Mark's readout down here." He reset the disc again. She followed his finger to the bottom half of the page and could see the difference as he explained

"These lines are for the carbon dating that is taken from the palm scan. One microscopic flake is analyzed to get a sequence reading from one day to the next. And look!" The specific line of Jason's chart was completely straight without any deviation. The line for Mark, however, right at the date change vertical marker on the screen, had a small bump in it. She now knew what Yosh must have felt, and the little bump in her heartbeat made her take a moment before she spoke.

"Continue."

"Well, that's just it. I mean Jessie is programmed to make the time allowance for when people clock out and back in. She gets her time reading from the government's atomic clock in Boulder, marries it to her findings, and verifies consistency. And boom! Like clockwork. Except for Mark that is."

"What exactly does the bump in Mark's line mean, Jason?" She hoped her voice sounded different than it did in her mind. This information, if correct, could change all their lives.

"I don't know. I only program these things and tweak 'em now and then, but basically sometimes, and only sometimes, there are lags, chronologically speaking, in Mark's carbon dating from one day to the next."

"Could the clock reading be the problem?"

"Dr. Merrill, that government ticker, as you know, is accurate to one second every two million years. And Jessie is directly connected to it."

"That's very interesting, Jason. Thank you. I'll study it."

"But it's not consistent, Doc. And I can't find a pattern at all."

Elizabeth stood there for awhile trying to return Jason's "tell me what you think of all this" look with her most enigmatic expression. After a beat, she ejected the disc and held it in her hand.

"Leave all this with me, and I'll see what I can make of it. Thanks again."

"Sure." Jason pushed his chair back, his tennis shoes squeaking on the polished wood floor. "You know, maybe it's..."

Staring at the disc she was holding and trying not to sound too dismissive, she simply said, "Thank you, Jason."

After he left, she returned to her desk, holding the shiny round disc to her stomach as if the answer would magically jump from it and still the queasiness she was starting to feel. She wandered the small universe of her office for awhile but ended up back at her desk, slowly sank into the chair, leaned back, and stared at the recessed lighting above her. Knowing she was avoiding the obvious, she swung back to the desk, reached for the phone pad, and punched in a sequence.

"Yes, Dr. Merrill."

"Janice, would you retrieve all of Mark's Class II project records for the last...oh six or seven years. I only want the time logs for his ocean work. Just inter-office them to my computer here, okay?"

"I'll have them to you in a minute, Dr. Merrill."

Elizabeth leaned her chair back and stared at the ceiling. She could feel the whispery thump in her ear of each heartbeat and started to count off the seconds until the bell sound on the computer would tell her that her concept of the world had changed.

Mark had gotten up well before dawn and had spent the entire morning in the ocean. For several hours he had swam around and tended the exotic gardens he had accumulated off the shore of his home. Still struggling with the events of the previous night, he had gone out to the deeper water. His favorite spot had become a large rock outcropping over the undersea canyon, about sixty miles west of the coastline. The light of the sun was dimmed to just a faint glow at this depth, and the current farther south and west brought fresh new information to all his senses. He would curl up in a sitting position in a small indentation above the blackness and spend timeless hours inside his thoughts. Even though no new answers came to him, it was time well spent. Feeling the energy of the sea, he returned to land.

It was almost 11:00 a.m. before Mark entered the lab from the ready room and was immediately intercepted by Staci.

"Mr. Harris..."

"Mark, please." He smiled and, without breaking stride, continued on to Elizabeth's office.

"Oh yes, I'm sorry...Mr. Mark...Sorry I, mean." Staci, having trouble in Mark's presence, both walking and talking, grabbed his arm and Mark stopped and tuned to her.

"Oh, I'm sorry, Mr...M...Mark, does that still hurt?" She immediately released her grip on his arm where she had imbedded the knife the day before.

"It never really hurt, and you need not think about it anymore. It was an accident." Mark smiled, turned, and continued towards the office.

"Mark!"

He turned to Staci again with a small smile at her aggressive tone and her success at finally dropping the mister.

"Yes, Staci. May I be of assistance?"

She stepped quickly to him and offered the bound AORI notebook she had been carrying.

"This is a summation of the work, so far that is, on the wet string project."

"Thank you. I will study it tonight."

"It also has, at the back, a list of further experiments I would like to do. They may seem a little strange when you see them. They aren't really lab work like the others. They're more..." She stopped and looked around the lab as if to find the encouragement for what she was about to say from the wires, beakers, and banks of equipment. "They are actually more in the realm of psychic or extrasensory studies." After finally getting that out, the floodgates opened. "You see, Mark, with the tests so far, I...we have proven that you have simultaneously experienced stimuli I administered to water environments, plants, and...and sea life outside your immediate area. Not only that, but also you, and I submit, eventually everyone can not just *feel* the experience of our environment, but...like you calculate accurately and scientifically what the effects are and also...like you...make causes that greatly influence, not only the immediate environment but reach far out into the world and..."

"Dr. Torelli!"

The voice of Dr. Merrill halted Staci mid-rapture, and Elizabeth's rare use of her surname left no doubt in the young scientist's mind that a two-person conference was to follow.

"Why don't we let Mark read your report, and after I have looked it over, we can decide on the next course of events."

There was no mistaking it. The *Dr. Torelli* and the tone of voice were a complete reprimand in one sentence. She thought, *what was I thinking*, and *why didn't I just take this to Dr. Merrill?* And a bunch of other excuses she knew Jason would call lame. So instead of offering any of them she turned completely to the doctor, whom was still standing by the open door, and meekly responded, "Yes, certainly."

Elizabeth easily shifted her gaze to Mark.

"We can go over that later, together, if you like, Mark. Oh, and, Staci, could I speak to you in my office for a minute?"

Elizabeth shifted her weight to the side and indicated the way into her office. Staci could only spin again to Mark and look at him blankly.

"Thank you, Staci. I look forward to reading your report." Mark looked at her as she stood there staring at him in silence. For a moment, it appeared she had not only forgotten what she was about to do but perhaps even where or who she was.

"Dr Torelli!"

Staci turned to find Elizabeth standing by her open office door.

"Yes, coming. Thank you, Mr. Harris. Coming."

She spun from him and directly into Jason who was walking to his desk. The collision knocked the digital camera he was adjusting out of his hands. Mark quickly bent and caught the camera before it hit the floor as Staci and Jason echoed "sorry" and "that's okay."

Staci walked to Dr. Merrill's door as Jason stepped to where Mark was examining the camera. The side of the digital recorder was open, and Mark had put his finger inside and removed the small data card.

"Oh, thank you, Mark. For some reason it's on the blink. I just hope I haven't lost all the stuff I shot yesterday." Jason reached to take the camera back.

"No, Jason, everything appears to be fine, including," Mark paused for a moment, with the two fingers of his right hand slowly moving along the small terminals of the card, "the two young women you recorded in the car next to you on your way home."

Jason's hands froze in mid air. The many things he wanted to ask hung somewhere in his brain and he just stared at Mark.

"I think it is dangerous to record while you are driving, don't you?"

"Yes...I...How could you tell? It's not even on." Now the floodgates were open. "How do you know it was on my way home?"

Before he could go further, Mark clicked closed the opening on the side. "Jason, some time ago, I found that when I touch the information gathering devices in things such as this I perceive what you would call a readout of the information it contains. I can only assume the silicone, or other of the elements, has some fluid qualities comparable with water and are therefore accessible to me." Mark placed the camera in Jason's hands, which were still hovering in front of him. "I knew the time from the readout in the memory storage, and the sunlight was on the young ladies' faces so you were going south. And I could read the highway marker as the car went past it."

Mark turned in time to see Elizabeth looking at him through the window of her office, and he smiled and turned towards his own office.

"By the way, Jason." Mark spoke over his shoulder as he approached his door. "The driver was especially attractive."

Jason numbly turned and, staring at the equipment in his hand, walked into the lab.

"Please, Staci, sit down."

Elizabeth closed the door and stood there with her hand still on the knob as she watched Mark speak for a moment with Jason. Mark then smiled at her through the glass and turned into his own office.

"Dr. Merrill, I'm sorry. I didn't mean to bypass you with my test results. It's just that I saw Mr. Harris when he came in."

"You can call him Mark."

"Yes, of course. I'm sorry. It's just that I saw..."

By now Elizabeth had circled around to the chair behind her desk and was smiling kindly at her young protégé.

"Staci, don't worry. I understand completely." When she saw Staci relax a little and ease back from the edge of her chair, she continued, "I have followed your progress very closely over the last few months as you know. I was impressed enough with your Ph.D dissertation to invite you here and, up to and including the present moment, you have never let me down." She could tell by the strange look on the young woman's face that she was completely at a loss as to why she had been summoned.

"Staci, when I first founded the AORI it was essentially Mark, Doctors Raggit and Lucca, and myself. Our work centered on oceanic research and our results could always be interpreted by the outside world, meaning Gasten and the board, as great discoveries made by good, even brilliant scientists." She saw Staci relax even more. "I have one test I use whenever we are close to finding something that will eventually go public." Elizabeth smiled now at the young lady, took a quick glance at Mark's closed door, and then let her eyes wander over the complex the AORI had become. "It's sort of like I visualize that cartoon game. Except that I call it 'Where's Mark?'" Staci's evaporating smile and widening eyes told Elizabeth she had lost her a little. "I try to see the entire project being scrutinized by other scientists, the press, and even the general public. If I can see something that could only have come from Mark's involvement, using his special abilities... in other words if I can "Find Mark" that changes the format of what we release or I drop the project completely... No matter how important it may be. Do you understand?"

"Yes, I think so. Are you considering the wet string project?"

"No, Staci. I think it's very important that we all go ahead and see where it leads. However, your priority is and should be the work, but mine is and will always be Mark." Elizabeth knew that she was about to include this young lady in a world that, up to now, only she had lived in. She had always known there was no other road for her to take, and Mark's anonymity was his only true security, but... "What we give the world from these labs are eventual products that contribute not only to the wellbeing and comfort of millions of people but they directly influence the creation of large new manufacturing companies around the world. Therefore, they affect the economies of many countries." She was drawn up from behind her desk by what she was feeling and turned, once more, to face the closed door of Mark's office. She no longer felt like she was a teacher with the goal of imparting something to her student. She was making Staci a sister in her world. "That's why we must have everything explainable beyond any one person's involvement. The people of the world are not just starved for goods anymore, or a better lifestyle, or anything like that. They have got all that, in some form or another, and they have found that they are still hungry. It's their hearts, Staci. It's their souls that are starving." Elizabeth made a silent reaffirmation to wherever Mark was behind that door and turned back to Staci, who only sat there with her mouth slightly open and her hands limply in her lap. "With what I believe you are about to confirm in your work, we will just jump from *real goods* to philosophy. For a large part of the world, it could even become religion."

"I had never thought it through to that application, Dr. Merrill."

"Well now we must, Staci." She came closer and looked directly into the young girl's eyes. This was the one time, the only time, she could have this conversation with Staci. If she didn't understand or if Elizabeth felt she wasn't ready for the responsibility, that was it. Elizabeth would be alone again. "If it is all connected, Staci—time, space, sentient, and insentient are all connected—and if the world thinks the only pass or key into the universe is Mark, what will we do? What will they think he is?"

There was no answer to that question and they knew it.

"Everything that has protected him up until now—the location of his home, the security that exists in the open area around it, and everything we do to protect him here—will be useless. The world will demand and find and use him. And I think destroy him."

But there was one course of action. They were together now. Elizabeth felt strengthened, knowing another would share him. Mark would be safe and his life would be sure. Now, with or without her, there would always be someone to care.

That evening, Mark sat in a lounge chair by the pool. He had just stepped out of the water, and the shining beads were still gliding off his skin and pooling in the small recesses of his muscles. The energy he had absorbed from the water filled his body and mind and made both feel strong. Although the sun had set hours ago, the moonlight was more than enough when added to the flicking rays from the large glass enclosed oil candle Elizabeth had given him. The candle burned on the table by the chair. He adjusted his eyes, the same way he did when in the depths of the sea, and picked up Staci's report from the table as he sat down.

He paused as the white of the paper grew in brightness, and everything around him appeared to his inner eye as though the sun had just come out from behind a cloud. He thought for a minute. Was that the feeling again? Was it his memory? Many times in the early days, when she was trying to open the locked door to his forgotten past, Elizabeth had described how different stimuli can make memories return. Did he remember smell? Was the comfort he felt then, and was feeling now, coming from some long ago page of his life? No! Mark was suddenly very alert. The smell was here. It was by this pool. It was by him!

He knew nothing was moving toward him so he remained motionless until he could target the danger. He knew it was danger, but he was not afraid. He could always handle the hazards he encountered. Just identify, locate, and react.

It only took him a moment to detect an outline in the shadow of the bougainvillea; an outline that, at one moment, was motionless then moved and grew over the edge of the railing at the far end of the deck. It was large and solid and stood out as foreign against the dappled stems and leaves of the shrub.

"What is it that you want?" Mark spoke as he slowly rose to his feet and, with equal smoothness, let Staci's report gently drop to the chair. The shadow grew as the form came forward, and soon it was no longer the outline of darkness but the shape of a man.

A few more steps before he can be considered a threat, thought Mark.

When those steps were taken, Mark was about to make his move. At the mere tension of his muscles, Mark felt his arms being pinned to his sides, and he was held motionless. He had not perceived the second person at all. It puzzled him how his senses had not heard or felt the man. He assumed it to be a man as the power that held him was considerable. He still felt calm and confident that, when he was able to identify these men and determine their intent, he would take whatever steps necessary.

The larger man approached until he was about nine feet in front of Mark. Mark knew this man was larger because he could feel the air on his neck from the one who restrained him and knew him to be six feet tall at the most.

"What is it that you want?" Mark repeated the question, this time slower and with a small smile because, based on the closeness of the man in front and unfamiliar way he was dressed, perhaps he spoke little or no English. The man stared at Mark with more intensity than he had ever seen. Over the last fifteen plus years, when someone would discover Mark's true identity, they would look at him differently. Sometimes it was curiosity and other times fear. But never had anyone looked at him the way this man did. All he could compare it to was some strange combination of anger and fear.

The man was big and stoutly built, and Mark took him to be only slightly older than himself. His dark hair was shining in the night light as though damp. His clothes appeared to be dry but the fabric? Mark could not remember ever seeing this material before. It did not fit snuggly; yet it adhered to the man's skin. It also never stopped moving even when the man was completely still.

Mark repeated. "What do you want?" It was as though the man was a little taken aback by Mark's calm detachment.

The stranger opened the top of the strange tunic he was wearing and, from his waistband, withdrew a shiny object about twelve to fifteen inches long. It reminded Mark of the old-fashioned pistols he had seen on television. Next the man pulled something from inside of his tunic. It was very small and appeared to be nothing more than a piece of cloth. Very carefully but quickly he unfolded the small square and placed it in the palm of his hand. All of this was in and out of the light and shadows and difficult for Mark to see clearly. Then the man shifted his position a little and, for the first time, the light fell squarely on the object in his left hand. Although resembling a type of pistol, it had none of the separate pieces that would identify it as such. It was one solid form... some sort of metal. From where he was, Mark could not identify the metal but was pretty sure that—based on what he could see and other information—he had never encountered its type before. Again that puzzled him. Since working with Elizabeth at the foundation, there had been times when he had to learn the names of certain elements and compounds, but they had all been familiar in some way. This time nothing triggered a response in him.

There was a cone-shaped opening in the larger end, and it was in this that the man inserted his hand with the cloth until it disappeared to the knuckles. At that moment, the casing on what appeared to be the barrel turned almost transparent and looked to be more fluid than solid. It retracted completely into the handle, revealing a razor-like blade. Something deep and long forgotten in Mark's life was suddenly activated and, for the first time, he could remember he felt fear, fear for his life!

The man started towards Mark. He held the weapon out in front of him and seemed almost afraid of it himself. Mark also felt the grip around his own arms tighten, and he sensed the respiration and heart rate increase dramatically in the man who held him. Just two more steps. Mark knew that the five feet or so between them would give him the room and the chance to throw off the one who had him pinned and to disarm the assailant facing him. As the man took the second step and Mark was about to move, he heard him speak for the first time.

"We have searched a long time to find you. We have traveled many shorelines." Now his face became more animated and his lip rose to a slight sneer. "Your time here has dulled your senses and dimmed the qualities of your people." The sneer was now a complete grin, but there was no warmth to it. "You are a weak keeper of gardens. Ja-Lil, it is to be, you must die."

Inside Mark's brain, it was as though a blast of the brightest light illuminated a place long dark. It was only for a moment. But in that instant visions came to Mark in blinding swiftness. A beautiful young girl's face, long dark hair, smiling. She is gone. Gone too quickly for him to call the image back! Now a man and a woman in their early fifties or so. He is waving. At Mark? He is gone. She is beautiful. Her face is over his, looking down. The long gold twists of hair fall against his face as she laughs and rocks her head back and forth. The beautiful face and mouth come closer. She is gone! Large strange shapes. Buildings? Just shapes? Shapes and symbols that puzzle him.

As quickly as the images came to him they were gone and then back again. Mark felt in those brief seconds like he was free falling through the shreds and edges of someone else's life. Then it was all gone and nothing replaced it. It was just the now. Him and the two strangers, the quiet night, and the danger! Mark knew now that he must act.

He flexed his arms to raise them above his head and break the grip of the one behind him, but he was held fast. Never in his life had he been unable to overpower another person, but one more attempt to break the hold told him it was not to be. The larger man raised the weapon to the level of Mark's chest.

"Your life is a crime, Ja-Lil. Your line must cease to be." He continued forward.

Mark summoned the totality of his strength and, with one twisting motion of his entire body, spun and flipped his restrainer into the oncoming assailant. For a second all was still. The strength that held him was gone. Mark, upon feeling his freedom, spun around and stood poised to act. To do what? He did not know. With their strengths being equal, he considered an escape to the sea. He was about to run to the wall and jump. At least if he made it to the water and out into the deep, he would have the advantage. The smaller of the two men, the one who had been holding Mark only a moment ago, slowly turned to face him. The left sleeve of his tunic was badly slashed, and a large gaping cut oozed blood from his arm just above the elbow. He brought his other hand up to staunch the flow. The free hand flexed strongly on the long diagonal opening. The compression did not halt the flow of blood, and Mark watched it run out between strong fingers. The man repeated the squeezing, and then Mark saw something. As the fingers flexed and released, the skin between them extended smoothly outward to the joint of the first knuckle. Mark was looking directly, for the first time he could remember, at another webbed hand.

The ground he stood on split beneath him. The crack became an opening. The opening widened as cement, deck, house, land, and the very air—everything except the space he possessed with these two men—raced into the distance and disappeared. Everything he could remember belonged now to another place, another world, another dimension. The connections he felt so securely to Elizabeth and the people of the institute stretched into such a fine filament that he could not feel their attachment for him. There was nothing in his universe but total darkness and that one hand pushing against red soaked fabric and skin. Thin snakes of brownish-crimson wandered over curved arcs of flesh that held his eyes like iron.

There was no controlling the systems in his body now. His heart raced, and the separation of beats blurred against the inside of his skin until he thought he would split open at every cell. His body had no weight but was pressed against the ground so hard he could not lift his foot. His mind was as black and empty as the world around him. A small speck of something was born into the black and matured in an instant into a feeling then into a thought—a thought which became a word "Who?"

One word typed indelibly on the black page brought the cosmos back to order. He was there on his deck by his house with these two men. He was standing in the glimmering moonlight. His breathing slowed and the muffled sounds he heard became the slap of the waves' crickets calling somewhere in the brush beyond the house and the rapid gasps of the young bleeding man.

Those little gasping tufts of air pulled his eyes off the bleeding arm and hand, and he looked into the eyes of the wounded man. What he saw there was what he had felt when he noticed the knife-blade. The fear was now married to fate. This young man knew he could die and he would die. In that stretched moment of shocked immobility, all three sets of eyes jumped from one person to another, almost begging the other to break the deadlock. The larger, older man very slowly let the knife loosen in his grip. Like a curtain coming down, the blade was soon covered with the flowing shield becoming solid. With the same deliberate speed, he slipped the weapon back into the waistband of his tunic. This serpent-like movement held everyone in its trance, and all was still until he reached down and grabbed the glass container and votive candle that was burning on the table. With a sudden eruption of violence, he threw it towards the house. It barely cleared itself under the rain gutter of the overhang and crashed in an explosion of crystal shards and liquid wax against the teakwood bench. In an instant, all of it was ablaze and small molten drops of flame were dropping to the cement patio.

The two assailants, using the diversion of the moment, jumped over the patio wall and disappeared. Mark's every molecule wanted to chase after them, but the sound of the growing fire turned him back. He grabbed a large towel from the back of the chair where he had been sitting and slapped it into the water. After he ran to the burning bench, he twisted the towel into a six-foot long, wet rope and hooked it around the armrest. Still watching the spot where the two men disappeared over the wall, he easily pulled the bench to the edge of the pool and threw it in. With one more quick movement, he drenched the towel again and threw it over the small flaming trail the bench had created. With the house safe, he ran to the sea wall and saw the last white explosions of water and foam as the two men disappeared into the ocean.

Mark ran to the telephone under the eave of the house. He picked up the receiver and punched the top speed dial button.

The seven-tone song quickly dialed, and he stood watching the few small dabs of flame above the surface of his pool like some floating candelabra. The phone rang six times. There was a click and then the voice of Elizabeth, "This is Dr. Elizabeth Merrill. I can't answer the phone right now, but if you leave a message I will return the call as soon as possible." Another beat as he shifted his eyes from the drowning flames to the waves breaking along the shoreline. Then the tone.

For a second he said nothing. What could he say? What was it that had just happened? What was it that he felt and heard and saw? The silence now roared louder than the surf. Never taking his eyes off the gentle rolling of the ocean, he took a deep breath. "Elizabeth, there are others. I am not alone. I will return."

Mark hung up the phone, ran to the wall, jumped over, and was gone.

CHAPTER FOUR

T he sun's rays filtered through the thirty feet or so of water and, by the angle of them, Mark was subconsciously aware of the chase being ten hours old. At this level under water, any turbulence that might be on the surface did not affect the signs and they were very easy to follow. Mark was excited and also extremely puzzled. These two were almost certain to be his kind, but why had they acted the way they did? Despite the speed of the pursuit, he was able to use his time in the water to collect and organize his thoughts. Putting the events of the last ten plus hours in perspective was important. Why would they want to kill him when he had no idea who they were? The killers' chilling words echoed constantly. "Your life is a crime. Your line must cease to be."

For the first time in his memory, he had to consider the blank parts of his life not being what he assumed they were. He had, since finding Elizabeth, always looked for and found the goodness in those he met. Over the years, there were many whose evil was apparent, but he took them to be the exception. Now he had to question everything about himself. All that was exciting about filling in so much forgotten knowledge was counterbalanced with danger. Was he a criminal? Why must he die? He was racing into the unknown where he might be targeted again for death.

He was sure from the moment they fled that the two men, somewhere in the sea ahead of him, were returning to their home. That thought pulled him through the water with as much force as his undulating body. Home! Was it his home? Were they his kind, his people? And if indeed they were the same race as he then why was the smaller one still bleeding? Why had the wound not closed?

The blood-scent in the water was a road map for Mark to follow. In the calmness of the ocean at this depth, although it extended rapidly in all directions, the strength of it hung in the water like a neon arrow. The sea water that Mark pulled in and out of his chest passed through both his smell and taste senses, and the information he gleaned spoke volumes. When the trail funneled from the surf to a direct path westward and on to the open sea, the wound was still wide and the man was losing blood at a great rate. At some point, a few hours into their retreat, the two had obviously stopped and bound the wound. This he knew by the concentration in one spot and then its diminution to a much fainter scent from that point on. But still he bled? Something was different about them but so much more was the same... Mark swam on.

Elizabeth stood by the open door to the patio and pool and stared. She had returned to her apartment late last night after driving back from the symphony fundraiser in San Diego. It had been so late that she hadn't checked her messages, only climbed under cool fresh sheets after showering. She had slept through the night. The bright sunlight and gentle breeze from the ocean that fluffed the curtains and washed over her had woken her. Taking her favorite big cup, the Limoges one covered with paintings of robins on branches and little colored bugs, she filled it with coffee. Treating herself with extra cream and two sugars, she walked out onto her deck. Standing there in the warm sun, the wind playing with the silk of her nightgown, she hummed a piece of the beautiful Barber she had heard the night before. She read through the entire newspaper and refilled the robin cup before picking up the phone and calling in for a message she knew was there by the beeping dial tone.

The fragile cup shattered when it hit the edge of the wrought iron table as she ran to her bedroom to get dressed. She had called him once from the apartment before going down to the garage, but when the message started she hung up and left. Two more times the message started when she called from her car—on what seemed an endless drive up the coast to the turn off to his house. The gate she opened with her beeper dragged irritatingly, and she smacked the passenger mirror when she squeezed through a second too soon. Nothing appeared wrong from the front of the house, and she parked by the gray pot that held one of the six orange trees that lined the walkway. Everything seemed right, but everything was so wrong! She felt sick and could feel Mark wasn't there when she let herself in with her key.

"Mark!"

The sound of her voice fell at her feet, and she knew no one would pick it up. But she tried again.

"Mark!"

The panic that had electrified her was strangely fading. The sound of his voice on her phone had removed her heart from her body. He was leaving and taking it with him. She couldn't live without it! She had to stop him!

That was how she left her home less than an hour ago and drove with the damn ocean teasing her to the left the entire way. Now in the house, his house, she knew he was gone and the panic was going and nothing was to be left but an echo of her heartbeat. Everything she saw and touched as she walked through the living room, past the large kitchen, and toward the backyard, she filed away in the place her heart had been. His jacket. The picture of them taken in Arrowhead. His chair. The light switch he had touched. Him...everywhere.

She stopped before going outside. Looking out from the coolness of the dark, she could see it was all wrong. The wind had scattered papers like a few days before. The towel on the deck, still circled with a damp ring, was very wrong. The beautiful sparkling diamonds weren't gems at all but ugly pieces of broken glass. It was all wrong.

She held the familiar curved brass in her hand, his again, before turning the handle and stepping out into the cool warmth. Violence still hung in the air. She wasn't afraid as she stepped over the broken glass and past the drying towel. She stopped by the flagstone wall. The sea was calm and beautiful under the cloudless sky. Beautiful and mean. He was somewhere out there and she knew it. Somewhere she could never go. She felt the edge of the top stone pressing against her waist. His again. She couldn't go any farther. She turned slowly against that edge and leaned back. She looked at the strange shape of the bench floating where the breeze had pushed it against the far side of the pool.

She looked down at the small piece of white that called to her eyes in the sun. She picked it up. Soft fabric and different than any she had ever seen. Maybe his? She didn't know. She opened it where it had been folded over and saw the small dark stain. Very familiar. It was a bit of dried blood. So it was not his. Not important.

She must wait for him. He said he would return, and he always did what he said he would do. He had given his word. *His word*. But what if he could not return? What if the sea had taken Mark never to give him up again? Then it would be time for regrets. All the times she had stopped herself from voicing her heart. The poems she composed but never wrote. These would be the regrets. But most of all she wished she had told him how much her life meant through him. But now she would wait. She would wait for her heart.

As the sun was setting, Mark was forced by the radical change in the trail's direction to drop to a much deeper level where the sun, even at midday height, could not shed its light. His eyes adjusted and, because of what he had learned from his testing at the lab, they immediately picked up the electric output of the various kinds of microscopic sea life. It was much more sophisticated, Jason had said, but very similar to night-vision binoculars. The outline of the sea floor started to come into view. At this depth, very little plant life was evident. Some of the bracken types of sea urchins were attached to the rock surfaces of this underwater mountain range.

Even with the two zigzagging along the midpoint and lateral line of the mountains, they maintained a consistent westerly course. Mark had explored these ranges numerous times over the years, and the familiar terrain added to his confusion. If they were headed to their home and they were taking the shortest route—Mark assumed the severity of the man's wound and amount of blood that he was losing would force them to do so—why had he never detected so much as a hint of their presence before? Mark continued to breathe in the sea at maximum capacity. Their speed over the two days had not diminished to any great extent. None of his sea friends could have maintained such a pace. The difference, Elizabeth had said, was that he did not just extract oxygen from the water to feed his muscles as did the fish, but his system had some way of drawing pure energy from the sea itself.

She came into his thoughts many times over the hours he had been following the men. He had gone over the message he had left on her phone several times. He had said so little. If he could, he would have told her more. She would know what he knew about the men on his deck. All he had left her with was that he would return. He could not have told her where he was going or even what direction he would be traveling. He did not know that himself, and even now the direction could change at any time. He had not told her about the attempt on his life. If more than these two men wanted him dead then perhaps he would not return to her. Long ago, he had tried to return to the sea and leave her and his other friends, but he could not. He recalled walking back to where she had watched him dive into the surf. The tear had still been on her cheek when he said he had not learned enough yet. Now here he was leaving her in order to learn. He could only hope—hope she would understand whatever happened. He hoped she would continue to help the world with her work at AORI. He hoped she would not be alone.

This chase that had begun as a sprint continued past its first full day without abating, and then into its second and third. Somewhere high above where Mark swam, the sun was rising into the fourth day since he had left the message for Elizabeth. Where he was now, time was measured by knowing the pressure of the tides and some sense in his body that was logging the change in magnetic pulls from north to south. Some time ago, they had passed under the river within the sea that ran warmer to the north and now the direction had slowly drifted south. Several times, Mark had made mental notes to report things he had seen for the first time to Elizabeth and his friends at the lab. Things of nature, like the plants Mark had witnessed growing at a depth where they should not have been able to survive or the almost pure mineral out-flow from the active volcano he had just passed at a depth of over three miles. He must also tell Jason of the faint electronic signal he detected from the twisted metal wreck on the ocean floor he swam by two days ago. After each of these discoveries, he also knew the information might die with him in secret.

On the sixth day, Mark started to close the gap between himself and those he pursued. The scent was stronger and they seemed to be following the ocean floor, which was several thousand feet under the surface now. Sea life was rare at this depth, although he felt none of the pressure that kept all mammals above him. Though they had slowed, he did not slacken his own pace. He wanted not to overtake them but rather get close enough to follow them to their destination. As midday approached, the sea floor started to slope ever upward, and he tracked their fresh sign around the boulders and hillsides as it now slowed considerably and wove its way through the more plentiful plant life. Mark slowed his own speed and was reading not just direction from the blood trail but the exact condition of the wounded man and precisely how many minutes it had been since he had passed. He knew the extremely stressed condition the bleeding man was in. The blood sign carried none of its former richness. Other signals indicated the shutting down of some internal organs.

As he rounded the outcropping of jagged rocks at the foot of a small hill, he pulled up suddenly. There was a pooling of information in this one spot. He swam to the largest of the stones and placed his hand on it. The younger one had leaned against it for awhile. They had stopped here for the first time since the chase had begun. He could detect the scent of the tunic, and it was the same as the one that had held his arms by the pool. He knew it was the wounded one. He also knew immediately that the body temperature of the wounded man had dropped considerably. The larger one had not rested but had moved in small circles a few yards ahead. Mark was very intrigued by how much sharper his senses had become since beginning the chase. Was it the extent he had pushed his body that sharpened them or these waters he had never been in before? Whatever it was, he could sense the vast difference in the signs of the two men. In fact, everything in him now had a greater clarity than before. His mind computed the input he received and knew they had stopped only for a short time. Then they had moved on but at a much slower speed, with the larger man swimming some distance ahead of the other.

Mark waited a few minutes himself. Not because he needed rest. He was waiting for one of those reasons he did not consciously understand. He was listening to and following a faint inner voice that was telling him to proceed slowly and expect anything. In fact, he felt stronger than he had in a long time. He had not pushed himself this hard in years and was encouraged to note that his strength seemed to increase with the stress.

When he finally knew it was right, he rose and gently pushed against the soft sand of the ocean floor. The small cloud swirled around his feet and settled back almost immediately. He rounded the base of the hill for about thirty feet, but he stopped almost instantly and dropped back behind a rock. From where he was concealed, he could see the two men. They had traveled not more than two hundred yards from where they had first stopped and the younger of the two was lying on the sand floor with his back against a large boulder. The larger man swam in small slow arcs in front of his wounded comrade. From where Mark lay, it appeared the smaller man could go no farther. He knew now would be the time to confront them and get some answers to the thousands of questions he had for them. He felt that with only one to pose him any real danger, he could avoid the knife blade so he decided to take the chance.

After the thought came to him to approach them, he stopped once again. The larger man had moved to his friend and appeared to put the thumb of his right hand to his partner's mouth. The younger man violently pushed the hand away and, with one more attempt being thwarted, the larger man hovered above his friend for a second, turned in the water, and with a push swam away. Everything these two did left only questions and no answers. What had the larger man just tried to do and why was he now leaving this dying man after carrying him for so long? Mark stayed where he was and watched the larger assailant swim until he was completely out of view. Knowing he could follow the disappearing killer anywhere now, he let him move out of sight.

He waited until all signals told him it was safe to move then he rose up and over the rock. At that moment, to his left where vision started, which was about one hundred and twenty yards, he saw the whitish-gray outline of what he knew to be a white shark. He knew also that the course the large fish had taken was dictated by the blood scent of the young man being carried by the slight current. The slow lateral movement belied the speed at which the shark was moving. It covered one hundred yards in just a few seconds and started its final attacking approach at about the last twenty yards.

Mark had seen this action numerous times. Once they experienced the blood in the water and identified its source, it was only seconds before they made their final move. He marveled at their lack of caution when attacking, which came from centuries of absolute mastery of their environment. Mark had seen them take seals, fish, and once a sea otter—although he had never seen one eat an otter once it had killed it. He had also watched many eat shell fish from the sea floor so he knew the immobility of the man and him being on the sandy floor of the ocean would not deter this great predator.

Mark had only a second now to plan his action and, although he did not know exactly what he would do, he instantly shot forward to intersect the hunter. The white had just dropped to the ocean floor, and the sand was billowing in the wake of his great bulk racing for the kill. Mark hit the fish just as the large jaw was opening, and the flesh rolled back to expose rows of triangular teeth. He did not strike the shark as dolphins sometimes did, but he came from behind and stayed to the right. The moment was timed perfectly and, with the eyes of the great white closed over, he did not see Mark approach. At impact, he jammed his right hand deep into the front-most gill slit on the shark's right side. The speed he had generated and his hand penetrating the fish's body completely deflected the shark from its trajectory. As quickly as he hit it, Mark reached his other hand as far as he could over the top of the great beast's head and found the gill slits on the left.

The fish was massive. Mark's reach from fingertip to fingertip was easily over six feet, but with both hands firmly imbedded in the slits and gripping the inner cartilage-like flesh, his face was pressed on the sandpaper-rough skin on the back of the shark's head. It was at least twenty-five to thirty feet in length and, based on his knowledge of small orcas and basking sharks, he knew this killing machine weighed 4500 pounds.

The shark's instinctual reaction when Mark grabbed it was to arc its body to the left and then turn to face its attacker. Mark used that movement and the moment to swing his leg over its back. His left foot just clipped the front dorsal fin and, thankfully, found the left pectoral fin. He hooked his toe next to the large dot on the shark's side. All this happened before man or fish could think, and from then on it was a battle of pure muscle and will. Essentially, all Mark had to do, or in fact all he could do, was hang on.

The giant fish, however, was doing everything! It could not know that the mystery thing that had attacked it had no intention of doing it any real harm. It employed every tactic that was in its genetic arsenal. One second it would be spinning at such a speed that Mark could feel the blood in his body being redistributed by the force. The next second all would change, and over two tons of pure muscle would be charged with spasms as it attempted to throw its rider loose so it could turn its knife-like rows of teeth on it.

Mark re-tightened his grip and held his face tight to that hard, slate-blue skin. He knew the strength of the big shark, but he also knew where his hands were and why. With a hand in the front gill slit on either side of its head, Mark had closed off the two openings the shark used to funnel water and life-giving oxygen to itself. Mark also pressed, with all his strength, along the remaining four slits. He was in effect strangling the large fish. Choking it. He had, actually, no intention of killing the beast, but as far as the shark was concerned it was a fight to the death.

The sandy ocean floor was being stirred into an underwater dust storm. Clouds would follow where the big tail and fin would thrust, and all that could be seen at times were flashes of blue-gray, pieces of seaweed, the tan of Mark's body, and glimpses of his yellow trunks. Although the action had started violently, in less than six or seven minutes, Mark could feel the starving muscles he was clinging to start to weaken. The fish would roll but not spin. It would sink for a moment to deeper water then as fast as possible race back into the cloud of sand. In a short time,

Mark could raise his head from the hard back of the fish and look at the pale glassy eye on its right side.

The shark stopped its fight all together and began to sink to the ocean floor. It drifted down and started to list to its left side. Mark maintained his blockage of the slits until he felt most of the shark's muscles finally release.

By this time the battle had carried them over a hundred yards away from where it began. As the fish came to rest on the sand, Mark released his hold and slid off the white's back. He stood on the sandy floor and gripped the portal fin that, only moments before, had been his lifeline. He began to push the semi-conscious shark forward. The deadly mouth was now slack. Life-giving, oxygen-rich ocean water began to flow over the gill membranes and life started to return to the fish. Mark walked the huge thing along the sand and could soon feel its energy returning. In a short time it was able to begin a slow sideways undulation, and when Mark felt sure it would not stop and sink again, remain motionless and die, he let go and the sleepy giant began to retreat from the battlefield on its own.

Mark, sure of his safety and that of the shark, turned his attention back to the wounded assailant. On approaching the man, he could see how the cut on the arm had been bound tightly in an effort to staunch the flow of blood. To some degree it had succeeded, but still a small amount of red could be seen flowing from beneath the bandage and disappearing into the seawater. Again Mark questioned, why had this wound not closed as his always had? The man was completely motionless and even when right next to him, Mark could not see any movement of the chest. Without taking in the life-giving water, the man would die as surely as the shark would have.

His eyes were closed and, as Mark came to a stop in front of him, they remained closed. Mark was given a sudden start when the man's voice came into his head as clearly as if they were back by his pool having a conversation.

"Ja-Lil, I am sorry."

Mark had never experienced anything like this before. Never had the language of any person registered in his brain! There had been odd times, over the years, when he assumed he knew what others were thinking and indeed guessed very closely when subjected to tests at the lab. The message between him and the other mammals of the sea were not words that other men would understand. In these cases he did, 100 percent of the time, know what was communicated, but it seemed to bypass language and registered directly as mutually possessed thoughts. This man was *speaking* to him!

"Ja-Lil, I knew it was wrong."

The voice was getting fainter, and something in Mark guided him in his effort to open his mind more to receive this new and wonderful thing. It seemed natural to think as he always had when communicating with other creatures in the sea. However, this time he tried to direct them. Looking into the young man's graying eyes, he thought, *I do not understand what you mean. Who is Ja-Lil?*

His question was not answered and he was not sure his thoughts had reached him. The man's eyes were half closed now and his head began to nod forward. Mark gently took him by the shoulders and, leaning him against the boulder again, knelt to better look into his face. The eyes, which were wandering without seeing over the landscape that surrounded the two men, fixed on Mark. The contact seemed to revive the man's focus and he locked on Mark's gaze.

"I have broken the cities sacred vow to protect your line."

With none of this making any sense to Mark, all he could think to ask was, "Who are you?"

"I am no one." An answer! Mark knew now that the young man was hearing him. Before he could pose another question, the weak voice continued.

"When you return, tell them it was my wish to end here. My choice not to be taken to the Tanta."

The voice was now so weak that nothing Mark could do would change its direction. It was getting farther and farther away. He was aware of something else now. A vague sense of darkness. Not everywhere but a small speck, a pin-point of heaviness, of blackness. When he felt the spot would turn into something that he could understand, Mark saw something. At least he thought he saw something. It was as if the man's body expanded ever so slightly. He knew it had not, for he was watching him very closely. But he *felt* it expand. Then there was a rush that felt like a sudden current in the water. It was water, lightness and darkness. It was energy. It was life! It rushed out from the man, hit Mark, and passed through him. Mark could feel it rush in a perfect circle out from the man and into the sea. It expanded as it dispersed, and in a second it disappeared just as the blood had faded and become one with the water.

It took some time for Mark to realize what had happened and to be aware that now the young man was gone. He had seen countless things die in the ocean. He had seen it give birth, nurture, and take care of its dead. He had not, however, felt a life in its essence as he had just now. Whatever had been this man's life, up to this very moment, was gone. What was left had only one function, and that value was to nourish the living. In a short time, all that would remain would be the clean bones that had once been this person, and the rest would return again to its source. He knew it was right to leave this body to the sea.

He also knew the door to any more information was closed and, therefore, the other man was his only option. But was it? Other choices were also apparent to Mark. He could return now as he had promised Elizabeth. That night on the beach he had told her he would always returned from the sea because of her. Even now, he felt the desire to continue his life on the surface. The pull was stronger, however, from another direction. Swimming somewhere just in front of him was the key to everything. If he followed, his past would most certainly be revealed. That knowledge would also dictate what his future would be. So there really was no choice. The only unknown was whether he would live or die. Would he, whatever he was to discover, be able to return to the surface and his friends, or would it end with him knowing all and them left with only questions? His mind played for him the clear image of Elizabeth giving him a smile and that little wave of theirs.

He smiled back into the darkness and he turned.

Sure of the direction—and that the man probably did not know he would be followed—Mark set out after him. In a short time, he had made up the distance lost by his encounter with the shark and incredible experience with the dying man. He saw him just inside the vision range, which in these strange new waters was farther than he had ever experienced. The man had slowed and no longer changed direction; he headed in a straight south by southwesterly path.

The last car had pulled out of the lot at AORI hours ago. Elizabeth sat in the captain's chair at the console holding the cup of cooling green tea in both hands. She had been staring at the security monitors; not out of concern but because she had no other place to focus. It seemed an apt analogy of her life now. Constantly changing vignettes of places that used to hold so much interest for her and were now just reminders of what was missing. She could see the patrols making their rounds and had notified them she would be working late so they avoided disturbing the Beachlab complex.

Reaching to the keyboard in front of her, she returned the wall to the map of the world and spun the chair around. The overhead lights in the main room were off and everything was bathed in the green and red power and stand-by lights on the hundreds of pieces of equipment. Elizabeth felt like she was looking through the glass wall that was between them into a giant underwater aquarium. She rose from the chair and walked toward the door. The motor under the floor clicked, the glass partition slid to the left, and she stepped out into another world. It was so different now. Just ahead was Staci's desk and computers. What would she do now? What could go forward if he didn't...? Stop! That was not where her mind should go. Countless times now in the past week, she had to stop herself. It can't be...*if*! Forget...*if*!

Thomas' area was more like a shrine as the time grew since he'd been in touch. As she thought about things, she continued to walk and now stood before the door to Mark's office. Since the first day back at work after the phone call, she had avoided this place. It was too close. Too much like him. Too painful. It was not entirely dark, but the chair and coat rack stood as dark sentries, outlined in green light from the monitors on his desk, and the two aquariums against the far wall. She griped the cooling pottery cup tightly and tried twice before successfully freeing one hand to have it rest on the handle to the door. Silently, it gave way to her pressure, and she went in. This was why she never came near before. *He* was here. She felt him. Everything but his voice said, "Hello, Elizabeth. I have been waiting for you."

She didn't cry. She couldn't. This pain didn't touch nerves or skin. It was beyond even where her heart should be. It was the lonely pain in the depths of her mind, and it was worth more than tears.

His chair rested at an angle to the desk, and she sat slowly until she could lean back and close her eyes. This was as close as she could get. It wasn't him, but it was *his* and that would do until he did as promised and returned. It was the shift in tone from the computer that opened her eyes. Clicks and hums were common background music here in the lab so she wasn't sure why this hum, that sounded exactly like the others, seemed so different.

She looked at the charcoal gray of the screen and the green dot to the lower left. The mouse laid waiting and she responded. The movement, as she touched it, made the gray quiver for a moment then disappear into the electric blue background. Icons and phrases she was very familiar with. Shortcut to this and shortcut to that, most with names of projects in various states of progress. The few games that he found to be no challenge to his logic at all and were never played again after being successfully won. And the *My Computer* and the *Recycle Bin* and just a folder... just a folder and a title. She saw the arrow creep up from the lower left towards the target. Her hand didn't seem to move, but the arrow continued on its arc, and her eyes never left the goal. Just a folder and shortcut to Mark.

The click opened the file. And it was just as it said. Just as he told her he wanted it to be in the car so long ago, coming back from Arrowhead. Long lists of things. Sometimes a feeling or a concept. Others were things. House. The Long Day. Whistles. The Dead Bird. She knew what it was. He had written as he had wanted to. He never told her, but then that's what she had told him poetry was sometimes. Secret little windows you open to let things in or out—for you and you alone.

As she scrolled down the list, she noted that it read like a beautiful poem itself. It was the shortcut to *him* and she smiled. Then he was there. Her heart was back. It tripped and stumbled to signal its return and pushed up and down inside her until she thought she would burst open. The arrow stayed on her. It stayed squarely in her middle, its point on the "a". The first click lined her name in darker blue. She watched it thinking,

Did it look like a name tag?
And
Did it look like a marquee?
Or
Headstone?

The second click.

Looking down
Inside, you found me.

Floating free, carried
By currents, feared, around me.
Stretching upward
Through dusty green
Feet in sand
Seeking sunlight.
Not thinking
Taking
Thankful
Closer.
The warmth of closer
My home embrace
I take your gifts of
Freedom
And rush before the tide.
As sea
You are a part of me,
Elizabeth.
Elizabeth.
Elizabeth.

It all fit just within the screen. The screen looked back at her, and she could trace the outline of her hair backlit by the glow from the main room. She sat in the chair watching the shadow drawing of herself, watching Elizabeth Elizabeth Elizabeth. The tear left a warm path as it trickled down her cheek.

For two more days, Mark and the man traveled together, but not together. Always the same distance apart as if tethered by a long mountain climber's line. The second day, the man followed a salmon road, an ageless invisible path in the sea that took them on a multilayer circuit of the Pacific. Mark knew it and had traveled it often but had not been aware it extended this far south. Towards the end of the day, the leader of this two-man expedition broke from the path and swam off to his right and around the base of the foothills that eventually rose into a moderate-sized mountain range. Several old volcanoes stood high, with their gaping mouths looking like frozen anemones. One towards the far end of the range still pushed liquid rock that left the opening with just a hint of pink to turn a dusty gray as it formed the embryo of some future island. Passing close enough to feel the sharp increase in temperature, the man stopped at the edge of a small valley where the water had cooled.

Mark held back about a hundred yards in the safety of a small arroyo of an ancient lava bed. The valley formed almost a perfect circle several miles in diameter. The foothills that rose in all directions held the ocean floor like giant stone hands. Mark surveyed the entire area carefully and could feel the comfort of the surrounding mountains. The feeling was familiar but obscured by the dark of his memory.

He watched closely as the man moved very deliberately to a spot on the floor by a large boulder and, while standing upright immediately to the side of it, held both hands out in front of him about chest high. His behavior was very strange. Why had he stopped here? What was this ritual? Mark never took his eyes off him. The man moved forward, not more than a foot, and Mark watched him...

He disappeared! Mark blinked once, almost as if the action would bring the man back into focus. But it did not.

Mark floated out of the lava bed, hoping the new point of view would show that the man had just moved behind something. But it did not. He could see by moving up and to his left that the man was not behind the rock...*inside* the rock! One moment he was there and the next he was not. The man was gone.

CHAPTER FIVE

Mark swam down to the lava flow and the eighty or so yards towards the large boulder where the man had disappeared. He stopped every so often, expecting, even hoping, he could catch sight of the man, confirming that he had just moved out of Mark's vision and not vanished into thin air. Within a few yards of the boulder, he slowed to a complete stop. From a distance, what appeared to be a small valley in the open ocean was really something else. Where Mark floated in the water, he could trace the almost invisible outline of a large arc; it swung from one side of the valley—where the sand dunes piled like frozen waves against the edge of the foothill—up and across at the height of several hundred feet, and then down to the rising ocean floor on the other side. From where he was hidden, when the man disappeared, it had not been visible and could not be seen until he was almost touching it as he was now.

After swimming along the edge of the valley in both directions for some time, he realized that it was a circular Dome that covered the entire open area. It seemed transparent, and he had the feeling he was enjoying an unobstructed view of the other side of the valley. From any position around its circumference, the Dome somehow optically reflected the corresponding terrain from the other side. That and its plastic-like consistency made it almost invisible to the naked eye.

Coming full circle back to the large rock once again, Mark investigated the composition of this Dome. Although it appeared transparent, he could not see inside it. One could assume it was completely solid, though Mark knew it could not be. The man had disappeared, and the only explanation was that somehow he had gone inside. Several times he swam to the top and hovered several hundred feet to look down. Again the view seemed unobstructed. The Dome reflected the ocean floor so perfectly that anyone viewing from his vantage point would assume the valley to be empty. This structure was the perfect camouflage. For the first time, he touched the surface. Quickly he drew his hand away. Not because of the feel of the substance itself but because of the mental pull he felt and sense of welcome it generated. It merely responded to the touch by giving slightly, but when he pushed again and exerted a lot of force the material resisted. The only matching experience he could call from his memory was the simple moon jelly, a jellyfish with a transparent but quite fragile float. In fact, if he were to make a report to Elizabeth on this giant Dome, he would have to say that it was...alive!

He knew he was at the exact spot the man had been standing so Mark began to precisely duplicate the actions he had made before he disappeared. He moved a little to the right and then to the left, and then extended his hands out and moved to the Dome. Where his fingers touched the substance, they were no longer met with resistance but easily penetrated the surface. He continued to move forward and, at one point, felt a slight suction or pulling sensation draw him in. One minute he was watching as his hands and arms vanished into the jelly-like mass and raising his foot to step forward; the next instant he was on the inside. He continued the single step and came to a halt.

He was standing in a small room. He looked back to where he had come through the wall. There was no opening or door or even an indication of how he had entered. He also noticed there was no water puddle on the floor. The airlock apparatuses he had used before carried some of the outside water in with the person entering, but here there was none. There was not even moisture on the wall to indicate that this was indeed the portal in and out. Then it dawned on him. He was also completely dry! Only his body and the suit he was wearing had come through to the inside. Every droplet of water, even the wetness on his skin, had been left on the outside.

He tried to think inside this, but he could not force his mind to do it. He did not understand but felt, deep in his life, no urge to question it. The sense of welcome rushed through him and expanded. He set his heart rate back to normal and calmed his system. Once settled, he stepped farther into the room. Everywhere, hanging from small fine outcroppings on the walls, were garments in differing hues of muted colors. Mostly the softer colors of the sea with pale greens or countless shades of whites and blues. Although he was perfectly still, the fabrics continued in constant motion like the gentle pushing and pulling of delicate sea grasses in a tidal basin. At the far end of the hall-like room was an opening with the choice of going right or left. Mark was aware of something else. Although he had left the water and was no longer wet, he was not feeling the gradual depletion of energy. He had an internal gauging system that would start to register how long he had been out of the water and at what rate he was using up his strength. He had always felt it and it had become merely a peripheral awareness. At some point, he would inevitably have to return to the sea to absorb its life-giving energy. However, now inside this dry area, instead of burning the fuel he had taken from the water, he could feel the ocean and its energy being absorbed into his body. Once again, the competing systems of comfort and tension vied for dominance.

Taking the first garment that looked like it would fit; he draped it over his shoulders. The cloth washed against his body and, at the same time, seemed to float just off the surface of his skin. Even when he held perfectly still, the cloth moved slightly as if responding to the gentlest of currents in perfect rhythm with the fabrics still on the wall. Closing the garment with the small metal clasp attached to the shoulder, he made his way out. Seeing that the way to the right ended at about twenty feet into a wall, he wondered why the passage would offer a direction that led to a dead end. Cautiously, he made his way down the opposite passageway to the opening he saw in the distance.

The floor was the same substance that made up the walls. It was soft under his feet and gave just a little with each footfall. It did not escape Mark's attention that there was no seam where the wall met the floor, the ceiling, or the walls. It was as though the entire building had been carved from a single piece of soft tissue.

It was not a long corridor he stepped into, and it emptied after about twenty paces into an area that Mark could see was occupied—as he caught a glimpse of someone or something crossing in front of him. Not sensing immediate danger, but not knowing what to expect, he carefully made his way to the opening. Keeping close to the wall, he approached the doorway. This time he let his senses heighten and his heart rate jumped to almost double. He was stepping into somewhere that offered only questions, but no other direction was possible now that he had made his choice. Looking down, he saw the floor change to a surface of fine, almost white sand. The light coming from the outside was much brighter, and the backlighting effect it had from his position in the darker corridor made it difficult to see what was out there. He took a small breath, straightened up, and stepped out. His little hallway opened into a vast city!

From where he stood, he saw two and three story buildings covering most of the valley floor. Some joined to one another as apartments would on the surface; while others of various sizes were free standing Walls surrounded some, and others opened directly to the streets and pathways. The colors that comprised the walls and roofs were different shades of the most beautiful-greens and light-blues, soft pinkish-browns and blue-grays. Each color blended almost imperceptibly into the other. Here and there was a sharp orange or yellow, but all in combinations that he could only describe as peaceful. No caves or overhangs where the roofs met the walls and no arbitrary straight lines and corners. Each one was unique but complimented those around it. There were no panes of glass in the windows, and every surface of every building appeared new and fresh like a youthful skin. All this time he realized he was also listening to a constant sound. Water noises were everywhere. The gurgling of tumbling water and the wispy spray that water makes when it flows smoothly and quickly. He could even detect that deep sound that great bodies of water make when they glide like a large river or like currents in the sea.

He saw the source of all these water sounds. Everywhere he looked, there were channels and streams. Waterways of endless varieties laced together all the areas of the city. Some ran under the walkways, and some paths would turn into bridges that spanned the wider streams. Long unsupported viaducts carried the water sounds overhead, across roads, and over buildings and released their contents on the other side into shimmering waterfalls to be collected in large and small pools and then directed onward. He traced the walkways and paths of various sizes laid out in irregular fashion across the entire valley floor. Across every walkable surface there was warm and dustless sand. Except this was not the sand of the ocean floor where he had stood outside in the water a few moments ago. This white sand was dry and covered a more solid version of the substance that made up the walls. Then there was the light. The entire ceiling of the Dome and, to a lesser degree, even the walls of the buildings were emitting light. It was of a phosphorescent quality. It appeared to have a definite source but was distributed throughout all the structures and illuminated the entire city. That's what it was. It was a city!

It was then that Mark realized what else was here. He had been so focused on the spectacular shapes and beauty of all the structures that it had taken him a moment to register that there were people! Hundreds of them! Men, women of different ages, and children. All dressed in variations of the garment he had on. He stared at the vision. There before him was an entire civilization. Moving and flowing in and out of the buildings and up and down the various walkways and roads in a gentle current of color and grace.

He started to move, feeling that he was not in any real danger, and he stepped out into the city street. The feeling was similar to passing through the wall into the Dome. He was being drawn forward. The control he was used to having at his disposal was fading. In its place, his heart rate increased again, and the reports from his sight and smell and hearing intensified. It felt like his movements slowed slightly as everything else grew a little in size and pressed in on him. He was moving in the direction of a group of people who were gathered in a large open area about fifty yards ahead of him. Each person he passed, he looked at closely. They appeared much the same as he. Some made eye contact, some simply ignored him and continued on. The smell was there. Not the specific smell but the general sameness was all around him. He only now noticed it, and it no longer seemed a dangerous thing. He also knew that the man he had followed was not near as that specific trail faded from the time he left the entry room. He knew this smell...this *feeling,* and it comforted him.

The buildings had no regular style, consistent shape or method of construction as far as Mark could tell. Each was unique but all blended together in perfect harmony. Like the corridor he had just left, the edges where smooth and rounded; each surface seemed to melt into the next. What was it about these shapes? *That one. That building there.* He could not force himself to look away. The doorway into the structure held him in place like cement. In an instant, it was gone, blocked by a face and a pair of eyes—a pair of eyes that locked on him.

Although he kept walking, Mark held the stare and turned slightly as he continued.

Who...?

Another building! The shapes! That one! The one on the right with large window openings! Mark felt a little dizzy.

An older couple stopped in front of him and stared. He slowed his pace again and returned their gaze. They both smiled, but the man's look was stronger. The kind eyes asked a silent question, and the woman slipped her arm around the man's and started to direct him away. Mark felt he should know these people. As he passed, a bit unsteady on his feet, he heard the man whisper, "Ja-Lil?"

Mark tried to walk on, but his legs were unwilling to obey any longer, and he stopped as he heard the echo of "Ja-Lil" return to his ears from behind. Then several more "Ja-Lils" from different parts of the crowd.

Those buildings!

Those shapes!

Suddenly in front of him was the face of a much older man. His eyes were kind, and he had a small smile on his lips. The thinning white hair and skin creased around the eyes and mouth. The sloping shoulders and slender fingers that now touched the face. *That face!*

Mark knew that face! Now his ears could hear nothing but "Ja-Lil, Ja-Lil, Ja-Lil" from all around. The kind old face was gone.

Where?

Many new faces came towards him from all directions. The shapes, the buildings, and the faces were all moving and spinning in front of his eyes. The water plopped and chortled all around him. Mark tried to walk away, to get somewhere and clear his mind. His body was not obeying his thoughts, and his thoughts seemed not to obey his desires. He had to get away! He had to find a place to be alone and think inside this! He wanted the water around him. He wanted to feel the silence of its weight. His blood was racing in torrents through his body. He felt the sand hit the back of his head.

It did not hurt when he fell. Looking up at the glow of the Dome made him feel somehow peaceful. Faces started to block out the light. People were bending down over him. They started to move in a circle above him, although they remained exactly where they were. The spinning feeling intensified. "Ja-Lil", "Ja-Lil." More faces blocked the light. Now it was almost dark. He felt strangely safe and still strong and wanted to rise up. More faces. "Ja-Lil." Dark shapes drew even closer. The spinning was going to throw him out of the city, out of the Dome. It was so dark now. He wanted to stay, to get up. His fists dug into the sand. It was totally dark now. Black. "Ja-Lil", "Ja-Lil."

Then nothing.

"Ja-Lil."

"Ja-Lil."

From the nothing came the sound and the sound kept calling until it summoned the light. Light. A small speck of light and...

"Ja-Lil."

Mark was falling again, completely out of control, out of this ball of blackness. Down this black tunnel toward that growing dot of light. The tunnel grew wider and brightened, and the dot became the whole. There was light everywhere. A gray shape was in the center of *the everywhere* and getting larger. Then it stopped growing.

"Ja-Lil?"

The shape became a face. The face became a person. A woman. It was the woman he had seen in his mind that last night on the deck by the pool. He knew this woman!

"Ja-Lil, are you all right?"

Mark stared up at the beautiful face. That face! Framed by gold. White ribbons bound some of the hair, and the rest of the deep golden curls swept down past the ears to gather at the neck. Her skin was smooth and lightly tan-colored. The blue eyes had golden rays, sparkling out from large black centers and her lips, that held a small upturn at each end, were a light rose-color. Mark stared a moment longer. The memory was there again. He had seen that face and felt the ends of that beautiful hair touch his. He had felt the warm rush of her breath long ago. Her lips parted again, and once more the warm sound of her voice called to his past. It came up from its dark airless corner and into the light.

"Mother."

"Yes, son. Are you all right?" It felt like he had been cold for so long and with a few words the cold was over. Her voice wrapped around him like a warm blanket. He now knew two Marks. One had never left this place. The other Mark had missed her so much. Never thought he would see her again. Forgot her. He was home!

"I believe so. Yes."

Myo-O placed her hand on her son's shoulder, and that kept him from trying to sit up. Her touch called even more old friends into the day. He had been held, carried, and cared for by that touch. She placed her hands on his chest, then his ribs on both sides. Her fingers moved to his neck and cupped his head behind both ears. Her eyes were almost closed, and her touch warmed his skin. She opened her eyes and looked into his. Finally, she bent to him and pressed her cheek against his cheek and then to his forehead. Once again, she looked at him. She started to speak, but then stopped. Her smile took the place of words. The small moment lingered. Then, putting one hand on his, she rose.

"Rest a while longer, my son. There is someone else here to greet you." Mark felt the warmth of her hip move away. He almost called her back. He felt like a young child who wanted to be picked up and carried away, but he knew she would never leave him. She stepped away and, behind her, he saw another person standing in the doorway. As this new figure came into focus, his memory opened another door, locked for so many years. She was a young woman. She stood a bit shyly with her weight slightly on one foot. Her hands were in constant motion as they fidgeted with the long sleeves of the aqua and green dress draped over her body. The garment appeared to have a hundred layers and yet to be no thicker than one layer of fine silk. With every shift she made from one foot to the other, the gown moved and flowed like the most delicate feather-like fins of the most beautiful exotic fish. Banks of dark brown hair, almost black, surrounded her face. Thick and heavy, it fell to the neck of the dress like a dramatic seashore, a place where both waves and rocks meet and vie to be the most stunning.

The strong cheekbones were flushed with pink, which only made the lightness of her skin more striking. Wide and set like crushed gemstones beneath the long dark lashes, were the most gorgeous eyes he had ever known. He stared into those dark eyes, remembering every moment that they had known each other. Their childhood days in the city and out in the sea. Growing closer than friends as they matured into young adults. Their eventual understanding that they were never going to part and realizing the bond of love that fated them forever. He remembered those eyes closing so gently as his followed, and their lips touching for that first kiss. He found that he had no voice to say her name. He wanted to and tried several times, but his words went no farther than his heart. All he could do was reach his hand out to her without taking his eyes off her. It was enough. She immediately came to him, the dress pressed against her, outlining her beautiful form, and flowing behind her in a tropical wake with every move she made. The memory and the immediate became one. In the space of a heartbeat, he saw everything he had known so well. Her arms that had held him lifted as she came forward. The fine muscle of her body carried her in power and grace more like she was flying. Then she was there. He could feel the weight of her on his chest, her arms around his as though she was trying to keep him from floating off somewhere. He looked at the beautiful hair now, spilling over her shoulders. Everywhere he touched her, his skin rang with joy at the homecoming. From under the warm wrap of her arms and hands, he gently freed one arm and touched her face.

"Tei-La." The name came from the depths of his life. With that one word, he wanted to tell her that he was hers. He wanted her to know how he had missed her. Even when he remembered nothing of this world, it was her he had missed. It was her he wanted to return to. It was her he loved. With both of his hands, he gently brought her face to his and, once again, he was falling into those eyes and onto those lips. How long the moment lasted, he did not know. Its duration meant nothing—for it was everything. It was forever.

"Ja-Lil." His mother's voice softly parted their lives. "Stay in here for awhile longer, until you are sure of your completeness." She smiled at Mark and Tei-La as they looked to her. He felt, in her warm gaze, more than a welcome or simply a mother's care. He felt a relief or a letting go. But as he was about to say something she gently turned and left the room. Tei-La's eyes found him once more, and she slowly lifted her head and carefully studied him. He could not leave her eyes and only felt the softness of her hand as it started to trace the contours of his face. Then another thing he had missed so much.

"Welcome home, Ja-Lil."

Her voice had not changed at all. Its richness washed through him and cleared away the last blurred corner of his vision. She studied him silently.

"You have been away long."

Long! Now he knew what she saw. He instantly viewed himself through her eyes. What she saw was a man—not a young man. Not the man who had left this beautiful woman but a different man. A man who had been gone...long.

People on the surface, he realized, aged faster.

"I was found on a shoreline after a storm. I had no memory or past to give the ones who cared for me. Their care and kindness protected me all this time until I could find my way here." He wanted to explain everything to her right now, but the violence that led him home had to be explained to himself before anyone else could know of it. Somewhere in the city was a man who wanted him dead and would try again. He must, for the time being, keep his secret. "I returned to the sea for my strength, but I lived with them on the surface. What you see is from my time there."

He had seen it a few times in the Domed city when he had been younger. Once he and Tei-La, holding hands, watched as the citizens of the city had a celebration for the return of an old man who was being taken to the sea because his life span was about to end. A younger man, who was to transfer his life-thought to the Tanta, was taking him out. Later, his father explained to them that the old man was actually the younger man's son. Mark remembered how they had both laughed. In fact, he smiled now as he pictured the two of them fighting to control their giggling, almost succeeding and then falling over each other as they remembered the young man carrying the little white-haired man to the outflow. Then the giggles stopped—not because of a reprimand but with the explanation. Realization had a sobering effect. The most profound thing becoming clear filled them with appreciation.

"It is simple enough," his father had said. And it was.

"You become one with your home, wherever that is. Ro-Hal's son left the city long ago. He lived on the surface until he felt his life had raced to its ending. He returned because he wanted his life-thought to reside with his father's line."

Mark's father could always make anything easy to understand. Mark had never once hesitated to bring any question or problem to him. Nor had anyone in the city. The king had time for the simple or complex and always left the questioner feeling proud for having asked. His father let him attend access times when, according to ancient city traditions, their home became the citizens' chamber. During that time, hundreds could come to ask for healing or guidance or to ask the king to confer assurance for their marriages. In fact, it was at a later access time when he and Te-La stood in the long line and eventually asked him to confer his blessing upon them. After that, as with all couples in the city, their official courtship began.

He remembered pages and pages of times with his father, each page a spotlight of memory leading to the next, until...

"Tei-La, where is my father? I must go to him. I have to explain and apologize for my absence!" The abruptness of his move caused her to straighten, and she sat there looking into his face. Mark felt a bit embarrassed for forgetting his father. He had always felt an almost mystic bond with him. From the time he could trace his memory, they had been able to think outside each other's thoughts. Not only when in each other's company but even when separated by vast distances. They were the only two of their kind he had ever heard of who could water-talk when they were in the city or on the rare occasions when they went to the surface together. Many times, his mother would come to him to ask where the king was or to relay some word of hers to him. He would simply make his mind become the mind of his father. That was the only way he could explain it when his mother once asked how he did it. With his mind set, the next thing he would hear would be his father's voice saying, "Yes?"

It was from his father, both by strict lessons and by example, that he had learned so many of the abilities he now possessed. The line of knowledge that had been severed was once again intact. What he knew now, it was as if it had never been forgotten. This drew his thoughts to the surface. These were the abilities that Elizabeth and the others at the lab had studied for so long and called gifts. He had been the student and his father the teacher. He had been taught to read his own body and regulate all of its functions. From his major organs to the cells of his skin. Before he left that last time to the sea he had, for the first time, been allowed to sit with his father on the day of the public chamber and read the health signs of those who came for wellness. Mark never failed to appreciate the sense of safety and wellbeing everyone—especially he—had always felt from his father's presence.

Mark let his eyes leave Tei-La. A voice from deep in his mind called for him to focus. He tried to place the feeling he had right now. He knew he must think inside this strange feeling. Then he realized. There was no feeling. That was what was strange. There was no place he could direct his mind to find the presence of his father.

"Tei-La, where is the king?" He dropped his legs over the side of the bed and was now sitting up. His head was clear and he knew his body was complete. He took her by the shoulders as he stood and asked again. "Where is my father?"

"You must speak to the queen." That was all she said. "The queen."

Tei-La had never referred to his mother by title since she'd been with him. When anyone in the city made reference to his mother or father, it was always the *king* and the *queen* as a sign of their respect. Tei-La was, however, to be his bride and therefore the daughter of his mother and father. From the time of their consent, she had called them by their names or *mother* and *father*.

He looked at her. Nothing he saw gave him a clue. She stood calm and straight, her gaze direct and her voice pure. He touched his right palm softly to her cheek and left her there.

Each room he entered was familiar, and as his memory sharpened, he knew where he was going and where he would find his mother. He crossed the reception room that stood across the hall from the resting room, took the stairs two at a time to the second level of the house. He went down the long hall on the right, directly to the room of his mother and father. The door was open and she was there. The naturalness of her beauty had always amazed him and filled him with pride. She sat on a wall bench with a small box on her lap. She had increased the light from the small protuberance that rose from the section of wall by her head, and in the white-green glow she was deeply studying what was inside. She didn't look up when he entered.

"You cannot feel him, can you?"

"No." The rising feeling in him was most like the sensation he often had that allowed him to react to something just before it was about to happen. Some physical reaction was kept in check only by her. She looked up at him with such open love it seemed to actually enter his chest and calm him.

"Sit with me." She moved the small wrapped object that lay on the bench beside her. Carefully she put it in the small box and placed them on the bench to her left. She took his hand in hers. "Con-Or, the One Who Knows, Of the Trilogy, the Keeper." He had never heard his mother say the quality titles of his father before. At functions of importance, the Elders would address him that way, or when the king would recite the oath of convergence upon moving the city he would repeat his quality names. This was the first time she had used these words when talking to him. Then she continued. "Your father, my husband, is no more."

The two Marks again materialized in his mind. The Mark of the surface had learned to feel a sense of loss that came with another's death. He had witnessed the grief experienced by his friends at the lab. He understood the importance of it because of them. Now he was, once again, the Mark of this city. Ja-Lil knew of the life-thought, of the natural sequence of birth and leaving. He knew of the long duration of his people and how natural the leaving was.

"It was not that long, son, after you had left for your last tour of observance and were overdue to return. Your father felt, even though you were not back, that you were still complete and told the Elders so. I did not suspect he was less than well. His life span ended in the night while we slept." She stopped for a minute and, when she continued, her voice was no more than a whisper. "I felt him enter my dream and kiss me gently." She sat quite still as if reliving that last embrace. "When I woke in the morning, he lay there beside me without life. That kiss was his goodbye." Her eyes searched Mark's face. "To both of us." She picked up the box and took out several small objects he recognized as being given to him by his father. She randomly chose one and held it in the palm of her right hand. It was a large red ruby. It was not cut and fashioned as gems were by Those on the Surface. It was irregular in shape but polished so brightly it appeared to emit its own light. "Your father found it in a small basin of rock in the tidal basin at the mouth of a river. Centuries of water and sand and motion created it. He told me that every time it was in my hand that I was holding his heart." There was no pain when she spoke, but Mark could feel the loving connection she still had for his father. "When I said goodbye to him, I summoned Man-Den so he could announce it to the city then prepare the body for enclosing. Since you had not returned, Man-Den took the life-thought of the king and delivered it to Nari- Tanta."

Placing the ruby in the cloth pouch and pulling the slender drawstrings to close it, she exchanged it for a piece of amber with a small insect in the center. Mark had seen this many times when he was young. His father had given it to his wife as a "piece of the surface of life." Often, he had invited her to accompany him during the times he briefly walked the lands for the placement of the sighting stones. Every time she would refuse, saying she had no desire. She would laugh and tell the king, "I would rather stay and be the magnet that draws you back." She held the clear brown object up to better see the light through it. The wings of the strange captive seemed ready to take flight. She spoke to Mark.

"The city had never been without One Who Knows so I sat in council with the six Elders and it was decided to wait on the appointment of the new leader. As your father had never felt you were gone, they decided to have the decision be mine. After fifteen solar cycles, I felt it was no longer right for the city to be without a king even if it meant our line would end. The people needed a center. I could feel them seeking and their desires called for someone. Man-Den had even suggested I consider breaking with the tradition of not remarrying in order that we at least have an heir for the city that would come from the wife of the king.

"As much as it bore the test of some logic, when I considered the emotions of the people, it was not a choice for me. The love that exists between your father and myself lives. We, none of us, could abandon another and be a true citizen. Apart from having no desire for another, it is not only the life-thought, but in the case of the king's line, the very blood itself that carries the vital information of our people. The blood is the key to the future of the city. Simply an heir was not the issue. If the line was not to continue, all that was needed was good honest management. I felt the citizens could best decide whom to lead and how. Man-Den, who had administered the Right and Left for your father, supported my wishes, and it was decided for the first time that the people would choose their center. Man-Den was beside me constantly and without him, the particulars of this time since the king's death would have been most difficult. We had set the date of the choosing for the beginning of the new solar cycle and preparations were made." She looked deep into Mark's eyes, and he felt so much of his father's presence in her. They were truly one, a single entity, as the binding ceremony said husband and wife should be. "I see now I needed more of your father's confidence and should have waited. It was as if you were summoned to take your rightful place, Ja-Lil. The next king of the city and the next of your father's line."

The time Mark had spent on the surface and what he had learned had expanded his view of the world. He had also learned that he had a responsibility to do what he could for the betterment of that world. That was all before he had returned to the city. With pieces of his memory constantly being opened, he tried to balance the new information with the growing awareness of his place in this larger equation. The most important thing was something he had never considered before. The city without a king. Not just any king or center but a king of the line.

"Mother, I have no knowledge of what it is to be king. Father never spoke to me about the qualities and duties needed to rule the city."

"My son, all the time you were with your father, all of your life, was preparation for it."

Now Mark realized the carefree times he remembered in the city, the preferential treatment he received from the citizens as the king's son, and his father's loving attention was the training for this moment. Everyone had hoped, if they even thought about it at all, that this moment would not occur for a long, long time.

Knowing he could never completely sever his connection with the surface, he also knew there was no other option but to remain here. He thought about the message he had left for Elizabeth, but he spoke to his mother.

"What do I do?"

CHAPTER SIX

Mark spent the rest of the day with his mother. They spoke mainly of the history of the city and of his father's line. Much he knew and more he remembered as soon as she gave it words. He was now the fifth in line since the placement of The Three. Of Those Who Walk and Those In The Air, he only knew the legends and she told him little. In his lifetime, and indeed the time of his father's father, there had been no contact with the other two civilizations. All knew the story of the passing of Those On The Land, but folktales and sagas were repeated and he was sure exaggerated about Those of the Air. They flew, they could vanish from sight, and they required no sacred treasures to perform great feats. He asked his mother simply for the truth of their history.

"With your father's life-thought, that will come," was all she said. He was told of the six Elders, the Sadhannas, who kept the life of the city. They kept a rotation of vigilance in their Kivs in the tower and from there all actions of the Dome were managed. The living Dome accepted this. The growth of the structures and all regulations of the environment that made life possible on the inside happened only through the cooperation of the Elder and the Dome. Depending on what was needed and how difficult it would be, from one to six Elders may have to enter the Kivs. The seventh Kiv was only used by the king and only on two occasions. First, after his anointing to establish his place in the Dome, and second to direct the moving of the city, which had only been done three times before. He remembered the excitement at the lab last year when news of the discovery of the "the largest living organism on earth" was made in the state of Oregon. A fungus-type growth that covered over two thousand acres was determined, by genetic testing, to be one large entity. When he saw now how that growth would be dwarfed in size and complexity by this city and Dome of living tissue, he smiled.

"Mother, there are still many dark areas in my mind." Mark was confident in his ability to learn anything that was taught to him. It was the things that could not be taught but would come from memory or instinct that caused him to continue. There also remained the things he knew but could tell no one yet.

"Ja-Lil." She reminded him sometimes of his father when she was serious as she was now. "Everything will come to you as it does to everyone, in pieces and in time. Much you will learn from the Dome while you are in the king's Kiv, but most will be yours with the life-thought of your father given by the Nari-Tanta." Again, the book of his memory was opened. When the dying young man had used the word Tanta, Mark only thought it a strange babble of his weakening mind, but to hear his mother mention the Nari-Tanta so much of their greatness came back to him. When he told her that small pieces of the particular history were still faded, she refreshed him on all the functions of the Tantas. He had recalled that they received the life-thoughts of all from the city. He had forgotten that any life-thoughts to enter the sea could be taken to them. The history of Those on the Surface that had died in the ocean rested in the Tanta if a citizen carried it there. The Tantas were a complete library of living souls.

"It is an outflow, my son. The life-history of a person resides in the body for some time once the life has left." His mother reached for his right hand, turned it palm up, and rested it in hers. "Here are the lines of the three." She traced the three creases in his palm that formed a triangle. "If you make the connection, you can receive the flow. You do not know what they knew. You will not see what they saw. And you cannot be what they were because you are not of their line. But you can hold them. What they were will reside in you until taken by the Tanta."

She quickly demonstrated how to connect by touching her thumb to his lips and placing it on his forehead in the small indentation of the skull between his eyebrows. "The flow will emerge from this spot, the Nuham, and you will draw it into yourself." While she was talking, she placed the triangle spot on her own right hand to Mark's forehead. "It is our greatest act of compassion, Ja-Lil, for it continues life from the past to the future."

He wondered how he could have remembered nothing of how to take a life-thought, but now recognized the actions of the larger man when the wounded one brushed his hand away. He briefly considered whether it was the right time to tell, at least, the Queen about the strange violent man who was a citizen. He was sure she would be able to identify him. But then what? If the two had not acted alone then there were others who wanted him dead. Her knowledge would put her in danger too. He must wait and watch alone.

The evening continued that way until it was time for sleep. Mark had never seen his mother as he saw her now. She seemed to radiate a light of her own as volumes of history passed from her to him. She would shift from a detailed account of some public matter and just how the king had handled the situation, to picking up an object from the box and telling stories of herself and his father. There was so much he hadn't known. Things he was sure if he had been there all along and if his father had not died, he would have eventually known. He felt it was not just knowledge he was receiving but something of his father and the joy of their relationship.

At one point, she said softly to him, "Without his flow, I give you his life as I knew it." All she had been with the king was being given to him, with love. As she looked at him one last time before retiring for the night, he thought she seemed tired and, at the same time, ageless and young. She picked up the box and gently closed the lid. Standing, she looked down at her son and said, "I love you." Holding the box to her chest, she bent and kissed his head and walked into the next room.

The following morning, as the Dome increased the output of greenish-white light, Mark rose and prepared to meet with Man-Den at his home. Tei-La had come to guide him. It was almost like seeing her for the first time. Her beauty startled him, and the softness of her kiss left a feeling on his lips that lasted well into their walk. They walked quietly for awhile and she would softly squeeze his hand every now and then.

"You are all right about your father, Ja-Lil?" They stopped at the waterfall in the center of the city. The Dome had created a tower of about one hundred feet. Seawater gushed out from the top and was caught by various sized outcroppings along the sides. From these gathering places, there were aqueducts that carried the water downward. This multilevel cascade was the source of a network of streams and brooks that meandered through the entire city and also fed into many of the houses and meeting places.

"My father was too young for his life to have ended. If I had been here, I could have checked him for completeness. Mother should not have to spend the rest of her time alone."

They continued now to a large pool, around which a few other people were seated and talking. Tei-La sat near the edge of the water.

"I know she does not feel alone, Ja-Lil." The softness of her response made him stop and sit beside her. She looked at her hands that were resting in her lap. He sat silently waiting.

"She and your father were one when he was alive, and they are still one now. More in them than almost anyone else in the city, I saw how complete love can be." She turned to face him. "I am sure she is still completely happy now. Their life together is what she has...always. Once you have that, nothing else matters. Not distance. Not even time."

He wanted to say something to her, but he could not find the words to match his feelings. On the surface, he had searched for ways to express his heart and who he was. Each attempt gave him a degree of satisfaction. Sitting next to her now, feeling her leg against his, the beauty of every poem he had read seemed shallow. The words he had written faded as they became smaller and smaller. He searched his heart only to find the feelings intense but mute. At that moment, she got to her feet.

"Ja-Lil, it is late and Man-Den will be waiting." With the moment broken, she kissed him quickly and stepped back. Behind her, he saw the eyes of many citizens watching them. In fact, wherever he looked people were observing them. He realized that from the moment they stepped from his house, heads turned slightly or people would hesitate in their walking and whisper to each other as their eyes followed the path he and Tei-La were taking. When he first noticed, he thought people were looking past him at something else so he paid no attention to it. He had never known anything but complete anonymity. Feeling it disappear, he longed for the freedom it had given. He felt self-conscious. He wanted to return the kiss before he left but did not want others to bear witness to his every move. They both were still for a moment before Tei-La smiled and repeated, "Go."

He moved off quickly, away from the city center to the wide avenue that led to the Elder's lodgings and behind that to Man-Den's home. The way was clear to him as if he had never forgotten it. Alone to think while he walked, his thoughts returned to the man who tried to kill him. He could think of no plan other than to wait for his next move. His mother or Tei-La would have warned him of any danger so they must have been unaware of it. To ask anyone else might be to ask the very one he could not trust.

Every step seemed to be greeted with a smile or a nod of the head. At one point, he thought he saw the kind eyes of the old man, but they were gone in a crowd of eyes staring at him. *Will they ever get used to me?* He tried but could not remember this phenomenon occurring when he had walked the city with his father so long ago. He actually felt this might be one of the hardest things to overcome if he truly took his place in the city and became its king.

"If?" he stopped suddenly at that thought. "If?" After the moments last night with his mother, he had never considered another course but to fulfill the function of heir to the king. But just this moment, without planning the thought, he considered ...if. *There is no if. I am my father and his line is mine."* Memories of the surface and the friends he'd left there had caused the *if,* but he knew what he would do.

In another minute, he stood before the house of Man-Dan, the Minister of the Right and Left. The large double doors were open. According to city custom, the doors of all the Elders remained open as a sign of their being in service to the people. Mark had only seen this door closed once, when his father and Man-Den had gone to the sea together and Roi-Den and his aunt lived with the queen for the two months they were gone. The Dome, with no one living there, merely sealed the house until they returned.

Mark climbed the stairs and passed under the relief emblem of the House of Man-Den. As he stepped into the waiting area of the house, he recognized immediately the blonde woman as she approached him with her arms wide in greeting.

He barely had time to drop his head and say, "I respect you, Len-Wei, sister of my mother," before she held him tightly to her.

"Ja-Lil, we have missed you. The thought of you not returning was a dark time for the city and our family. And how many times have I told you not to be so formal with me?" Pulling away she continued, "I am not my husband." When she leaned away and looked at him, he could see in her eyes what he had seen in others.

"Yes, Len-Wei, my years on the surface have passed the time for my body more quickly."

"I can see your father in every line of your face, and it makes me glad in my heart."

"You and Man-Den are well?"

"Thank you, yes, but Roi-Den was most troubled by your absence."

Roi-Den! Like a blast of sound, the name came to his ears and with it a complete and wholly formed history. His best friend in the city. The one he had grown with and schooled with. He was amazed that so large a part of his life could have been omitted when he was remembering so much.

"Where is he? Is he well?"

"He is scheduled to return from travel in a few days. I have sent someone to prepare him for the shock of your return."

"I know how you think, Len-Wei, if you send a messenger it will speed his return home to you, true?"

Her smile was her answer as she walked Mark to the other end of the greeting room and said, "Man-Den is in his chambers. Please, go in."

Mark walked through the rooms he had played in so often and felt strange to be here as the king. Or at least as the soon-to-be king. He turned the corner and stepped into Man-Den's main room. As he entered, he saw the back of a man as he was leaving from a door at the other end of the chamber. The large man at the table spun around quickly.

"Please do..." The voice, which had been loud and hard, stopped dead. Man-Den stood there motionless staring at Mark. Though Mark had always considered his own father to be a big man, and, most likely, the memory of him made him even larger, the man staring at him now was every bit as big as the king and even thicker in body and muscle. The dark yellow hair had not a strand of gray, and the thick features of the face were still full and without many lines. The face still commanded respect and a little fear. The piercing gray eyes, with their brows of almost black, widened and then blinked several times as though some small speck of something had flown into them. His hands hung limply at his sides, and Mark could detect the beat of his heart from the large veins. For a moment, he thought the big man might drop to the chair that was directly behind him.

Mark nodded his head. "Minister of the Right and Left, I respect you." Since the minister had not responded, Mark stepped to him. "I understand how I appear to you. It seems everyone needs a little time to adjust to it."

"Ja-Lil." A large smile preceded his embrace as well. Reaching forward, Man-Den put both arms around Mark.

Mark could feel the hardness of the big man's arms and chest. "The resemblance to your father is wonderful." He then put both hands on Mark's shoulders and, with a little show of effort, he was almost lifted off his feet. Mark could not remember his uncle ever being this physical with him before. "Welcome back to the city! Please sit down. We have many things to discuss. Some will bring joy, and the others we we'll make the best of."

Over the next few hours, Mark listened as Man-Den told him of being summoned by his mother and his care of the king. He arrived at the house just minutes behind the returning messenger to find the king as Myo-O had.

"I could find no face of pain or discomfort, Ja-Lil. Whatever had failed in him, left him at peace."

He then went on to describe in detail preparing the king for enclosure. The ceremony that had been done for every passing king of the city was followed to the letter. The Elders had carried the body to the room before the chamber of treasures. There, Man-Den had removed the garments the king had worn when he died and laid them out for Ja-Lil's return. The line of kings was continued not only by blood but also by action. Mark would later put on the very clothes and be the next king, just as one second leads to another.

Man-Den then washed the body and wrapped it in the ancient royal cloth, and then the Elders were summoned to witness Man-Den's taking of the king's life-thought. Following that, they removed the body to the chamber of kings where it would forever rest. That completed the final ceremony for Con-Or fourth king of the city. He would now stay wrapped in the yards and yards of almost transparent cloth in the honeycomb chamber until the convergence.

Mark had gone with his father one time into the chamber. The king had taken him there after the celebration for the last moving of the city.

"It is one of the few times I see value in looking to the past," his father had said as the Dome opened the wall to the chamber. The air was different in that room, he remembered. It was cool and had a scented aroma. Not at all what he had expected. They walked to the far wall where he could see the round tube-like individual chambers. There were four of them in a line and each ended in a curved solid finish. Starting from the right-most chamber, which had no cover on the end and was empty, the king motioned to it, saying, "Here is where Con-Or will rest, the One Who Knows, Your Father." He then looked at his son and, with a smile, finished, "But not for some time."

He then stepped to the next tube, and when he laid his hand on the curved end for only a moment, a line appeared. The cone drew back and Mark saw for the first time the face of his grandfather. And he could *see* the face. The cloth wrapping bound the body securely but was of such a fine material that the body seemed covered by glass. "Here lies Dar-Soc, my father." Mark could see many of his father's features in the wrapped face. The hair, although mostly white, was thick and fell in waves much like the king's. One by one, the Dome opened the ends of the remaining chambers as his father introduced him to his line.

"Poi-Dan."

"Draa-Pic."

"When I am at last laid here," his father said, and stepped to the center of the room, "the Dome will create another chamber to await you, my son." It was only after being on the surface that Mark now appreciated the feelings of the living for the dead in the city. Here each person celebrated their life and the lives of all others. Each day and each encounter cleared all debts of gratitude and left no regrets for the next. Therefore, when a citizen died, there was nothing but the celebrated memory of the value they had created while alive. The knowledge that their life-thought continued uninterrupted left no need for the feelings of loss or sorrow.

Man-Den ended his story with the last of his responsibilities. "I then entered the meditation-of-oceans for your father's repose and after took my friend's life-thought to the Nari-Tanta."

Man-Den then fell silent. He appeared to Mark to be exhausted after reliving the story. He sat quietly starring at his hands before him on the table. Mark rose and went to him.

"You were a good friend to my father. I trust you will honor me by continuing as my friend and councilor."

The minister sighed and rose to face him. Even now, he stood taller than Mark by at least three inches. Mark still felt the awe he had experienced as a child for this man. There was still respect for this person his own father had loved so much.

"The age of the surface is on your face, Ja-Lil, but it is the face of your father. You are the line and you are the king. I only hope to serve you as I did him and your mother."

He walked Mark back through the house and was joined by his wife as they reached the front entrance. She slid her arm through her husband's and put her small hand on his wrist, which remained motionless at his side.

"For the next two days you have much to do in preparation. In the king's chamber is the book I spoke of. Follow it and you will be ready." Man-Den stared for a long time at the city's new king. As his eyes made their way up and down, Mark thought how strange it must feel for the man to be looking at the son and seeing the father. The minister regained his bearings and continued clearly, "I will then take you through the final anointing, and we will go to the Kivs."

Mark left and felt, as he walked through the city to his home, that his life was now being led by his father. But this had always been so even on the surface. He had always felt responsible for the oceans and all they contained, but now that included the city.

CHAPTER SEVEN

After reporting to the minister, Mark went to the king's chamber and read completely the ancient book that detailed the different ceremonies he would follow for the next two days before becoming the king of the city. That night, still remembering the meeting with the minister, his mother and he ate outside in the garden. The gentle sound of the water drifted up from a channel that ran along the back wall, under it, and into the large stream in the avenue beyond. Vines and fine strands of sea kelp grew in profusion from the sandy floor. Several large sea fans occupied the corners of the garden, their rough, rounded sections of yellow and purple reflecting the night-light that seemed to float down from the Dome like a glowing mist. A canopy of sea grass and bell kelp laced the arbor they sat under. Hundreds of red-ball anemones clung to the strands with their tentacles extended, each tip displaying its little ball of orange and red. Here and there, throughout the enclosed patio auger, snails inched along in their twisted shells, and sea urchins and sand dollars comfortably sat in their tiny sand dunes. Just under a cluster of small-coiled garlands of white whelks, a large reddish-brown fanworm waved its eight-inch feather-like gills, absorbing life from a sea current, which came, moisture free, from the Dome.

They talked for several hours under the faint evening glow of the Dome. They remembered for each other everything they could of her husband, his father. She later left him at the door of his room with a gentle kiss.

"I feel he is happy you are here to guide the city, Ja-Lil."
She gracefully walked down the corridor to her rooms. The way
she moved was more like floating. The way sleek boats move
on glassy-smooth water. He heard, just before she disappeared
through the door, "Everything is complete now. Everything will
continue."

Mark lay for a long time on his bed but could not sleep
yet so he rose and went out into the city. The glow was almost
completely faded now and only the few maintenance walkers
were on the street, making note of where re-growth was needed
on the waterways and paths. Tomorrow this information would
be passed on to one of the Elders, who would direct the Dome's
action. One passed him as he walked down the great avenue,
nodded to him with a "Sir", and then he was alone.

He felt good in the quiet. He mentally counted the hours
since he had last been in the water. He was going on his second
day. No feelings of weakness. He was actually stronger than be
had been in a long time.

He was going no particular direction, but just walking where
his feet led him. He still could not figure out why someone in the
city had hunted him down and tried to kill him. He did not want
to inquire about the identity of the man who died out there in the
sea. Everything would have to work backwards from when he found
the killer. He was going to, however, eventually find his family and
deliver the young man's final words. It seemed all he could do, for
the time being, was move forward until new circumstances would
dictate his actions. So far, he had encountered only friendly souls
here in the city. It seemed there had never been any crime or
conflict, and secrets were nonexistent.

As he passed from the grand avenue to a side street, the buildings on both sides and the many over-walkways shaded even the faint light from the Dome.

The quiet was suddenly occupied by a new sound other than his own soft footsteps. Mark stopped to listen but was greeted only with the echo of the distant waterway that ran along the grand avenue. After turning full circle and finding he could see nothing out of the ordinary, he continued on. A few more blocks into the narrow lane, he again thought he heard something behind him. It was faint and soft but definitely the regular compression of sand. Rather than stop again, he felt that if someone was following him, he would wait until they got closer before acting. He dropped his height by bending his legs a little. By shuffling each step, he softened his footfalls and continued on. Now he could clearly hear someone. Slowly they were making ground. He could tell that it was only one person and judged by the lightness of the footsteps that it was not the large man who had attacked him before. He calculated by the person's walking that he would soon be able to turn and grab him. But then he heard,

"*Ishnan abatta yddap ama ama.*"

These words came from such a secret part of what he now had as his memory, he almost spun around to confront this ghost. But words rather than actions came from him by instinct over which he had no control.

"*Klac torri belhorra ri tenso dan.*" These words! *Their* words! Their most...

"*Mil enso narama nylarc atui.*" The ghost behind him recited it perfectly and then said, "That is all I know, the six lines he said there were."

Mark turned. He knew the voice was not correct, but only he and his father knew this chant. It was theirs and no one else's. His father had taught it to him out in the ocean to avoid the "accidental ear" that may be in the city. Over and over, he had said this was to be their bond, their secret. Mark had kept it so deep inside his life it seemed to him to be his very heart. And now someone had stolen his treasure. He found himself facing an old man of small stature, an old man who was looking up at him. With those eyes!

"You are the one I saw when I entered the city. I can remember you from before, but I do not know why. How do you know what was only between my father and me?"

"May name is To-Bay. I am your father's only friend."

"Then you lie because everyone in the city was my father's friend."

"Your father told me often, "Believe in everyone. Trust no one." The old man smiled gently and gestured for Mark to follow him out from under the walkway where they were standing. In a low whisper, the old man said, "Open areas are the safest." He then walked into the wide circle that joined six small streets. He sat on a bench in the center. "The king taught me only the first three lines of your poem. He told me of your times together when you learned it, and that it was the only way I could make sure it was safe for me to make myself known to you." He paused a minute, and then seemed to look deeper into Mark's eyes. "I am your father's only friend, and the keeper of the secrets."

From the moment he had stepped through the wall and into the Dome, Mark had only encountered people he knew to be honest and of good heart. All seemed open and appeared to have no secrets. Now this old man was talking in riddles and was wary of everyone. Mark wanted not to trust him, but he did value his own instincts, and they were telling him it was okay. And he knew their poem!

"You must tell me how you know the poem and why my father taught it to you."

"Please, sit down for it will take some time."

Mark joined him on the bench, aware that no one, if they talked quietly, would be able to hear a word.

"I don't know why the king chose me," To-Bay started. "I had seen him as we all did in the city over the years, and twice I had gone to the people's chambers for wellness. If I passed him in the street, I would nod, as is the custom, but we never spoke.

It was the festival of the deep moon many years ago. The Elders were on the platform with the king. In fact, you were there too in your mother's arms, as you had not yet gained your feet. The king had just spoken, and Man-Dan was reading from the book of ancients. I was deep in the crowd listening when more and more I felt my attention leaving the voice of Man-Den. I chided myself for my laziness and tried to concentrate on the ceremony. I looked at Man-Den and saw his lips moving, but only heard the drone of his voice. I happened to glance at the king and saw he was looking directly at me. Our eyes locked, each upon the other, and I could not pull my gaze away. The king just kept his kindly connection with me. Then the most incredible thing happened! His voice was in my mind. Not in my ears. I was not hearing him. It was in my mind! He said, 'To-Bay, do not be startled. It is indeed I talking to you. Following this celebration, I want you to meet me at the Elder's lodging. Tan-Ue will be in the Kiv, and all the others will be completing the ceremony in the sea. Tell no one and do not be seen.' I remember I could only stare at him, still not believing what was happening. Then he told me to nod my head if I understood, and I did. He then smiled slightly, nodded his own head, and turned away to follow the ceremony. He never looked at me again the entire afternoon. When it was over, everyone dispersed and I wandered the city trying to construct any reason this had happened. Finally, with no answer but ready to serve the king, I went to my house to wait for evening."

Mark sat next to To-Bay long into the night and heard the entire story. To-Bay had gone to the lodging. He quietly entered expecting to see the king waiting, but all was still. He walked around to the backs of the chairs where the Elders sat in council at the round table. In front of each place was the carved hollow that held the recoding gel. Each speaker placed the palm of their hand in the gel, and all they said was absorbed in the fluid. Anyone in the city could place their hand in a similar gel in front of the large meeting hall and read the history of what was said and seen. To-Bay waited.

"After a time, a voice said, 'Thank you, To-Bay my friend, for coming.' I spun around to see the king entering the room alone.

"It is not in your mind. This time I am speaking to you. Only those of my line can converse in the mind when not in the sea or at a long distance. I am sorry if it disturbed you."

"Why did you speak to me at all?"

"I must ask you to bear a great burden. For me and for the city." The king approached the little man, putting his hand on the thin sloping shoulder. The king then fell silent and just looked deep into the old man's eyes.

"It was the strangest feeling, Ja-Lil." To-Bay searched for the right words to explain. "I knew he saw all of my life at that moment. Everything. Good and bad. I, right then and there, wished I had been a better person. I just had a feeling there were parts of me that disappointed him. The things that I wasn't proud of.

"But then he smiled at me and said, 'I have looked inside your life, To-Bay, and could find no place that was not light. So I will now explain to you what no other living citizen but myself knows.'"

Everything To-Bay was telling Mark was true. He knew it! He could hear his father when To-Bay spoke of him, and he felt the king in every description. He sat and listened in the warm night, comforted by the regained presence of his father.

"To-Bay, I will tell you what all citizens are aware of but only as a vague legend. At the time of the first settlement, all three trilogies were together—the Air, the Land, and We of the Water. At the river mouth to the inland sea, we began our cities. There was much to do when they first were placed, and the three kings ruled as one. There was much communication between our peoples as we waited for those here to become teachable. They developed quite slowly and for that time, we traveled the seas and logged all those who walked upright. After a time, we decided to make ourselves known to the people around the inland sea in slight ways, in keeping with our training from the ancients."

"I thought our forefathers were the ancients! The beginning started with us." Mark could not help voicing what he and the entire city had always believed.

"I will tell you everything I was given by the king," To-Bay continued. "I can tell you nothing else. I sat in the lodging with the king most of the night and this is what I heard: 'we taught, protected, and nurtured until they began to use the gift of culture and society. For many years, the early people knew us mainly by our actions on their behalf and only on rare occasions by us interacting with them. They came to regard us first as spirits of the natural workings of their world. They gave us names. Some of them were gifted in many ways, and some of them we communicated with more openly. Sometimes they gave us powers and abilities that we did not possess, and they came to consider us gods. We continued to teach. When the people became many we, of the Trilogy, separated. That was when they moved the city for the first time. From the shore and into the deep water. It was there that we discovered the life form that became the Dome. Its final loyalty is to the line of kings. When the Dome eventually covered us, and we began the living city, we seldom ventured from the water. From then on, only the rare messenger would take stories from one of us to the other.

"'Those of the Air, after a time, left their visible forms and continued on only as the energy of the life-thought, although they maintain the capability of both. They have at times, and can at any time in the future, manifest. They will certainly all appear at the time of the convergence, but we have not spoken for two of my generations.

"'You are here, my friend, because of the path of Those on the Land. Because they could walk with the people and their differences were not apparent, they became the living teachers and Elders of the people. At the second generation of the king's line, something happened that we could only surmise. By whatever cause, the royal bloodline for Those of Land was cut off. The king died before an heir was conceived. The ceremonies and rituals of the ancients and the use of the treasures that had served the people became actions and ceremony only. They no longer had the ability to be effective and their powers lay dormant. Their purpose died with their king. Generation after generation continued and Those of the Land became one with the people. The rituals became more and more distorted, and eventually the people of that world had to be abandoned.'"

To-Bay came out of the reverie of his tale and spoke directly to Mark.

"Your father told me it was most important that you know the power of the treasures is carried only by the blood. Only by the blood."

"You are tiring, old man, we can continue at another time." Mark could tell the strain of caring for this information and now releasing it to him was exhausting To-Bay.

"The honor you father entrusted me with is not a burden, Ja-Lil." To-Bay went on with the tale of that night so many years ago. He told Mark as well as he could the uses of the treasures and their origination. He assured Mark, from his father, that the gift of speaking to the mind would come when he took his place in the city. In the midst of listing history, To-Bay stopped for a moment.

"The king kept on until he was confident I could repeat all he wanted to give to you, Ja-Lil, but at one point he seemed to be resisting or thinking about something else when he started to talk about the queen. It did not resemble the information he had been giving up to that time, and he never asked me to repeat it. It was almost as though he were talking to himself. I could not forget it, however, and so I repeat it to you."

Mark waited

"The king sat quietly for some time. I said nothing. He then started so softly I could barely hear his words.

"'I loved Myo-O from the time we were first aware of each other. I have always felt our oneness was a continuation from long before the time of the settlement. Here we are, living the love once again, but not remembering the one before. She is the strength the people cannot see. She nurtures the good in the city by drawing it out from the people. My son...our son is how she and all that is good in us can go on. Because of that, my heart is free and without cares or regret. I hope when the people see the three of us together, they can see the good in their future.'

"Then he stopped and looked at me as I listened and smiled before continuing the history of the city." The old man looked at Mark with a small smile. "Ja-Lil, I give you that as a gift from your father."

To-Bay then gave Mark a detailed explanation of the many processes of giving wellness and other functions the king could do by virtue of the blood. Turning to Mark, he shrugged his shoulders a little. "The map I can give you, but your father said the knowledge would come with the life-thought." Mark followed the gestures as To-Bay showed them. What had looked so random when he had watched his father, he realized were actually precise motions that were needed to be effective. He memorized the different spots on the head and body for the drawing of various areas of darkness and pain, and then he learned how to rid himself of the debris. He was amazed at how many things he now knew his father did every day without anyone being aware. This part of the schooling took almost the rest of the night. Mark knew the Dome would soon begin to brighten when To-Bay took a deep breath and slapped his hands to his thighs.

"And then, Ja-Lil, the king was done. He told me of the two other times the city was moved and ended the evening by charging me with my duty.

"'To-Bay,' the king said, "'if anything is ever to happen to me, I give you the life of my son and therefore the city. Watch him closely and, when you think him ready, teach him what I have told you. Each of the kings before me has had one such as you, and they have lived out their time in the city without ever being known. They never had to discharge their duty and the line has continued. If I die and he dies with me or is not complete, I charge you to use the goodness in your heart to find the most able in the city, man or woman, and teach them this. That is the best we can do.'

"After that, he repeated, 'the heart is the city. Tell him, To-Bay, to be confident because the heart is the city.' He then bowed to me and he left. For years after that, I was to see him in the city. Sometimes alone or at other times with your mother and you. He would acknowledge me as he would any other but nothing more. It was as if we had never had that meeting.

"One time, when you were in your thirteenth year, I was in the city center around midday when his voice once again clearly came into my head. I looked around to find where he was, but could not find him.

"'To-Bay, I am in my lodging. I am speaking to you for the last time.'"

He then taught me the three lines of the poem, saying it was the way you would trust me if I should ever contact you. He said to tell you that you would use the second three lines at a time in the future. His last words to me were, 'I trust the city to you, my friend.'"

The old man stared at the ground and then up at the Dome high over their heads. He sighed.

"It is over. I can do no more. It was a dark day when the king died and each day since I have been deeply sad."

"Death is natural, To-Bay. You sound more like Those on the Surface that do not understand."

"No, no, no." To-Bay looked at Mark. "You do not understand. Death is natural and even good, but the king died too soon." He stood up and started to shuffle away while he continued. "You have very full days ahead. Be very careful." By then he was at the edge of the circle and disappearing down the dark lane.

Mark went back to his home. Later in the morning, he was to meet Tei-La and spend the day in the sea.

TV GUIDE

®

30¢ Local Programs Dec. 3-9
¢ʰ

TV Writers Wrestle with
Their Consciences
Page 6

Patrick Duffy of
'Man from Atlantis'

As the Man from Atlantis, he's learned to talk underwater and outswim dolphins at 30,000 feet

By Dick Russell

Inside the huge saucer-shaped tank at MGM Studios, a swimmer descends through a porthole and begins his graceful glide through the waters. But this is no ordinary swimmer. He moves with hands at his sides, undulating forward in the manner of whales and dolphins. When he pauses, he brings his body upright; no bubbles escape his lips. His stomach and chest pulsate, as if he is breathing water into his lungs. Examine him more closely and you notice that his fingers are joined together with webs and his eyes are an otherworldly fluorescent green.

The swimmer is Patrick Duffy, 28-year-old star of the new NBC series, *Man from Atlantis*. Portraying the survivor of an ancient underwater civilization, he is known to the scientists of the "Foundation for Oceanic Research" as Mark Harris. Since washing ashore last spring in the first of four pilot films—and being revived by comely costar Belinda J. Montgomery (as Dr. Elizabeth Merrill)—he has now become the bane of villains bent on melting the ocean's icebergs or extracting its precious metals.

For Patrick Duffy, the role is not without occupational hazards. Consider his emergence for a lunch break one recent day on the *Atlantis* set. Whereas his character lives on a diet of kelp and plankton, the dark-haired, classically handsome Duffy is not so blessed. Sitting down to a hearty fare of pot roast and fruit salad, he reaches for his fork—and sends it crashing to the floor.

"Don't ever get webs and try to eat," he said, staring disdainfully at his hands. "I feel like my wife should be here to cut my meat."

The hands, designed by the same makeup man who created Spock's ears for *Star Trek*, are fashioned of latex. The webs are sculpted into a mold of Duffy's hands. For each day's shooting, five coats of rubbery latex are hand-painted over the mold, powdered and slowly worked off the mold onto Duffy's fingers as they dry. The process takes more than an hour every time. Which is why he lunches in his webs.

That's the painless part. As an Atlantean with supposed gill-like membranes in his chest cavity, Mark Harris can't survive much more than 12 hours on land without beginning to deteriorate. For Duffy, this meant learning to "talk" underwater and to swim like

It's a whale!
It's a fish!
It's
Patrick
Duffy!

Flipper. When you haven't even been in the water for five years, that's not the simplest of tasks.

"I didn't even own a bathing suit," Duffy was recalling, struggling all the while with his lunch. "I had to do the audition in my underwear."

But he wasn't a complete stranger to the sea. In 1965, while still in high school, he had taken lessons from his older sister and become a certified scuba diver off Puget Sound, Wash. To become the Man from Atlantis, though, he needed more specialized lessons—this time, from veteran stuntman Paul Stader—on how to swim the way a good Atlantean should. The desired underwater stroke, which Patrick describes as "an undulation from head to toe," had rarely been attempted by anything but a marine mammal.

"In a whale or a dolphin, the backbone runs continuously right to the tail," explains Duffy. "In a human being, it stops at the pelvis. So it's tiring, especially in the base of your back, and really not too good for you to swim that way. It's not painful; you just know you've been doing it after a while."

For sheer speed underwater, though, Duffy calls the strange wiggling motion "the only way to travel." Under →

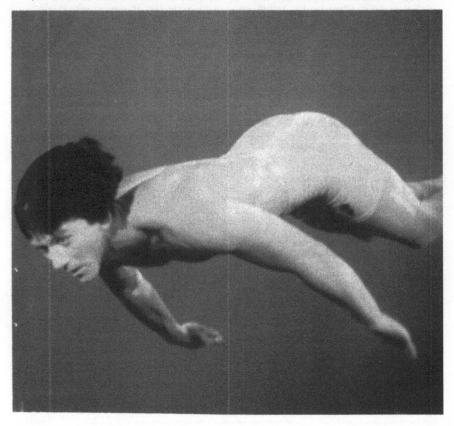

continued

Stader's coaching, he managed to master it within minutes. Next order of business was learning to breathe and "talk" as a comfortably submerged Atlantean. "Everyone told me it couldn't be done," says the show's executive producer Herb Solow. "You couldn't 'talk' in water. Paul Stader said it could work, with some training. But none of us thought it could be done to the extent Patrick has. We all felt he might learn to say hello, but he says whole sentences down there."

Duffy doesn't actually talk underwater. In a bizarre kind of dubbing process, he mouths the words he'll say later. Those words are then given a watery echo effect by the technicians at the mixing controls.

"It's a weird feeling," says Duffy. "When most people hold their breath, their cheeks puff out and their eyes squint. I have to keep my eyes open, put water up into my nose and mouth, and talk. What I do is hyperventilate,

32

which saturates my lungs with oxygen, and then I exhale, so I have a negative buoyancy and can stay down there. You inhale just enough water to go up into your nose and sinuses, so that no air bubbles come out. Then you stop the air in your throat, rather than your mouth, so you can open your mouth and keep taking water in and out. This makes it look like you're breathing."

The most grueling ordeal of all has been Duffy's adaptation to his new eyes. On land, Mark Harris wore sunglasses at first to protect his light-sensitive vision (a practice since discontinued). At ocean depths, his catlike eyes allow him to see in almost total darkness. For this, Duffy's own hazel eyes must transform to a deep fluorescent green. It's accomplished by wearing a pair of painted scleral contact lenses that fit under the lids and cover the whole exposed portion of the eye—a duty described by the show's lead-

TV GUIDE DECEMBER 3, 1977

ing villain Victor Buono (Mr. Schubert) as "acting with golf balls stuck in your head." The lenses are about the size of half dollars.

As an Atlantean, Duffy must also keep all body hair constantly shaved off his arms, hands, chest and legs. Using a razor, he was doing it twice a week ("I took the longest showers you ever saw; I'm probably solely responsible for the water shortage in Los Angeles"). Now he's switched to electric clippers.

The question is, when the Man from Atlantis's 13-episode contract with NBC comes up for renewal, will Patrick Duffy's alien adaptability have proved worth the struggle? Science fiction, despite the fourth Atlantis pilot's No. 1 rating in the weekly Nielsens, has never fared exceptionally well on TV. Nevertheless, Atlantis's Herb Solow, once part of the production team on Star Trek and Mission: Impossible, is convinced viewers are ready for the

remarkable realms inhabited by Mark Harris. "The obvious reason is the success of 'Star Wars'," says Solow. "The less obvious is that audiences have gotten tired of sameness."

By choosing Duffy as his Man from Atlantis, Solow hoped to break through the "pattern of sameness." At first, he says, NBC wouldn't hear of it. The network wanted to cast a name athlete in the stereotypical well-muscled, All-American, bionically inclined mold.

"What I tried to get the network to understand was that the story deals with an alien," says Solow. "Patrick was built like a water person—long, muscular, slim—and he had a certain air about him. When he walked into a room, people seemed to look at him and say, 'Gee, I wonder where he's from'."

Where Duffy's from takes in a long, circuitous route to playing a guy who can outswim dolphins at 30,000 feet. His past bears something of a Ren- →

continued

aissance Man stamp. You name it and he's done it—everything from carpentry to clownery.

Born and raised in whistle-stop towns in Montana, where his parents owned local taverns, he moved to Seattle at age 12. There, he and his father assembled the family house from scratch. After high school, he was selected for a special drama program at the University of Washington and stayed on to become the state's first "actor in residence," performing with touring troupes and teaching high-school classes in movement and mime.

On one tour he met his future wife, Carlyn, then performing ballet with the First Chamber Dance Company, and joined her group to teach therapeutic exercise. After that, it was on to eking out an off-Broadway actor's living in New York, "furnishing our apartment off the street and surviving doing carpentry gigs."

When his agent opened a Hollywood office in 1974, the Duffys followed. Patrick drove a florist's delivery truck for two years before landing a key role in the San Diego Shakespeare Festival. There he caught the eye of a few producers. After playing in an episode of *Switch*, Duffy wound up as Julie Harris's nephew in "The Last of Mrs. Lincoln." Next came *Atlantis.*

The big reason for NBC's initial reluctance about Duffy—his physique—required another hurry-up regimen to get him ready. "Patrick was 10 pounds underweight," recalls Herb Solow. "When I first dragged him over to NBC, we had to put a padded sweater on him." Stuntman Stader proceeded to get Duffy going on a protein-enriched diet and a daily hour-long workout schedule of weights and isometrics.

He has since gained 20 pounds, and today carries a healthy 185 pounds on his 6-foot-2 frame. Before leaving for the set each day, he continues to arise at the unholy hour of 4:30 A.M. — cramming in the weight lifting, the

liquid protein and a half hour of chanting the ancient words "Nam-Myoho-Renge-Kyo."

Both Duffy and his wife are adherents of a form of Japanese Buddhism. Carlyn, who now teaches classical ballet at a Santa Monica school, first came upon the religion 10 years ago while performing. Though the Duffys were married in a Buddhist temple, Patrick describes it as a "life philosophy more than a religion. It starts to tap a deeper wisdom that everybody has anyway."

With the additional energy he gets from chanting twice daily, Duffy says he needs only about five hours of sleep, providing he catches up on weekends. In another unusual pastime, he's also a collector of antique toys and children's books (though a number have been appropriated by his two-and-a-half-year-old son Padraic). But as for the legendary lost continent of Atlantis, Duffy merely shrugs: "I know very little about it—except everybody seems to get me either seashells or books on Atlantis for gifts now."

In Duffy's world, the bad guys are folks like sea-siren-kidnapers and 9-foot giants named Thark. But there are plans to take advantage of Duffy's other skills —like fencing and mime—in certain episodes. "We've made Patrick more of the dominant force in the show," says Solow. "In the submersible vessel he sits in the main chair, giving the orders. In his world beneath the sea, he's in charge."

If it doesn't always work out that way in real life, well, what's a guy to do? Take Duffy's vacation voyage to Hawaii just before the season's filming started. There he was, snorkeling away, when "I looked up and saw this huge sea turtle come swimming by. I tried to catch it, swam just like Mark Harris does. But I couldn't seem to make it understand that I was the Man from Atlantis. It just high-tailed it right out of there." **END**

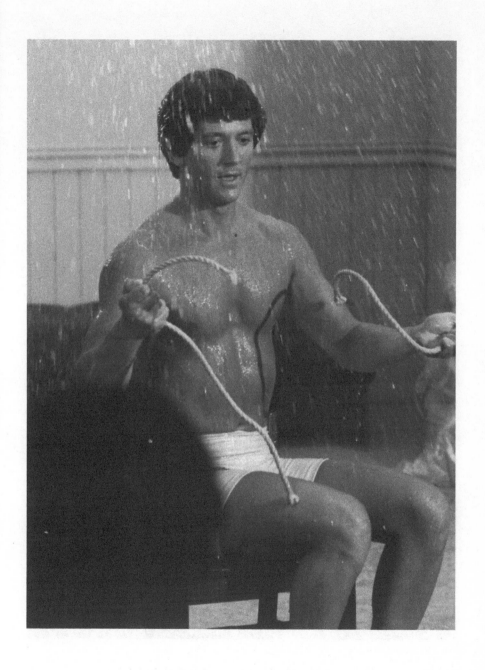

On set With Kareem Abdul Jabbar

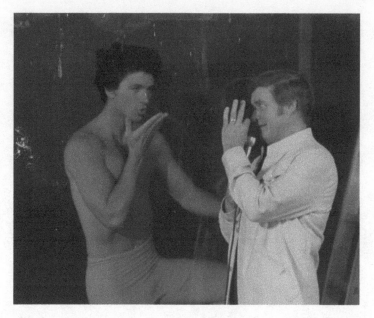

Behind the scenes when Mike Douglas did a special on
Patrick Duffy and *Man from Atlantis*

Patrick Duffy with *Man from Atlantis* co-star
Belinda Montgomery

Magazine clipping from Patrick Duffy's
personal collection

THE MAN FROM ATLANTIS

A stranger in the world of humanity who has no memory of his past, his people or his own world; a water-breathing man with physical limitations on land—Mark Harris nevertheless keeps his wits about him as he seeks his roots and tries to bring sanity and justice to the alien universe of Man.

As given life by actor Patrick Duffy, the man from Atlantis shows young manhood at its most capable—with eyes that see through subterfuge, a quick mind unwilling to distort the truth and a body like a well-tuned instrument of action.

While his non-human perspective allows us to see ourselves as others might see us, his attitudes and behavior serve as a fine model for human honesty and purposefulness. ★

Above: Mark Harris, the man from Atlantis, with spiny sea friends. Right: Mark relaxes in his own version of a waterbed.

Feature in *SF Heroes Magazine*

MAN FROM ATLANTIS

Series
Premiere
September 22nd
NBC-TV 9 pm ET

NBC Promotional Postcard from September, 1977

Watch "THE MAN FROM ATLANTIS" Every Week on NBC

CHAPTER EIGHT

The Dome was brightening as Mark returned and entered his home. How natural it felt to him now to refer to this large pinkish white building as home. The entire time on the surface, he did not know it existed, but now the conch shell emblem of his line welcomed him from over the doorway as if he had never left. The one solid piece of his past had stayed with him all those years on the surface. The spiraling circle with small wave-like lines under it was on the piece of clothing he had been wearing when he was found on the beach. Though the clothing had been discarded before anyone knew where it (or he) had come from, Elizabeth remembered the design and had it put on Mark's new swimsuit. It became a sign for him that he had a past even if it was temporarily lost to him.

Every piece of the living walls seemed to be telling him how glad they were to have him touch them, to elevate the light, or to place his hand on a seemingly solid wall only to have a seam appear and a door develop.

There were many things he could do in the time he had before Tei-La was to meet him, but he felt drawn to the king's chamber. He knew the clothing worn by his father when he died would be laid out along with the ring and pendant. So many times his father had told him the story of the ring and piece of metal that hung by the woven gold thread from his neck.

"Since the settlement, this pendant has been worn by all my father's fathers, Ja-Lil, and someday I will pass it on to you." With the ring, there was a wonderful story. Sometimes he would fall asleep hearing of Poi-Den, two kings before his father, who went wearing the pendant of his station to the land along the great river. It had been decided at the Great Tallon, which was the gathering of the royal lines of the People of the Air and Water, that someone must try to connect with any remaining royal blood they could find of the Landed Ones.

Poi-Den was chosen. He swam far up the wide river and confronted the remaining People of the Trilogy. But this time the Elders were still trying to preserve the life thoughts of their people even though the royal blood of their line was gone. They performed ornate rituals of removing internal organs of the dead and preserving them. All their efforts had created was an elite class of priests who cloaked the futile rites in ceremony and mysticism.

He arrived at the city of the Stone Mountains and, once he was identified, was welcomed by the remaining Landed Ones. Many still remembered him and others of the settlements. The Elders prepared a great celebration in his honor, and for eight days they met in council and debated. They presented theories of how the royal line could be rejuvenated with the offspring of one of their daughters and Poi-Den. Though, as Mark's father told him, there was no history confirming such a thing would activate their treasures in the future.

Each night Poi-Den would return to the river to rest before coming back to the council in the morning. On the ninth day, the Landed Ones took him captive. Desperate to regain their lost powers, they watched as he weakened but continued to send woman after woman to him in an attempt to attract him into fatherhood. Mark's young mind would drift off, seeing the weakened Poi-Den, close to death and being rescued by Shause.

The King of Those of the Air had become not-seen and walked into the giant stone prison, picked up the king, and flew him over the walls and into the clouds. From that time on, all contact with Those on the Land was cut off. Shause delivered Poi-Den back home, and he gave him the ring to be handed down to all future kings of the city. At the convergence, it was to be given back to the Air King to use for the return. When Shause left, Poi-Den and the Elders began the long move of the city from the circled ocean, north into the cold sea, and on to the shore of the large island. Never again was there to be any contact between the three of the settlement.

Mark approached the wall of the king's chamber and placed his right hand on the spot that protruded from the wall. A long line appeared beside it, and the wall separated into a doorway. As he entered and touched the knob on the inside, the darkness evaporated into a beautiful gray-white light. He stood at the doorway and waited. Silently the opening became a wall again, and the seam disappeared. Here was the last minutes of his father. On the dais, in the center of the alabaster block to its right, were the ring and pendant. Various other tables and stands around the room displayed the personal things that had adorned the king's life. Each one, even at a distance, spoke to him of emptiness. Of the king being there but not there. One a ledge to the right of the larger dais was the string of small shells his mother had made for him. She had secretly gathered them on their various trips out to sea. She had called them her trip treasures and had one for every time they had been together. The string of shells had been lying by his dinner plate one night when they all sat down to eat, and Mark heard even now the happy laughter of his father as he jumped up from the table, lifted his mother from her chair, and they danced around the room. Right then and there, before they ate, he made her tell the story of each shell and its corresponding trip. Mark had sat and watched with joy in his heart as his parents included him in their remembrances.

On another stand were small things Mark recognized. Things he had worn as a baby or items he had found and given to his father as gifts. Each one lay with great care and respect in its special place, and Mark knew each had held a special place in his father's heart. The small star shaped barnacle was treated with the same reverence as the two gold coins he had discovered on a trip to the ruins with Roi-Den. He found the presence of his father everywhere and he expected to see him around the corner and welcome him home. But he knew that was not to be.

He stepped farther into the chamber and walked to the dais. The white cloth of the sleeping garment seemed to float above rather than rest upon the carved coral table. The over layers of the body tapered to the sleeves and ended at the large folded cuffs at each side. Looking down as it resting there, he proudly remembered how grand his father had been. A true king. Not just by his muscular frame and handsome features but also by the grandness of his heart, his compassion, and humanity. How could, he wondered, such a positive force be stricken from the inside and die? If he had been in the city, even with his limited abilities, maybe he could have detected the problem and the king would be alive. Still the king should have felt his own illness. Mark had always had the ability to detect the condition of everything within himself; the only explanation was that his father had known there was a problem but had chosen to keep it a secret from the queen and the city. But that theory did not hold up after all he had learned from To-Bay and the king's concern for everyone in the Dome. Mark realized all knowledge had its limitations and, if the puzzle was never answered, the future always lay in wait with its surprises. What this unfortunate piece of the past had done was put the future in motion. He knew he must create what good he could from it.

It was some time before he could bring himself to touch the fabric, but he found it comforted him to rest his hand on it. He sat on the bench at its side and gazed at the very thing he would put on the next day to continue the royal line as king of the city. He lifted the sleeve in his fingers and watched the light dance off the silk-like threads. Then, like a small voice from a distance or the way one perceives the light through their lids before waking, something on the sleeve above the cuff called his attention. In the light, it looked as if it could be a shadow or a gathering in the threads, but he knew it was not. He turned fully to the dais, picked up the sleeve, and held it to the light. A spot. Barely visible to the eye. But when he turned the fabric it was definitely a spot!

Why a simple spot, one that could not normally be noticed, would grab his attention so fully and seem so important he did not know. But it did! He very carefully reached his hand inside the cuff and inverted the entire sleeve. There, plainly visible and about ten inches up from the top of the cuff, was the spot. Much darker on the inside. The instant he touched it, he knew exactly what it was. Blood! His mind was racing. Blood! The king's blood! So many things said it could not be so. Blood would not have escaped his father's body. It could not! The skin would have closed before. He had lain with the queen that night. He had kissed her in the middle of the night. In the morning, he was dead. Where had the wound come from? More than at any time in his life, Mark focused his mind. He now had to think inside everything that had happened to him since fighting with the two men by the pool several days ago. So far, it was just information, but these events and, perhaps more that he did not know yet, had a sequence. Everything started to form a path he now followed, but the destination was still unknown. He must not let the calm welcome of the city mask the danger it posed for him.

Mark left the king's chamber a short while later. The door closed to its solid form as he passed through, and he knew the light in the room behind him was dimming as he stepped away. As he approached the door to his room, he could hear his friend from the other side of the house.

"Ja-Lil, Ja-Lil."

Mark continued on and turned as he heard the footsteps round the corner.

"Ja-L..." Roi-Den stopped motionless in the doorway, his mouth half open with half of Mark's name still in it. "You are old."

"Der," Mark completed the word, and saved his friend from embarrassment. "Older? Yes, I am older."

"I knew the effects of staying on the surface and mother had said it had affected you, but..."

"Roi-Den, it is like the waves on the surface. Underneath nothing has changed. You and I are still the same."

"Ha! We were never the same!" Roi-Den crossed the room in two jumps, grabbed Mark, and swung him around laughing. "You were always bigger and stronger. And you could swim faster. Just like your father."

Mention of the king stopped Roi-Den, and he released Mark. "I am sorry you were not here when your father's life ended, my friend."

"Thank you, but soon we will unite through the Nari-Tanta and all will go on as before. As for you, welcome back from your first tour."

"My second!" The young man's exuberance made Mark smile as he watched his energy carry him in a circle around the room. "I volunteered for this second one right away. I thought maybe I would come upon a sign of you in the southern waters. Ja-Lil, the ocean is so beautiful in the deep waters! Have you seen it there?"

"Yes, I have been to the southernmost depths with my father." Mark had to speak quickly to respond before his friend went on.

"I want to go next to follow the warm river to the north, all the way to see the ice there! Father went there with the king on their very first tour." Roi-Den seemed to conceive of a plan in mid-sentence. "We could do that! We could go together."

Now the plan, as he was designing it, hit a small obstacle. "Could you do that now, Ja-Lil? I mean now that you will be king, could you leave the city and take a tour? Who would be..."

"Roi-Den, I have no idea what will be from one moment to the next right now." For the first time with Roi-Den, Mark started to feel more than the superficial effects of age. He felt the weight of each decision. He had to envision the consequences of every action he would take from now on. The pyramid of responsibility in the city ended with him. This was like the shared responsibility with Elizabeth when he was at the lab or working with his friends on land. It had seemed natural for him there, but now he knew it was more than just the time he had been away that separated him from this good young friend. "We will have to wait and see."

"Of course." His cousin took but a second to find the next perfect plan. "Let us go now! Not for a tour, of course, but just out." It was full speed ahead. "We could just leave the city now and take the day and go to all the places we used to explore when you were young! I mean we...when we were young."

"Roi-Den, we will have time, much time. But I have already made a plan to go out today."

"I will go with you."

"I am going with Tei-La. And if you would like, please come with us."

"Roi-Den." The sound of a third voice stopped their conversation. Tei-La was standing at the door, and neither of them had heard her enter nor knew how long she had been there. "I will have little enough time alone with Ja-Lil when he becomes king so I am going to claim this day for just the two of us."

Mark was only slightly surprised when he viewed the two of them as an outsider. She embraced his friend warmly as she spoke, and as they separated and held each other by the hand, she said, "Welcome again to the city. I am glad you are back safely."

Roi-Den planted an energetic kiss on her cheek and backed out of the room, raising his hand in a wave to the two of them. "I have to report to my father about my tour anyway. Have fun with each other. I mean enjoy your... uh... bye." Then he was gone.

Mark stepped closer, and she reached for his face and pulled it to her lips. He loved the fresh smell of her skin and the soft aroma of her hair. His arms reached around her thin waist, and he felt the firmness of her body along his. His mind could not stay on his feelings for her and was constantly shifting to tomorrow and to his father. He knew the water would clear his thoughts, and he wanted to be out there. He wanted to be out there with her.

They walked across the city to the gowning room holding hands. A few of the citizens followed them with their gaze, smiling a little. His return to the city comforted them. They knew he would now be there for them and that nothing had changed between him and the queen to be.

They entered the room, just as two young men of the city were leaving on their tour. Mark did not now know where they were assigned. That responsibility was Man-Den's since the king had died and, starting tomorrow, it would be his. In fact, all decisions concerning the city and its people would fall to him. From tomorrow into the future, whatever definition that future would take. The two men nodded at Mark and touched their right thumbs to their foreheads before turning, placing both hands on the wall of the room, and then passing through and into the sea. They would be gone for several months, covering assigned areas of the seas and oceans before returning and logging in their observations for the convergence.

Tei-La crossed to the wall of gowns that hung over the bench and pulled off her garment and hung it with the others. She was strong. The definition of her muscles told him she had not slackened in her schedule of swimming and working with the others. Even when they were younger, it was she who would almost drag Mark to this room, and then out when he would have rather stayed in the Dome. Her legs, arms, and back were well formed, and through the light swimming garment, Mark could tell her stomach and chest were hard. Hanging his own garment next to hers, he stepped to the wall and, with outstretched arms, they passed to the outside.

He had missed that feeling. The weightlessness of the water, the comforting pressure it exerted on him, and the real feeling of drawing in strength with each lungful of liquid. They both held there just outside the wall. They were only a few feet away from it, but already it was vague in its outline and transparent in substance. It was very dark, and they left the lit inner Dome. Their eyes adjusted instantly, and they could see the beauty of the open sea. Tei-La slowly circled Mark, her hair flowing like dark ribbons behind her. The suit she wore moved in the water like the delicate fins of the lionfish. It trailed behind her, while in front it outlined the curves of her breasts and hips and highlighted the muscles of her stomach.

She swam a complete lazy circle and faced him once again.

"Where shall we go?" What was so beautiful in her voice when she spoke in the Dome or on the surface was made even more so when her mind spoke directly to Mark's.

"Ja-Lil," she smiled, "you look like you're in a trance. Where would you like to travel?"

"It is good that you can only listen to my words and not my thoughts." Now he was smiling too. "I think I could make the color come to your face and you would swim away without me."

"Never, my love. Losing you once was enough." She now started to swim backwards away from him. "Come, let's go to the ruins where you asked me to wed."

With a languid rotation, she turned and slowly made her way towards the low mountain range to the north. Mark came along side her, and together they made the climb up the foothills and closer to the surface.

Soon the plants became lusher with access to the sunlight. They crossed onto a plateau after a few hours and soon were at the entrance to the kelp forest. At first, they stayed at the level of the sand and rocks at the bottom. The bases of the kelp trees were bare there, and the beauty of the giant tritons, Spanish dancers, and hundreds of other types of sea life were highlighted by the faint shafts of light that penetrated from above. Weaving their way through the forest, they would constantly stop to watch when a butterfly or spotted eagle ray rose from the sand at their approach. As with most life in the sea, these creatures would detect no threat from the couple and settle to the bottom again under a fine covering of sand. In many cases, these rays or the moonfish and eels would turn and come to them, and for minutes they would swim together touching and exchanging information.

Mark had always had a heightened sense of communication with most creatures of the sea. All the citizens lived easily with the life in the open water, but Mark noticed early on that all the beings in the ocean reacted to him and his father differently. They would come to him if he made his wishes known. On many occasions, as a boy, he would impress Tei-La by having one of them take a trinket or even just a sea flower to her and place it in her lap. On trips or tours with his father, he had seen the same reaction but to a greater degree with the king. Perhaps that too was in the blood. All these things, he had never given thought to before.

"Look, Ja-Lil, there is the road." Tei-La had stopped at the thinning edge of the forest and was pointing up to the side of a small rise. The tracks were still there as he remembered. They seemed to start from nowhere. The ruts, made by who knew what, were deep in the surface of the hill; they started at the jagged edge of the rock cliff and had been formed ages ago by an earthquake of great magnitude. Far below, he could see the faint outline of the road extending for a few yards then disappearing under the sand and debris.

They swam over the chasm and met the tracks at the edge. Following them, they knew of the approaching ruins by the series of carved stones that sat to the side of the road at regular intervals. The carvings on them were still discernible, although the lettering and symbols were strange and unreadable. They came to a halt when they were at the outer gate that lay in rubble some two hundred yards from the city. Tei-La swam next to Mark and stopped with her arm around his waist.

"It's so beautiful. It is still my favorite place in all the sea."

He felt it too. From here, they could see what it once was. It sat on the small hill well situated, he thought, for beauty and defense. It had a command of the sea in all directions. The details in the buildings and walls that remained standing spoke of people who were artists and master craftsmen. The sea life that had taken residence over the centuries only served to heighten the old ghost's beauty.

Together they moved down the main roadway and into the center of the city. The large well and fountain in the square was now the meeting place of baler shells and hermit crabs, and the coral mounds seemed to fit naturally in the beds around it. Mantis shrimp and other small creatures of the sand darted away as they came to the low carved base of the well.

They sat and looked out at the submerged countryside over the tops of partial walls and through windows open to everything.

"You can feel them, can you not?" Ja-Lil asked. She was so much like him in her heart that he knew what her answer would be.

"Yes." She sat there as though she were listening to the sounds of a town full of life. "Yes, I can. The children are here in the streets, playing in the fountain. There," she said, pointing to the listing side of the building, "a mother calls to them from the upper window. The men are arriving from the fields with their tools for a cool drink, and their women will bring them food. It makes me sad to think that it was all here, so full, so alive. Then so quickly it was gone."

"They built all this to be enjoyed and to protect them. Their only danger came from the earth itself. Their gift is still here and perhaps then so are they."

"Did your father tell you anything of this place?"

"Only that its end came long before Poi-Den moved the city here."

"I hope," Tei-La rose off the stone slab, pulling Mark up after her, "that our children and our children's children come here often. To where the great king of the city, their father, asked the queen to marry him!"

Mark watched her as she floated in the mild current. The feeling in his chest was almost as if his heart was expanding. So many reasons he loved her. Her compassion for the past and her determination for the present and the future were only a part. He swam a small arc to admire her from several angles. Her eyes followed his route and, just before her widening smile told him she was about to ask what he was thinking, he grabbed her hand.

"Come." He led her off to search through the familiar sections of the ruins.

At the rearmost edge of the city, they looked over the crumbling outer wall to a gently sloping hill that stretched out to the south beyond vision. The once deep-water channels were almost filled in with sand but still visible.

All traces of the crops that had occupied the fields had long since vanished. Only the stone walls that separated one field from another remained. The rays that filtered down from the surface were deepening in their angle. The color, which increased its yellow tint, seemed to gild the edges of the plants and creatures that inhabited the slope.

"Soon the sun will be gone, and I have much to do tomorrow." Mark turned off in the direction of the Domed city. "Let us return."

Tei-La had just lifted up off the pile of large fallen blocks and was about to join him when a sudden increase in the activity of the sea creatures on the hill caused her to stop.

"Wait! What is that?"

Mark stopped and followed her pointing finger to the crest of the southernmost part of the slope. What looked to be a large shadow loomed just above the horizon and seemed to grow as they watched. Suddenly, it more than doubled in size and in another moment, Mark recognized the blurred outline of two whales. The closest he knew to be a black right whale. Now with the return of so much of his memory, it seemed a little strange for him to put names on all these lives that he had always shared the water with. Over the years, people of the city learned the general title used on the surface for many of the creatures. They had come to call some dolphins, squid, jellyfish, or plankton. Most had learned to identify urchins, sponges, stars, and giant floating kelp. He had now, however, spent years with his friends at the lab on the surface, learning the official names they had given to thousands of fish, plants, and mammals.

The black right was followed closely by a very large blue whale, although this smaller female was not blue at all but a slate-gray except for the white edges of her flippers and flukes. The smaller fish on the hillside moved out of the path of the oncoming duo, more in concession for their size than fear.

"The Tanta in front is not well." From the moment his mother had mentioned the Nari-Tanta, he knew he would never again refer to the most revered of ocean mammals by anything other than their ancient title. "He is not that old. It must be something else." From the slow rolling motion of the leading whale and the way he would drop all the way to the floor of the hill and take small mouthfuls of the sand and spit them out again, Mark knew what was about to happen. "Have you witnessed the transference?"

When she shook her head, Mark gently pulled her behind the stones. "If we are quiet and act with respect, they will not mind. We will watch."

The black came to rest just to the side of the water channel closest to Mark and Tei-La. His large under belly sat heavily in the sand, while his fluke beat a slow steady rhythm, raising gentle clouds of dust that caught the light of the setting sun. For awhile, nothing changed. The blue female hovered motionless about ten feet directly in front of him.

"His time has come." Mark was behind Tei-La with his hands on her shoulders. He knew the importance of this moment. That they were here at this precise time to see something that so rarely happened was another sign to Mark. The entire sea itself was rewarding their love. "When he is ready, she will move to his side."

Everyone since the first settlement knew the history of Tanta. After the first placement of the Trilogy, a great many tours were undertaken while they waited on the development of the Landed Ones. Almost immediately, the immense capacity of the giant mammals of the sea was discovered. With their ability to contain limitless living information, it was natural to give them the name Tanta. Tanta, in the language of the city, was the word used for most containers or vessels. Most specifically, it was the name of the vessel used to carry the Trilogy to the original placement. From the very beginning, the Tanta was the final repository for all life-thoughts and information—logged into the recording gels since the placement and before. When a citizen died, the life-thought was taken to the sea and given to a Tanta for keeping. If on a tour, one were to find a life that had ended in the water, they would take and hold that person's life-thought to deliver it, when possible, to the Tanta. His father had often told of times when he and others of the city would hold hundreds who died from the wars on the surface and how, throughout the world's oceans, these surface-ones now resided side by side with the ancestors of the city.

The black's tail slowed and eventually lay flat on the sand. The golden beads in the water drifted to cover the broad, pointed fluke in the dust.

"Now." Was all he whispered to Tei-La.

It was almost impossible to detect any muscle movement in the big Tanta's body, but it began to glide smoothly to the black until he was eye to eye on his left side. Then all was quiet once again.

Mark and Tei-La remained still. The vibration came from inside them and from without. Through his hands, Mark felt her entire body begin to move in a smooth, almost imperceptible rhythm, and he knew his was doing the same. A sound was simultaneously coming from both places as well. Originating from deep within their bodies and mirrored from its source on the outside. Tei-La wanted to turn her head to him but found she could not look away. Waves of sound emerged from the very water and sand all around them. Mark had seen it before and knew it was originating from around the two bodies in front of them.

The sound was not the normal conversation between whales, even of those two different species. There was no clicking or songs.

Nor was there the communication that he had, over the years on the surface, tried to describe to Elizabeth and the others. These were the words and songs of something else. Of someone else. It was the lives, thousands of lives of nameless men and women who'd perished in the sea. The life-thoughts lived once again, if only for an instant, as they came into being through the water while passing from one Tanta to the other.

The symphony of lives reached a crescendo and held for a moment before shrinking into a beautiful echo. Silence drifted back to the ocean floor like the gold flecks of sand. Mark whispered to her, "Now you really have them. All those men, women, and children."

The big blue began to roll her right flipper and drew herself away from the ailing black. When she had left a gap of several yards between them, she halted and let herself sink to the sandy bottom. The black, after seeing this act of respect, rose from the bottom and, behaving exactly as Mark told Tei-La he would, made three complete circles around the body of the larger blue whale and continued on to the surface to breathe before swimming away. When he was long out of sight, the blue Tanta also left the hillside but in a different direction.

"He will now find a place to end on the shore."

"But why do they always go to the land? Why not find their end in the water as we do?" Tei-La had always wondered this when hearing tales of transference and the death of a Tanta.

"They are returning just as we do. They came from the land, and when their work is done they try to return."

It was a silent swim back to the Dome, and they both remained deeply affected by what they had witnessed. They did not see, when passing back through the ruins, the faint flutter of a swimming tunic as the man pulled behind the columns and watched them fade into the distance.

CHAPTER NINE

Their silence continued when they left the changing room. Everything needed between them was being accomplished—not with words but by simply holding hands as they walked through the city streets. When they came to the set of small avenues that branched from the main street, Mark halted at the one that led to Tei-La's home. He turned to say goodbye, but she put her finger to his lips and said, "I will go home with you."

They stepped into Mark's chambers as the light in the Dome was lessening. Mark placed his hand on the nodule by the door and the room brightened. She walked in and stopped at his bed as he brushed his hand on the edge of the door. The wall closed completely and the seam grew together. It was so clear to him. This was what he had always wanted. The times on the surface when he remembered nothing of this city or these people, he wanted to return. Return to her. He walked to her as she waited for him.

As she turned at the bed, her head leaned slightly to one side and she looked at a spot on the floor in front of her feet. He took the last step in and their bodies touched. At first, they barely brushed against each. She felt like a breeze that lightly danced over parts of his skin. Her breasts and then her hips. He did not reach out for her, or she for him. Their arms remained waiting at their sides. The breeze pushed forward and he responded. As he pressed against her, she placed her hands on his hips. As her head tilted up, her eyes found his and everything he wanted to be true, was. They kissed. Their lips parted, and her hand came up to the clasp at the shoulder of her gown.

"Tei-La, wait." He did not know why he spoke or what he was going to say next. He looked down at her lovely face and could find nothing that was not perfect. In all of her, there was nothing that he did not want and want forever. But he had spoken. There was nothing left in his mind to say. It pained him to see the look that came into her eyes. A question that he could not answer and the beginning of a pain that he could not heal.

"Why?" she asked.

Yes. *Why?* His brain could not find a response. There was no answer to that question. *Why?*

"You are so beautiful. I love you so." He knew all this to be true, and he knew she believed him when he said it. So why?

"You are beautiful, too, my love." The question and pain started to fade as she spoke, and she reached again for her clasp.

"Tei-La." When he saw his hand on hers...when he stopped her once again from opening her clasp, he noticed it. It was *difference*! His hand. Her hand. The difference!

"Tei-La, you are beautiful. So beautiful and young. And I am different then when last you knew me." That was it. He had said it. There was no more in him to say. Since his return, he had been seeing her. From his eyes. Looking out at her. Seeing her hair, her face, her body, her youth! And he saw it all with young eyes. The eyes he had left with so many years ago. Eyes like hers. But he was no longer young.

She was seeing him as he stood before her—not as the young man who had left the city long ago.

"I am different, too, Ja-Lil. The same amount of time has passed for me as for you."

"Tei-La, you can see the difference."

"No, Ja-Lil, I see the future. And right now, you can see only the present. If you stay trapped by what you see, you will be denying us the future"

"So much changed when I was gone. I am back a different age."

"You were never away, my love. You took me with you—not in your memory but in your heart. I have aged every second with you. Look at me with your heart as I am looking at you. The only important things are those that cannot change. Not your strength, your body, your family, or even this city. Eventually, all this will be gone. Oh, Ja-Lil, have you not felt that we have always been in love, always together!"

Of course, he had felt that. Before he had left the city, he knew they were continuing on together from ages past. He was not discovering what he saw in her but rather remembering it. Like something lost being found. He loved her so much that he had to give her this chance to go. "Are you sure you love me as you once did?"

"My love does not have quantity only value. Do the tall love more than the not as tall or the fair deeper than the more plain? Your father and mother are great rulers of the city, but their love is no greater than that of the common citizen." Tei-La held him in her gaze quietly for a minute then walked to the foot of the bed. When she turned to face him, her look was steady and her voice strong. "I will tell you what my love is then I will say no more. I will tell you what it is, but I cannot describe it. It is the mere shadow of the greater thing you can never see or touch. But never doubt it is there. Please tell me the love I felt from you is also the shadow of something true and not some ghost invented by a foolish girl."

She did not go to him nor ask him to come to her. She didn't have to. Mark stepped to her and softly said, "My wife."

This time she was not stopped. As her hand found the clasp and it opened, the gown slid from her body and floated to the floor. Before him stood the most beauty he had ever seen. Her skin reflected the glow from the room like a marble statue, and her hair seemed to shine from within. She reached to his side and found the chord that held the tunic together. As she pulled it, his garment opened and lay draped from his shoulders. She reached inside, and he felt her hands around his back and down to his hips then up to his chest. Slowly, she kissed him and he felt the warmth of her embrace touch more and more of him.

She slid her hands up to his shoulders. As their kiss deepened, his garment fell from his back. She floated into his arms, and he carried her to the bed. Time stopped and what was the past came rushing forward and they controlled eternity. Nothing mattered but their two bodies becoming one and their love continuing.

His hand left her shoulder and she did not wake. He had been watching her for a long time as she slept. He had held unanswered dialogue with her. He told her how he would love her as he had seen his parents love. He would respect her life as his own and hold it sacred. But most of all he thanked her. For loving him, for waiting for him, for being. "My love will cast a warm shadow over your entire world."

He slid out from beneath the covers so as not to wake her and stepped into his garment. Today was the day he would take responsibility for the city and all the people. He would assume his place in the line of his family. The entire day would be taken with the ceremony before the six Elders, the Time of Deep thoughts in the king's chamber, him entering the king's Kiv in the Dome, and finally presenting himself for confirmation before the citizens. Before leaving the room, he quietly walked around the bed and bent over her. He kept his face close to hers and breathed the wonderful scent of her. Soon he kissed her forehead and walked to the wall, touched it, and stepped out before it was entirely open.

He walked around the king's chamber for a long time before approaching and kneeling before his dais. He closed his eyes and brought before him all the images of his father he could remember. He felt the fabric of the sleeping garment under his hands and could detect the slight odor that was a combination of both his father and mother. He would wear this robe to be anointed king and it would signify not breaking the line. It would be different from when his father had worn the ceremonial garb of his own father. Mark's grandfather had lived a long full life. His wife had been dead sixteen years when he at last felt his time approach. He dressed in the royal coronation robe he had worn at his wedding. The Dome had constructed a small balcony over where the conch emblem is now, and on his final day, he had welcomed the end in front of the entire city. His full life had drawn to a close in a citywide celebration, and Mark's father wore the garment the next day in a continuation of the ritual.

How different this was to be. The king dying so young with no one to see and laud his life. His last act of a loving kiss in the night for his queen. Now his mother would carry that kiss and its memory for the rest of her life. Everything seemed to reflect his love for Tei-La, and he made a quiet promise to have her in his mind and heart at this last moment.

Mark rose and undressed and put on the garment, the ring, and the pendant. He whispered, "*Ishnan abatta yddap ama ama...*" He continued on through the full six lines of their poem. He did not know why, it just made him feel close to his father and correct in his attitude. When fully dressed, he opened the wall and walked to the greeting room where he knew Man-Den would be waiting to escort him to the hall of the Elders.

"Ja-Lil, son of the king." Man-Den greeted him officially, as he would not be the king until he emerged from the Kiv. "I see your father even in the way you move. I have asked your mother to stand for you before the Elders. I hope you approve."

"Yes, of course." Mark was glad she would be there and was going to ask her himself as was the custom of the one who was about to become the One Who Knows.

Myo-O stepped into the room behind the minister. She looked lovely in her queens' robes and the woven gold-wire breastlet. When she caught sight of Mark in the robe, she stopped and quickly grabbed Man-Den's arm. "Oh."

For a moment, Mark thought his mother was going to slip to the floor, and he started forward.

"No, it is all right. You look so like your father when I last saw him in that robe. I almost felt his kiss again."

Man-Den held her hand in his and supported her until she regained herself. "This line will continue, my queen, and you will always be the heart of the city." He smiled down at her. "Now to the hall."

With Man-Den leading and the queen on his right, they walked across the large room to the front door. Three on one side and two on the other, the Elders waited outside. Every citizen was out on the street, but not a word was spoken. Many had never witnessed the exchange of kings, but the older people had a sadness that they were to see it twice in their lifetime. Man-Den stepped forward to make it three Elders on each side, and his mother took Mark's arm and they began the long walk to the hall.

It was strange to see the entire population of the city there, but to only hear the sound of the water as it flowed through the channels and ran from the fountains as they passed by. Everyone was completely still. Some held hands and some simply stared, but all heads followed the group as they made their way onward. Mark kept the poem repeating over and over in his head. The voice in his mind sounded more to him like his father's than his own, but it felt appropriate for the moment. With the voice and that warm steady hand of his mother's around his arm, he felt his family was somehow complete. The faces of the crowd continued to drift past him, between the bodies of the Elders, as they walked to the hall. Most he remembered or had seen since his return, but some were complete strangers and it was on these that he seemed to linger a little longer. Not really expecting to see him, Mark still wondered where the killer could be and how he could avoid detection for so long.

The entourage left the main avenue and continued by a shallow canal on a street he knew well. From the time they turned, he began to look ahead to the large building. The front door could be reached by the little bridge that arched over the water. As they drew closer, he saw Tei-La. She had left his home sometime after he had entered the king's chamber that morning.

He tried in vain to will the group of Elders into slowing their pace a little. She was there standing on the steps just above the bridge with her father and mother and the other two families who shared the building. He knew it was not so, but it appeared to him that the Dome had increased the light just over or around her head. From the moment she was visible through the crowd, he could not take his eyes off her. She stood a little in front of her father. Her hair was pulled up from the nape of her neck and bound with pearls strung on a golden wire. The green- blue gown hung from her left shoulder and was swaged under her right arm. The skin of her neck and chest and arms radiated the light in white golden rays back to him. On a cord that was almost invisible to the eye, she had strung the clasp she had worn on her gown the night before. She touched it gently with her fingers as he drew directly in front of the bridge. Her eyes sparkled and her lips parted a little as if she were going to speak. He wanted to break off the parade and go to her and take her in his arms, but he would not. She obviously was aware of how he felt, and she smiled at him and his heart rate jumped.

He then felt his mother's hand squeeze his arm slightly as she whispered, "Yes, she is indeed beautiful."

They had passed the house now and he didn't turn his head, but he knew she was following him and felt as he did.

The number of people increased as they neared the Elder's hall, and soon Mark could see the building and its open balcony where in a short time he would stand and be presented to the city as its new king. He and the group did slow now as the crowd pressed into the street and left very little room for them to pass.

Man-Den had reached the steps with the first of the Elders and was going up when Mark glanced to his left and there, about four or five rows back, he saw To-Bay. The old man's face gave nothing away. From both of their actions, no one could have known that Mark and he had ever met, but Mark knew To-Bay was also reciting the three lines of the poem he had been given by the king. Mark nodded just enough to show that he had seen him, and To-Bay responded with the smallest of smiles. Mark now knew this was how it had been with his father. No matter how alone he might have felt at times, there had always been To-Bay. It all continued on. Now he would always know this friend was there for him and more importantly for the city.

The two lines of Elders stopped at the door and remained motionless. Mark had studied the book of ancients in his father's chamber and knew every action he must take for the rest of the ceremony. He stepped to the door and placed his hand on the wall. The seam appeared and the door pulled back to reveal the inner receiving room of the hall. Mark did not enter but stepped back as the Elders filed through. Next, his mother released his arm and followed them into the building. He would wait outside alone with the people until—as it had been done since the second king was anointed—he was invited into the chamber. Every act from now on would symbolize the fact that the king serves the city and holds his position as an honor. The king must exist because of the needs of the people.

He stood at the top of the stairs and had no idea how much time passed. He could feel the sea of faces looking at his back in silence and he was asking himself, *what is it I can do for you? I can only promise to try.*

"Ja-Lil, son of Con-Or, the Elders of the city ask that you enter." Man-Den stepped just outside the door enough to catch the brighter light from the Dome. With the darkness of the inside surrounding him, he looked twice his normal size.

"I am a citizen of this city. What is it they want?" Mark recited these lines with both hands extended to the doorway and his palms turned upward.

"The Elders ask that you enter and respond to the needs of its people."

With the formal exchange of entry done, Man-Den backed into the shadows, and as he disappeared into the darkness, Mark then stepped inside the room.

The brightness from outside was blocked as the door closed behind him and the seam disappeared. The large circular room was on the three levels. The main floor was thirty to forty feet in diameter. At the front of the area where ten o'clock would be on the face of a clock were two eating areas extending out from the living wall. They were not the ordinary ledges as was common in the city, but larger free-standing chairs elevated with two steps leading to them. Both had full armrests. Mark's mother sat on the left seat, and the one on the right was conspicuously empty. That was where his father would have sat while Mark went through the crowning ceremony.

Myo-O looked small and alone without him and was not aware that her hand rested on the empty chair as if hoping to find her husband there. In the center of the floor was the emblem of the Trilogy. It was a circle inside of a reverse pyramid. On the outside of the circle at each point of the pyramid was the sign of each of the Three. The emblem for Those of the Air was on the left point at the top of the pyramid. It consisted of a circle inside several dots of various sizes. To the left of the circle were glyphs, which Mark could not decipher. Under the circle was the emblem of Those of the Air, which Mark and everyone in the city recognized. It consisted of two interlocking sine curves encompassed by five dots. On the right side was a similar circle, which held dots of different sizes, but these were in different positions. The glyphs were unique also and on the right side of the circle in the two o'clock position. Those of the Land, whose circle this was, had their sign at the bottom. On a flat line that went up and down, there rested an arc under an inverted V. At the bottom was the emblem of Mark's own people. A third circle, with the exact diameter of the other two and dots placed seemingly at random. Under this circle was the conch shell pattern of concentric circles, with the three waves underneath which represented Those of the Water. Mark stood at the outside of the circle with his city's emblem in front of him.

Man-Den, after backing into the room, made his way past the emblem of the Land People to the set of nine steps extending up along the wall and ending on the second level. On the protruding stage directly in front of Mark sat the six Elders on simple chairs behind a long semi-circular table that faced the open area. In front of each was a basin-like hallow, which held the recording gel. Man-Den went to his chair on the extreme left. On the second level, there was a walkway around the entire circumference of the room. When the door had sealed, the walkway extended across the former opening. Directly behind the seated Elders was a single chair with no desk or table in front of it. It had been placed on a series of platforms until it was completely visible behind the seated men. This was where the king sat for all official functions concerning the city and its citizens. Behind the throne, if you could call it that, as it was the simplest chair in the room with a half back and no armrests, was a much smaller set of stairs that led to yet another walkway. This much narrower walkway was at least thirty-five to forty feet above the floor, and it ran right and left around the room to a nodule that would open a door onto a balcony to the outside. It was to be on this balcony that Mark would be presented to the city for the first time as their king.

Mark had never actually been in this building. It was solely for the functions of the king and the Elders and was only used for their official acts. As a young man, he had stood outside while the hearings for banishment had taken place, several other times when decisions were made for the expansion of the city. He had looked forward to officially entering the hall as heir to his father's position after that last tour of the oceans. Had the accident not happened and his memory not vanished, he would have sat on the chair where his mother now sat and observed the activities of the Elders at every function from then on, until he became king. Now here he was, first entering the hall and about to become king. He glanced at his mother and was met with her warm smile and gaze of pride. He knew how she felt and could only hope the spirit of his father she held in her heart was feeling the same.

He also knew that somewhere in the back of this building were the Kivs, and that after his anointing he would go there and enter the king's Kiv.

Mark's taking in of this new but familiar place was interrupted by Man-Den's voice. He had placed his right hand, palm down, just touching the surface of the gel in the basin in front of him. A faint glow coming from the liquid reflected off his face, and Mark knew every word and every vision in Man-Den's eyes was being kept in the memory gel.

"Who is it that would present this man?" The ceremony was now starting according to the ancient traditions. The queen rose from her seat, came down the steps, walked to Mark, and placed her hand on his left shoulder.

"I am Myo-O, wife of Con-Or, and mother to this man." Mark could hear or maybe just feel the odd mixture of pride and sorrow in her voice. "It is I who present him here."

"In all times past," the Elder on the far right spoke, bathed in the glow where his right hand touched the liquid, "it has been the duty of the father to present his son to the council."

"And so it should be now. But my husband has left this city before his time and now rests with his fathers in Nari-Tanta."

"The royal blood line is more than tradition; it is the very existence of the city." The Elder second from the right raised her left hand while speaking as all of them on the dais did.

"The blood of the king is here. It is in this man." Mark could feel her hand growing stronger on his arm. "My blood is there also, separate but inseparable. Just as one day I will be one with my husband in life-thought so I am one with him now here." Her left hand pressed against her chest over her heart.

The second Elder from the left raised his hand. "We take this man and your word as we would from the king." He smiled at Myo-O and continued, "There is no difference in the word, blood, or love that you bear this city or its people. Tradition is only of value if it serves the truth. Thank you, Myo-O."

Mark's mother stepped in front and turned to him. With her hands on both his shoulders, she kissed his cheeks and whispered in his ear. "You are every bit the king your father was. You will serve well." She paused here and looked into his eyes. "We love you." He felt, beneath her words, there was so much more she was saying. He didn't know what it was but felt the love she professed and the echo of a sadness he knew came from her being alone.

"I love you, mother." When he said those words, he realized it was probably the first time he had told her that since he was a very small boy. They walked back to her seat where Mark bowed to her as she sat, and then he returned to his position at the base of the circle.

"Ja-Lil, in the time with your father, was your training complete?" He now turned his attention to the Elder who sat next to Man-Den as she spoke. Mark knew none of these men and women were aware of To-Bay and his function.

"I do not believe anything is ever complete. I can see now that everything my father did with me, every moment of time we had together, was training. I know when I leave the king's Kiv and receive my father's life-thought from Nari-Tanta that I will know what the king's of this city have always known." He felt confident now that his father would have responded the same way. "Beyond that, any knowledge of mine will be defined by my effort."

Silence filled the room. It was not strained or uncomfortable. Each Elder looked to the others and then to Man-Den who rose and stepped to the front of the bench. Behind him, each of the Elders had risen and raised their left palm, keeping their right on their basin's surface.

"Ja-Lil, fifth of the sons of the line of kings, step to the center."

After a quick glance at his mother, who returned his look with a smile, Mark took the several steps that carried him to the middle of the circle.

"In the book of the ancients," Man-Den's arms were out front with his palms upward, "let it be written that Ja-Lil, son of Con-Or, on this day continued as king of the city and protector of the people."

As Mark stood there, the Elders rose and, led by Man-Den, descended the stairs and walked to the circle. They formed a large ring, facing Mark with their hands to their sides and their palms on him. He waited as each one recited their oath to the city and to him as their king, and when they were done, he stepped from the center and walked to the stairs as they followed. All of these moves were traditions that were recorded in the book of the ancients, but Mark felt now that his actions were guided from the inside. He now led them. He had to. This was his function from this time forward.

He went up the first set of stairs and around the bench to the steps at the back. As he rounded the bench, he could see his mother as she rose from her seat, bowed to the dais, and began backing out of the room. Their feet made no sound when they proceeded up the living stairs to the uppermost walkway. They started down it and, from where Mark could see, the wall opened at the front of the main floor and his mother passed through. It quickly closed behind her as they reached the section directly over it.

The men behind him stopped as he put his hand on the nodule that emitted the faint greenish light. The seam appeared and the wall opened to a width of two doorways exposing the large porch that overlooked the main part of the city. From the moment the opening began, Mark realized how quiet it had been in the large room. Now he heard the growing water sounds from the various canals and waterfalls rushing up and into his ears. He stepped to the railing and, behind him, the Elders stood with their hands folded in front. Below him were all the people he had passed on his way here. When he saw them a short time ago, they had been friends and strangers and equals. People he felt at one with. He looked at their faces now, and there was a difference. Each one was a person he was responsible for. He would feel their pain, and their happiness was his responsibility.

His mother stepped into the crowd and looked up to where he stood. Beside her were Tei-La and her family. The center below him and all the small streets and alleys extending out from it were filled with the citizens of the city. There were no appreciative noises and almost no one was moving. The Elders, with Man-Den, stepped to Mark, three on a side. When they were seven across, the Elders turned toward him. Then together they put their right thumbs to their lips, touched them briefly to their foreheads, pressed their palms together, and bowed to him. The crowd erupted. The ceremony by the Elders confirmed the new king. There was no water sound now.

The force of the cheering pressed against Mark's eardrums until he heard a slight hissing sound, and the vibrations echoed deep in his chest. From below him, Mark heard his name being chatted in waves through the city. People were yelling, "Ja-Lil", clapping, and swinging each other around in impromptu little dances. His mother stood uncommonly still with her hands folded in front of her. Her gaze locked on her son, and a loving smile crossed her face. Next to her, Mark saw Tei-La put her fingers to her lips and then extend them to him.

As this show of approbation washed over him, he felt a strange mixture of emotions. He was proud to be his father's son because this show of love was a true reflection of what they had known and trusted about the former king. He instantly made a determination at the very depths of his life to live every moment as if his father were always watching him. His other feelings were a composition of excitement, worry, and perhaps even fear. These faces, looking up at him, were not just fellow members of his city; they were individuals who from now on would look to him for guidance, encouragement, and healing. They would line up outside his door now and file through his chamber. His responsibility was to give them answers. He marveled, remembering his father sitting in that room years before, at how calm and assured he had appeared, and how gently he had embraced each person. As he spied Roi-Den in the crowd, jumping up and down and waving his fists over his head, he realized how different they were now. He would no longer have that wonderful freedom his friend still had, the freedom to live his life only for himself and his family.

With these impulses acting on him, Mark also knew he would not trade his position for any other. Was it the blood that coursed through his system talking silently to him? Was it his genetic mission as all tradition in the city said it was? He didn't know the answer, but he did know that it felt natural and good and right. He felt he was Ja-Lil, son of Con-Or, the fifth in the line of kings of Those of the Water.

CHAPTER TEN

Mark left the balcony with the Elders and proceeded along the upper walkway to the rear of the building. The closing of the door silenced the cheering of the citizens that continued after Mark's brief speech. When they reached the point directly opposite the door to the balcony, he stopped by the two nodules on the wall. He paused. Another moment like so many others over the last few days. Significant life altering moments in time. Some had been painful and others had filled him with joy and wonder. Now he paused because he knew he was about to receive, actually take into his very life, the history of his people. Mark placed his palm on first one nodule and then the other. The only time both were touched was when the king was entering the Kiv. All other times, when the Elders rotated in the Kivs for the maintenance of the city, only the nodule on the right was activated. By touching both, Mark had sent the signal to the Dome that his Kiv would be occupied. In fact, this time all the Elders would enter their Kivs, which was only done on the occasion of the crowning of a new king or moving of the city.

The seam appeared and the door opened. A long well-lit corridor ran over one hundred feet directly to the rear of the building and onto a large opening the group walked towards. Mark had never been in this building, let alone the large room that held the seven Kivs of the Dome. Just after passing through the doorway, the group was standing in front of the outermost wall of the Dome itself. It was shaped, at this particular spot, like a double wall and rose before them in two levels. Mark could make out six areas behind the wall of the living tissue. Each cubical would accommodate a single person in a standing position. The wall itself glowed with a bright greenish-blue, and the interior space seemed to be filled with seawater. To the left of these Kivs was a short set of steps that led to a small balcony and another Kiv situated directly above the lower ones.

Man-Den stepped forward and turned to Mark. "Ja-Lil, every king of this city, since we left the shoreline and entered the sea, has learned the history of our people from the Dome." As he spoke, the other Elders stepped each to their specific Kiv and stood in front of it facing Mark. "We will all enter before you and make ready the Dome for your introduction to it as the new king."

Mark simply nodded, and the six men turned to the solid wall. They touched their thumb to their lips then to their Nahum. Then, palms outstretched, they extended their hands to the wall and, similar to entering or exiting the city, they passed through the wall and into their Kiv. Mark could make out through the opaque nature of the wall that they were immersed in the liquid. Their hair and garments lifted slightly and floated a bit away from their bodies. They slowly rotated until they were facing out and then became motionless, suspended at the centers of the Kivs.

Mark went to the stairs and climbed up to the ledge that passed in front of the king's Kiv. Duplicating the action of the Elders precisely, he ended by extending his hands until they touched the wall. The softness of the tissue began to envelope his hands and arms and he felt himself drawn into it. The transition was rapid. The next instant he was inside. It was not water from the ocean as he had thought, but rather fluid of the Dome itself. He recognized the quality of the recording gel—very strong in the liquid. As he drew it into his chest, he felt a sensation he had never known before. It was puzzling. He tried to analyze the input he was receiving, but everything felt so much a part of him he could not think inside it. He realized this was because he *was* inside it. And it was inside him at the same time. He could not tell where he as an individual stopped and where the environment around him began. His body no longer felt wetness or warmth. The outermost cells of his skin was the same as the next particle of fluid that touched it. There was no separation. He actually became like the temperature of the seawater on the outside as well as the coolness of the air inside the Domed city.

He soon realized that he was no longer looking out at the wall of the Kiv he had just passed through, but different visions were taking over his consciousness. Sometimes, in the past, when he had been dreaming a long and involved dream he would wake and know he had dreamt only minutes. The sequence of his dream, however, was long and covered sometimes days and weeks in great detail. What was happening to him was somewhat like that. In his mind, he could observe what was happening within the city, not just now but before and in an ever-increasing expansion of time. He was everywhere. In a single instant, he saw today, his anointing, his mother, Tei-La, and all the citizens of the city. In the same instant, however, he also saw his father lying without life on his bed next to the queen. There were all the king's since the city passed beneath the surface and their people. The secession of Elders since the days of Draa-Pic were there with their complete history. Not a minute of time was omitted—not in the life of the city or of any individual. In that momentary existence of time, Mark knew all life, every birth, death, and all moments in between. He was there while the first king and Elders moved the city from the shore to the depths of the great inland sea. Ages later, he saw Poi-Den as he took the Dome on the long trek to the west and northward. He witnessed the entire interaction with the Landed Ones over that time and the setting of convergence markers. The stories his father had told him were no longer the lore of the city. They were before him and around him. They were, in fact, his life.

The Dome and he were one, and they communicated freely all that they were and what they had experienced. There was no time. There was only the energy of emotion that defined life itself.

Mark now understood why the king had the title of the One Who Knows. In this moment, Mark was with his mother and could see her in her solitude sitting quietly in her place of meditation. He was with Tei-La as she walked along the street by the large canal. Nothing omitted. He encompassed all.

He felt an immense respect for the life of the Dome. This living thing that held and protected all their lives existed only for their wellbeing. It sought nothing in return. It lived and grew and extended itself at the request of the people. Mark offered his appreciation for the dignity of this great living thing. He knew the Dome received this sense of respect.

Depending on the extent of what was needed, the Elders would enter their Kivs in whatever number necessary and together, with the Dome, walls would grow, homes would be built, and anything needed would be done. What he now felt at the depths of his life was that it was not his life. It was not the city's life. Nor in fact was there any one individual life. It was all one, and every part was just that. A part of the life.

He had no idea how much time he spent in the Kiv. He only knew it was not a dream and yet all of history had occurred. His mind focused and, with a sense of gratitude, he extended his hands and passed through the wall and onto the landing outside the Kiv. Walking down the steps to the lower level, he arrived just as Man-Den and the others, excepting one Elder who remained inside, emerged from their Kivs.

"We honor and respect the fifth in line of the kings." Man-Den spoke as he and the Elders bowed to Mark. "I will take you to the hall of treasures and the Dome will allow your entry."

"I know of the hall from my father, but not of what is in it. Man-Den will you join me and explain what you can?" Many times as a boy, Mark had listened as his father told stories of past kings using certain treasures to accomplish tasks that were beyond even their prodigious strength. Although he remembered the stories, he had never been schooled on the instruments and their uses.

"I am sorry, Ja-Lil, only one of the true blood is allowed to enter. It is not just tradition but fact. The Dome will not admit anyone who does not have blood of the royal line."

"If I enter surely then you can accompany me."

"The Dome will close the entry on anyone if they try to pass."

In all his experience with the Dome, Mark never considered it to have volition of its own. He had assumed that it responded to the will and wellbeing of the citizens and specifically to the influence of whatever Elder occupied the Kiv at any given time. Mark knew that many families in the city had the specific job of guarding the king and his family, but he now realized his greatest protector was the Dome itself. It would react, if not with intelligence at least with instinct, in his best interest. This explained to him why he always felt so calm and assured when he was in the city.

"Then take me to the hall and thank you."

Standing in front of the wall, which would lead to the hall, Mark watched as Man-Den and the four Elders left for their homes. The nodule in front of him glowed a gentle-green, but he did not immediately place his hand on it for entry. Everything he did now would be following in the footprint left before him by his father. He could still vividly see in his mind the image from the Dome of the king lying so peacefully on his bed with his mother. In a minute, he would enter this room where only his father and three others had been before him. He could not remember feeling moments of great sadness in his life. Indeed, he was not sure it was sadness that he felt now. It was more a sense of loneliness. He missed his father, yes, but his loneliness was more the type you feel in a crowded room when you know no one. Mark was aware that from now on, in this city he loved so much, he would always be separate from all the others. That he really would be alone. This was the feeling his father bore all of his life, just as the kings before him had done. But his father had the queen. Mark had a deeper and more profound sense of appreciation for the bond between his father and mother. And of course he had Tei-La. She was there now. She flooded his mind. He could see her, feel her, and smell the scent of her so clearly he actually glanced as if to suddenly see her standing behind him.

He would never be alone. This swell of emotions he experienced for his father would pass and the memory would soften its influence on him. He would have the strength that Tei-La would give him. He would only be as great a leader for his people as her support would let him be, and he knew her love was absolute.

"I am ready," Mark said in a low voice to no one, and he placed his hand on the wall.

The seam began, and it appeared to Mark to move slower than other door openings elsewhere. It was as if the Dome was aware of the importance of him entering this room. The division was complete, and the wall retracted into itself. As Mark entered, the light in the room brightened.

"The treasure hall, Ja-Lil," To-Bay's long lecture of several nights ago reverberated in his ears, "contains all the relics of the ancients. All have a purpose and all can only be wielded by one of the line."

Standing in the room and not moving, Mark could see over a dozen carved stone stands of various heights on top of which were different objects.

"Some have not been used in several generations," his father had told To-Bay, "while others are used on a regular basis."

Slowly Mark approached the closest carved podium. It was the purest quality of marble and stood about five feet five inches in height. From the stepped base to the top, it was covered in finely chiseled relics. Grapevines formed frames around replicas of pillared buildings, fountains, and busts that he guessed to be Mediterranean in style. Resting on top were two bracelets; one of silver and the other of gold. In the center of each was a gem, which he could not identify. In the gold bracelet, there was a stone the size of a small acorn, almost white in color. At first, Mark assumed the light from the ceiling being emitted by the Dome was pinpointed at the stand. As he came closer, however, he was aware that the brightness he perceived was coming from the stones themselves. In the silver bracelet, the stone was orange and red except for the center, which pulsated in shades of orange and yellow.

These would be the "Hands of Healing and Closure." It appeared that this father had related to To-Bay the items in the hall in order so that one would see them as they went through the room. "You will know each time the appropriateness of entering the body or not. For often the healing can come from without." The second-hand instructions Mark knew would make logical sense when the time dictated, or he would know by instinct after he accepted the line of the life-thought of his father from the Nari-Tanta tomorrow. He took the ornaments in his hand and, as soon as he touched them, the light from the stones intensified. The white light and that from the reddish stone joined in a prism-like effect, and the reflection of the myriad of colors bounced off the walls.

The effect jarred his memory to a time long ago in his father's house. Mark had been sitting in a small chair to the left of the king as citizens came through for healing and guidance. One particular older woman spoke to his father of the pains in her chest that were increasing daily. The king had her sit in his chair while he held her hands and fingers, and later cupped his hands around her feet and ankles. Mark had watched the king lead her to a small anteroom and, from where he sat, Mark saw the reflection of the rainbow of lights. Colors he had never seen before chased each other up and down the walls and raced over the parts of the ceiling and floor of the small room that he could see from his chair. He remembered so clearly the change in the woman when she emerged from the room with the king. Her face had filled out. Gone were the wrinkles that lined her brow, her mouth was no longer pressed into a tight line, and she wore a small smile. She had made a point of coming over to where he sat, and she touched his forehead gently.

"I bow to you too, my future king," she had said, nodding her head slightly. As she left the room, his father also touched his head as he took his seat once more.

"We can take away pain and often give joy, my son. It is only time we're powerless about."

The gems dimmed to their original luster as he replaced them on the podium and stepped to the next. He stood and stared—not at the article but at the space of two or three inches between it and the table over which it hovered. Two wooden handles extended from the sides of this ceramic-like ball. Two small openings that held crystal-like stones were under the handles, and a third layer of stone was imbedded on the other side directly opposite the first two. In the Kiv earlier, he had seen his father's father with this very thing, walking through the city to the ready room. He knew it was for the placement of the convergence markers his father had told him of.

"Immovable and light as air." To-Bay had described it. "It will have the weight of the world when touched by others."

Mark made his way around the hall, carefully taking in every aspect of each article and remembering every word To-Bay had used to describe them. With each piece, the image of his father grew stronger and, save for his voice, Mark felt his presence like a strong hand on his shoulder. Pondering the gold box filled with white sand, which was inscribed with a simple circle and a single dot in the middle—a symbol that To-Bay had described only as "primary start"—Mark placed it back on its stand and turned to the next pedestal. The sound of his own voice startled him almost as much as the object he was staring at. Resting in two cupped holders on the gray-green marble column lay the very knife that had threatened his life on his deck weeks ago.

Yet it couldn't be. How could this weapon, which To-Bay had said his father described as a tool that could be used "...for internal healing or cleaning" have been removed from the hall and operated by someone who was not of the bloodline? He circled the stand to see the knife from all angles. The shiny casing covered the entire blade and the whole thing looked as if it had not been touched in years. Mark took it in his hands. He felt traces of the same fear he'd experienced that night by his pool. This tool could end his life or the life of anyone in the city, in an instant. He had seen how the wound on the younger man had never closed and his life slowly drained from him. It was merely an object now, weighing maybe one pound. It had no visible seams, and it rested benignly in his hand like a small, carved sculpture. Holding the round hilt-like cup in his left hand, he slid his right palm inside the opening. He wrapped his fingers around the smaller interior handle and, as his grip tightened, the round covering became liquid-like and retracted back into the handle, revealing the blade. As he looked at it, his fear was replaced with wonder. It was completely in his control. He knew it was never meant to be used as it had been, to harm someone. The words, healing and cleansing, still rang in his ears and he knew he held in his hands the possibility of life or death.

Still the mystery remained. It was virtually impossible for this or any other thing here to be removed by anyone other than himself or his father. Replacing the knife, he examined the remaining items and left the hall for his home.

CHAPTER ELEVEN

H e stood there in the corridor as the wall closed behind him and the seam silently disappeared. Now he had many more questions about the city and its people. How had the knife left the hall and returned? When he was in the Kiv, thousands of faces flashed through his mind. Until this moment, he had not thought about it, but now he realized the two men who tried to kill him were not among them. How could that be? They were definitely of the same people as he. They had possessed the knife. Where was the surviving older man? Mark had seen him actually enter the city so his life should have been recorded by the Dome. Ultimately, how could he have activated the knife if he was not of royal blood? These questions would have to wait unless the answers were forced upon him. He would now go home, change from his father's clothes, go to the Nari-Tanta, and accept the king's life-thought, hold it, and then return it after the knowledge of the ancients was transferred to him.

The citizens he passed on his way acknowledged him, but he already felt the change in their attitude. They gave him the space of deference, did not approach, and after nodding or smiling, they turned their faces away. He knew they did it because they did not want to intrude, but it reinforced his feeling of being separate. He knew the feeling would only grow stronger as the years went by. Upon entering his house, he went immediately, before changing, to his mother's quarters. She was still where he had observed her while in the Kiv. He paused just inside the doorway to where she sat in meditation. Her eyes were closed and the Dome's light fell in a warm circle around her. He stood there feeling so happy for his father. He could feel, looking at this remarkably beautiful woman, how humble and grateful the king had been to call her wife and share his life with her. She spoke without opening her eyes.

"My son is now my king."

"Your husband is your king. I will always be your son." He walked to her as she opened her eyes.

She turned to him and smiled. "Ja-Lil, I have decided to join your father. I have wanted to from the time of his passing, but I remained here because I knew his heart so well, and his heart was the city. Until you returned, I stood for him in advising Man-Den and the Elders, and through that I believe the people felt they still had a king."

"I understand." And he did. Completely. "I will inform Man-Den and will tell the people. Tomorrow, I will take you to join my father."

She kissed the palms of both his hands and returned to her platform as he left the room.

Walking back along the streets after changing from his father's clothes, Mark tried to put his feelings in perspective. He had observed, over the time he had spent on the surface, how the people there reacted to death. He had come to understand their sense of loss and their sadness at being alone. It was the anger that bewildered him. Their seeking of some kind of retribution for the loss of the one they loved. It must have been, he finally concluded, that they felt all was over and any connection they had with the departed was severed. That loss of hope and power caused them to react with anger.

Approaching Man-Den's home, he had a growing feeling of elation. His mother was going to where she wanted to be. She was continuing in the direction she had chosen when she married. He knew the city would celebrate her and her life.

He met Roi-Den on the street, and in the short distance to his home, told him of his mother's decision.

"Ja-Lil, I knew it was going to be sometime. How wonderful for you to have them together again." Roi-Den led Mark to the minister's quarters where his aunt and Man-Den rose to their feet as he entered.

"I am afraid it will take some time, Man-Den, before I am used to this. Please, sit down," he said.

Mark sat quickly to stop further shows of respectful tradition for his new position.

"Ja-Lil has wonderful news, father." Roi-Den jumped in immediately. "The queen has decided to join his father at the transference tomorrow."

Len-Wei lightly clapped her hands together and from that little gesture, Mark knew she was happy for her sister.

"No!" Mark looked at Man-Den who had just spoken. The man's face had none of the joy of the others. His skin was flushed and his darkening eyes were rimmed with red.

"She must not!" By now everyone was staring at him. He returned each gaze, one by one, looking almost as startled as they looked by his outburst.

"The queen must stay with us. She is needed in the city, Ja-Lil," Man-Den said.

By now his voice had softened a little, and he stood and walked to the small window overlooking the courtyard. "She has been invaluable to us in your absence, and I should imagine you would want to have her guidance while you adjust for the time you have been away."

"My darling," Len-Wei went to her husband before Mark could reply, "she is only doing what any of us would do. She will lie forever with the one she loves as you and I will one day. Many times others have chosen not to remain apart, and we have always agreed and supported them." She leaned in to kiss Man-Den's cheek, but before she could he stepped to where Mark sat.

"I must speak with the queen immediately, Ja-Lil," Man-Den said.

"You may not."

"What..."

Mark had been looking into Man-Den's eyes from the time he first spoke and now had answered him; not as Ja-Lil, the friend of his son, or citizen but as the king. "She entered her meditation as I left the house, and I will be ready by morning. I will take her life-thought and you will inform the people of her passing." Mark rose as he spoke. It was not a request he made, and all three of them, for the first time, saw him as the king.

"Of course, Ja-Lil." Man-Den now smiled, looking at both his wife and son. "I meant only to pay her my respects and thank her on behalf of the city, as is my office."

"Thank you, minister; she will be aware of your feelings when I take her tomorrow. Now I must go." Mark nodded to Man-Den as the minister bowed to him. Then he kissed his aunt and walked to the door with Roi-Den.

"I could go with you tomorrow, Ja-Lil. It is my responsibility to always protect your family and your line just as it was my father's." Roi-Den gave a wink to Mark as they walked outside.

"Thank you, my friend, but I do not need protection tomorrow, and we will have time enough when I return." Mark remembered the many times they had gone out into the ocean together, and although the young man went with him as his friend, he also went as his protector. Neither ever spoke about it and, in fact, Mark had always felt that he would be the one to protect his friend if trouble occurred, but Roi-Den still assumed it as his responsibility. The gratitude Mark felt...he knew he could never fully repay, but he knew also that he would never forget.

Walking into his mother's chamber, he knew she had already started her preparations so he took his position at the side of her bed where he would spend the night. He watched as she lay there. She had put on the royal gown she always wore on great occasions of the city and had done her hair the way his father always liked. She lay with her arms folded across her chest and the queen's amulet around her neck. Time began to expand outward in all directions. He was at the same center of space as his mother and moments pulsed out and away from him.

When he took her life-thought tomorrow, he would remove the charm with the six small gems of different colors that were imbedded so they could be seen from both sides. He would give it to Tei-La and that would confirm her as the next queen of the city and as his wife. He knelt by the bed and closed his eyes. Soon his thoughts centered deeper and deeper into his memory, and he spent the night somewhere between sleep and awake, reliving the history with his mother and father.

His eyes opened just as the light in the room was brightening. He wasn't sure why, but before he rose or looked at his mother, he repeated the entire poem his father had taught him. It was the most personal thing his father had given him, and it felt right to offer it now. He got to his feet and looked down at the queen. The beautiful color of her skin had not changed. She almost seemed to glow and her skin still remained warm to the touch. The only indication that she would not, at any moment, open her eyes and bid him good morning was that her chest no longer rose and fell with her breathing. She had entered that final sleep with a small smile on her lips, and he could tell that the memory she held at the last was of his father.

He carefully removed the queen's necklace, placed it around his own neck, and kissed her on the forehead. He knew what he was to do next, but for a minute he hesitated. He had never accepted a life-thought, although the practice was common and many he knew had done so. Roi-Den had carried one from an uncle of his when Man-Den was away on a tour years ago, and he had said nothing about it to Mark—other than it had been completed. Mark remembered thinking how out of character it was for Roi-Den to say so little. Knowing how his friend loved to talk and found almost everything worthy of discourse. Although the transfer was normal, he then realized it was also deeply personal. This transfer was even more so. This was his mother, and he would deliver her to his father and a Nari-Tanta he had never seen. Perhaps hesitation had more to do with his time on the surface and of the importance they gave to life and death.

The moment passed, and he sat on the side of the bed touching his thumb to his lips. He touched her forehead with it, and then placed the palm of his right hand over the spot. His hand lay there with his fingers under the ringlets of hair gently touching her scalp. There was no specific thought process, no incantation. It was the wanting. He wanted to take and protect the life of his mother. His desire made it so. If there was a feeling, it was the sensation of warmth he sensed in the palm of his hand and, following that, an energy. The energy went from a feeling to having volume, and he could sense it filling him. Also, it had joy. For no apparent reason, he began to smile as the sense of his mother filled his being. Where it went in him, he could not tell, but it was a complete part of everything he was. It took no longer than fifteen or twenty seconds and, when done, nothing seemed to have changed.

He opened his eyes, which he could not remember closing, and focused on the face of his mother. The glow remained and the warmth, but he knew her life was within him. It gave him a feeling of honor, and it was not solely because it was his mother's life he held. It was that he was responsible *for* and *to* a life, and now he had the mission to see it safely to the Tanta.

He left the house knowing the Elders would prepare the queen's body for the royal chamber in the tradition of the city, and he made his way to Tei-La's home. Man-Den and the Elders had informed the city and every face he encountered reflected the happiness they felt for his mother as they greeted him on the streets.

"It is so wonderful, Ja-Lil." Tei-La kissed him several times as he came into the reception chamber of her house. "Every person loved her so. She will be celebrated forever."

"When I return today, the city will have their new queen, and I will be as fortunate as my father." He held her close and felt her push against him as he kissed her again. It was an endless chain of beginnings, with each ending leading to yet another beginning. That's why he had to see her before he left the city. They were the next beginning—although they had always been—and his parents were ending, although they would always be. There was no other one for him and could never be. "I love you."

"I know."

She touched his face and kissed him softly, and he left for the exiting chamber without looking back at her.

He swam out into the open sea with no particular destination in mind. He knew he had to find a Tanta, and it would be they who would communicate with the Nari-Tanta. He had never received the life-thought of another, and now he traveled with his mother's very life within him. He felt no different; he could not tell by any sensation of her presence. Her actual life *was* but now did not exist. She was dead but also, within his life, she was alive and in fact would live forever. It was easy to think about these things here in the vastness of the sea. The water was not just full of living things like plants and fish and mammals, but for him the ocean itself was a living force and he was a dynamic part of that life.

He traveled in a northward direction, and the sea floor rose gradually until the total depth was only a few hundred feet. Marine life was abundant in this area and it was not long before, in the distance, he saw the rounded head and white markings on the underbelly of a small whale he knew to be a pilot whale. The language was very familiar to him and he clicked in the high decibel range of the species. The small male turned immediately and swam easily to Mark. The communication took only a few seconds and, with the location fixed in his mind of where to wait, Mark swam off as the pilot whale turned to deeper water and disappeared into the grayness.

Mark had never been to this part of the sea, but his father had described it and the transfer on several occasions.

"The Tanta will find you only when you have readied yourself. The proper one for you will follow your call," the king said as he was describing the location of the area. "Once the Tanta has arrived and signaled it is ready, you can approach and complete the transference."

He did not need to define the action or the song of the call. All citizens knew the language of the sea from birth, and the rituals came as natural as walking and swimming. Landmarks or topography did not blaze the path Mark followed to the site. He slid along in the water guided by the current, gravity, magnetic pull, the echo bouncing back to him, and a host of other stimulation that he could not put into words. When it all matched perfectly with descriptions given by the small whale, he was in the center of a bowl-shaped area of seabed the size of a soccer field. The walls around it climbed steeply to almost a hundred feet, and the floor was of white sand with little vegetation.

He had no idea how long the wait would be or how far the Nari-Tanta had to travel to get to him. There was a circle of rocks in the center of the field. Some were small and smooth and round and others slightly larger and on end so they stuck up out of the sand. Mark swam to it and settled to the sand in a seated position, with his legs crossed, and waited. He became less and less aware of his surrounding as he stilled his mind and repeated the calling song of his father and felt it race out into the water in all directions. He would reach the end of the song and he would start the notes of the call again until there was no start and stop but a continual circle of the melody. It was all there together. He was the water, his father and mother were the sand, and the song connected it all.

At some point, he began to separate things again and, as the rocks and fluttering strands of sea grass came into focus, he was aware of a sound other than his own. He could see it was not so, but it seemed to vibrate the sand all around him. It was low in register and pulsed through the water and through him. It grew in strength and he could pinpoint the source as coming toward him from over his left shoulder. It was a beautiful sound and generated a feeling he could only describe as comfort. He felt like he used to when he would be in his home and could hear the voice of his mother and father in discussion. He couldn't hear the words, only the distant hum of the two sounds combining and filling the space in the house. He would, at times, feel they were everywhere that there sound was, and therefore all around him. Roi-Den told him of the same feelings, and he knew it was probably common to young people.

The sound began to modulate, and then the light around the bowl dimmed slightly. He could definitely feel his body vibrating with the deep song as a grayish darkness fell on him. It traveled like the shadow of a cloud that had moved across the sun's light. He followed it as it raced along the sandy floor, and then he saw the rounded snout of the Tanta glide about twenty feet over his head. It was enormous! He had never seen nor heard of a blue whale reaching these proportions. The width of the darkness it created easily covered over one half of the sandy sea floor. It moved through the water without any physical motion. It slowed almost to a halt directly over Mark as he sat there and began to turn sideways. It hovered, suspended in the water like a huge ship of some sort.

Even his father had not known how old this Nari-Tanta was. He had delivered his own father's life-thought to this very being long ago. There were others like this one in the history of the city, and when they died their holdings were transferred to a younger Nari-Tanta and the cycle continued. This giant cetacean was easily over one hundred and thirty feet. He wore the marks of his long life on his skin. The blue-gray hide was covered with many scars and had a yellowish covering on much of it, which Mark knew came from living in the cooler southern waters. His long white-tipped flippers hung down almost touching the sandy bottom, and the large eye looked gently at Mark.

Mark sat silently looking up into one dark eye. The hum of the Tanta changed and he began to follow the song of Mark's father. Mark followed the call and rose from the sand and pushed up, coming to rest across that kind gaze. The sound from the whale became the words they heard in their minds. Mark put his palms together and extended them to the Tanta.

"I am Ja-Lil, son of Con-Or."

"Yes." The voice he heard from the whale was like no other. It came from all around Mark and entered his mind without the foreign feeling that usually accompanied communications from other sea mammals. And at the same time, it felt like it came from within him.

"I hold Myo-O, wife of the king. She has quit this life to be joined with her husband and reside with Nari-Tanta."

The whale held Mark with its gaze for some time before responding.

"I hold not the king Con-Or nor was I aware of his passing." This experience was so different from any Mark had had before. He was not sure he heard this last statement of the Tanta correctly.

"Several years ago, Man-Den from our people brought the king's life-thought to you here."

"It is not so." There was no surprise or confusion in the voice, unlike what was racing through Mark's entire being.

"My father died and Man-Den took the life-thought. To whom would he give it if not to you?" Mark could feel his heart pounding faster as he tried to make sense of all this.

"I do not know. The answer would be with Man-Den. Leave Myo-O with me until you deliver the king."

"Of course." Mark knew the Tanta was correct and that his mother, no matter what was to happen in the future, should reside here with the line of kings. He knew exactly what to do next for the transference, but so much of his brain was occupied with the shock of what the whale had told him. He would find the answers and he would find his father. These were the vows he made to himself as he swam to where he could touch the large mammal with both hands. Looking into the eye that was half the size of his entire body, Mark put his right hand over the small opening between it and the base of the large flipper. Covering the ear hole, he put his left hand near the bottom of the eye. The moment both hands felt the rough texture of the whale's skin, he willed his mind to completely relax. It started at the tips of his fingers and moved up and into his hands. The current of energy went through his skin and expanded until he could sense its presence throughout his whole body. It was then that he felt the life of his mother. It seemed to gather itself from all parts of him. As the essence came together, it seemed to gain substance. He could feel her becoming real inside him. When it felt like it might take real physical form inside his skin and rip him apart, it left. He felt it go as it traveled with the retreating energy, along his arms to his hands, and into the whale.

He knew she was gone. He felt smaller than he had ever been, and in the next instant, he felt normal again. He pulled his hands away, clasped them together, and closed his eyes.

"She is with me," the whale said.

"Yes, thank you. I will bring the king to her soon." Mark was already backing away from the motionless giant. He could not remember feeling this kind of confusion and anger before. It was not the anger of loss that he had witnessed in Those on the Surface. It was the anger of betrayal. Why would Man-Den, the Minister of the Right and Left and his father's most trusted advisor, not complete the transfer. There was no explanation.

There was only what he must do. He swam fast, not really racing, but with determination. The landscape went by without him really noticing it. Was Man-Den lying and had he not even taken the king's life-thought? If that was so, then it was too late. The life-thought of a person would dissipate into the environment over a short period of time after death. Also, a person could release their own immediately if they willed it as Mark's young attacker had done. If the king's life-thought was now gone then the line of the king's and their history was broken, and at the time of convergence the Nari-Tanta would not be able to deliver. All of this made no logical sense. What could the minister gain by any of these actions? Mark swam on with no answers, only a mountain of questions.

He traveled along the foothills and over the dark channel that ran east and west for hundreds of miles. He left the ocean floor to clear the hot geysers that spewed highly acidic liquid from the earth's interior. Dropping again to the sandy bottom, he made his way through the little valleys of low mountains and their jagged outcroppings. Still, he swam with his focus on what he imagined would transpire with his return to the Domed city. Passing under the overhanging ledge, he started to turn toward the sea lane that led to the city.

He didn't see what hit him because it came from over his right shoulder. His peripheral vision caught a shadow of the shape just before impact, but he could not react in time. The blow hit him along the side of his chest, and the force of it sent him smashing into the rocky cliffside. What had he seen? Anything? He didn't know if it had been a shark or an inanimate object. He knew he was not badly damaged, and his mind switched from its overview of his body and tried to focus outward. With his vision blurred, he tried to be aware of where his attacker was going to strike next. From just above him, he saw the large boulder falling through the water and got his hands to his head in time to deflect the downward thrust so it just grazed his forehead.

Now his eyes focused, and he darted out from under the ledge into the open where he knew he had a better chance to maneuver and survive. This time he saw him. The same man again! At that moment of recognition, he was also aware of the scent. It had been there a moment before the attack, and he was upset with himself for not reacting more quickly. Still not completely recovered from the first two blows, Mark braced his feet on the sand to receive the next attack. The man had a large rock in his hands and was racing downward from the overhang directly toward him, using the gravity of the stone and the thrust of his swimming stroke to create power and speed. Mark concentrated hard on the approaching figure. He still hadn't regained the sureness of his body and wanted to avoid this assault to give him another minute to gather his strength. Mark stayed his ground until the man was no more than ten to fifteen feet away. Then he saw him pull the stone toward his chest to give a bit more velocity. Instead of trying to deflect another blow, Mark feinted slightly to the left then pushed off with all his strength to the right. The man couldn't react fast enough to redirect the force of the rock and, though he tried, the blow missed the target, which was Mark's head, and instead hit him squarely on the left shoulder.

The pain shot along his arm and all the way down to the base of his spine. Even as he felt it, he knew neither the arm nor the shoulder was broken. He turned several somersaults in the water as he tumbled away, stopping further solid hits, and came to a halt twenty feet from the man. The electric surge from the impacted nerves in his left side exploded all through him. Color deepened and he could feel the blood racing to his stricken shoulder. His attacker was not launching himself again but stood in the water watching Mark as he regained his balance.

"Who are you?" Mark could only feel a tingling now over his entire left arm, which hung limply at his side. "Why are you doing this?"

The man said nothing. Reaching to his belt, he pulled out a glove and slipped his right hand into it. He then opened his tunic and there, for the third time in his life, Mark saw it! His attacker drew out the sacred king's knife and inserted his gloved hand into the opening. The shining cover withdrew to expose the deadly-sharp blade.

"How did you get that? Only the king can open the treasure chamber!"

The man answered by slowly swimming forward. Mark had no choice but to retreat. He knew the man's strength was close to his own, and with his left arm useless, his only option was escape. With the shock of seeing the weapon out here in the open sea, and then to watch it obey one who was not of the blood, Mark had not paid attention to where he was. Before he could correct his direction, he realized he had backed up against the solid rock face of the overhang. The stone wall made a definite V and he was squarely in the deepest recess of it. He was trapped! The only way out was to go through or around the man and the knife. There was little chance of success, but Mark felt if he were cut, perhaps even badly, there was a possibility he could make it to the city and the healing bracelets before he lost too much blood. Thinking that it might make a difference, he planned to rush by the man exposing only his left side. It would leave his good right arm protected and the blade might be deflected from entering deep into his body by striking the arm bone or a rib. It was a small consolation, but it seemed his only chance of surviving at all.

His attacker filled the exit lane of the little cul-de-sac and continued to move toward him, and Mark saw a smile on his face. He knew he had him trapped and was confident of making his kill.

Now. It has to be now, or there will be no room to get by him. This thought came to Mark as he felt the vertical face of the rock against his back. With a strange vision of Tei-La's face briefly before him, he knew not seeing her again would be his main regret if he failed to make it back to the city. Mark crouched a little, braced his right foot against a boulder, and was about to launch himself. Before he could move, the man was hit from behind at full speed by Roi-Den. The man obviously had not seen him and neither had Mark. The weapon flew from his hand as he was driven forward into the sand.

"Ja-Lil, are you all right?" By this time, Roi-Den was on the man once again, lifting him to his feet and pushing him up against the rock wall. Before Mark could respond, the man grabbed Roi-Den by the back of his neck and spun him around and into the rock. When they were face to face, the larger man hesitated for a moment and seemed unsure if he was going to continue the fight. The halt was only for a fraction of a second then he tore off a piece of rock from the wall and drew back his arm. Before the man could land the blow that was aimed at his jaw, Roi-Den had dropped down and launched his shoulder into his stomach. Both men pushed through the water, and the force of Roi-Den's charge drove the larger man down into the sand.

"Do not let him reach the knife!" Mark was now holding his useless left arm in his right hand.

"Go back to the safety of the city, Ja-Lil. This one may not be alone." This was no longer Mark's youthful friend, but a man who knew his duty to protect the king and was confident in his ability and his decision.

Mark swam around the two fighting men as their swirling bodies stirred up the sandy bottom and obscured the violence of their battle.

"Beware of the knife, Roi-Den."

Locked as they were in their fight, he was sure neither of them could find the blade, which sheathed itself as it left the man's hand and fell to the sand. It was now lost in the whirling storm of sand. Mark left the two, worked his way out of the little valley, and made for the city.

The elevator door opened directly into the dark foyer, stabbing the blackness with a shaft of yellow light. The two bodies were outlined in the doorway as if it were one person with two heads. The kiss was brief but welcomed by both.

"Would you like me to come in for awhile?" He spoke quietly and kindly.

"Not tonight, Gasten." Elizabeth put both hands to his lapels and gently smoothed them. "I had a wonderful time. I know I have been a bit down lately. I don't know why," she lied, "but thank you for being so patient."

She stepped into the room and the point of yellow light bounced off the silver heels of her black-velvet pumps. Turning to look at her from inside the elevator car, Gasten smiled and made a little wave. "I'll give you a call on Monday. We'll talk about the trip," he said.

The doors came together and sealed the room in total darkness. She could hear the elevator descend into quiet, and she stood for a long time enjoying the cool comfort of solitude. With a little sigh, she walked the familiar four paces in the dark, thinking like so often, *I'd really do all right if I were blind.* At the juncture of nothing and the faint gray of the living room, she reached out and her finger landed directly on the switch. With the several lamps connected to the switch and the deep-dish hanging Tiffany in the center of the room, she made the mental king's-X as the radiance of the colored glass made her glad she had sight.

She stepped out of the shoes and walked over the hardwood floors to the welcome comfort of the carpet by the bar. Slipping the gold chain from her shoulder, she set the small black bag on the marble counter and poured a small glass of port for herself. She turned and leaned against the curved smooth edge of stone and stared out the glass wall to the single boat's light that was on the water. It had been months now since Mark had gone away. And there was still no sign of Dr. Thomas Raggit, though she'd searched for him. She and Gasten had been seeing a lot more of each other outside work. The longer Mark had been away, the more (once the shock of his leaving wore off) she looked for comfort in her other relationships. Gasten was always there but never imposed himself on her. He was kind and gentle, and she found herself having fewer and fewer reasons to keep him at a distance.

A few lunches then dinners followed by nights at the opera or the theater and soon she was looking forward to his calls and invitations. But there was always Mark. Or at least the possibility of Mark. Still standing there, she started to smile. "How long will you wait tonight, Lizzy?" She had been talking out loud to herself more lately, and she felt it was almost like having a third person there to add a little objectivity to her internal debates. She knew the answer to that question tonight, however.

She would change into her nightgown and robe, which she did. Then she would wash her face clean until the skin glowed and tingled, which she did. Then she would take her drink and her laptop out into the warm night breeze on her balcony, which was where she was now, sitting on the overstuffed cushion of the wicker loveseat, just so the infrared signal of the computer would reach her desktop outside. She chased the jammy aftertaste of the Boplaas around her teeth with her tongue while she opened her laptop and accessed Jessie at the lab. With fingers sure of their path from repeated nights of this very same thing, she quickly was connected to Mark's poetry files in his office.

"Therapy time." Her voice was soft and carried lightly into the dark night. She wondered though, was it therapy or a mild form of torture? She felt close to him when she would sit here alone and read the words of his poems and paragraphs. But the closeness also made her aware of how far away he was. It was a comfort like reading history. It happened long ago, in the past, and here she was in the present so it must prove that life really did go on. But it was going on without him, and deep in her life she wasn't sure she wanted it to.

"The bottom line is," she hated it when she used phrases like that, "this is all I have." She clicked on *Tides*.

The water grows
And pushes back the sand, the birds
And time.
Waves grow down
Leaving the fragile white lace of memory
Weaving on the shore
Standing with my feet
Pressing in the cool of your last visit
I welcome you.
You have
You are
You give me life.
And then you go.
And somewhere else receives
Somewhere I am not
Sometime, I don't know when
Somehow, I will never know
And I welcome that
Somehow.

She steadied the laptop while she curled her feet under herself, and the coolness of her toes felt good on the backs of her thighs. Settling down, she stared at the typed message from him staring back. Taking the last sip of ruby liquid, she let it rest on the back of her tongue a moment before allowing it to drift down her throat and warm her. "I will talk to Gasten on Monday," she thought. "Tuscany in the spring really shouldn't be missed." She smiled a sad smile and made a little finger wave at the words on the screen. "I will welcome that, Mark. Somehow."

CHAPTER TWELVE

M ark could raise his arm a little and feeling was coming back to his fingers as he extended his hands and passed into the city. Grabbing a robe as he strode through the ready room, he was still putting it on when he stepped out into the street. So many things had been racing through his mind on the way from the fight to the Dome, but it boiled down to two big questions. Why and how? Why didn't Man-Den take the life-thought of his father? Why would he keep all that a secret from his mother and him? Why did this man, who Mark could never remember having met before, want to kill him and try on two different occasions? Also a question almost as big, was how? How could the knife, one of the royal treasures, be taken from the chamber? Only the king or one of the royal lines could be admitted to the room by the Dome. When he was gone from the city for so long before, that person could only have been his father the king. Now, since the king's death, only he was granted entrance. But yet the knife was out and, not only that, the killer had activated the sheath and exposed the blade. That too should only be possible by one of the royal line.

Soon he was well into the city. People were acknowledging him as he walked, but he didn't respond. He was aware only that, as he passed, many of them stopped and stared at him, their voices fading into the background. He knew, somehow, the key to all the mysteries would lie with Man-Den. His house was Mark's destination and he crossed the bridge over the shallow channel and turned onto the small avenue. He saw Len-Wei as she was coming out the door.

"Ja-Lil, I am so happy my sister is..."

"Where is Man-Den?" By the time he spoke, Mark had already passed his aunt and entered the house.

Almost running to catch up, she informed him that her husband was in his study chamber.

"But he has closed the wall. That is why I was going out because when he does that he cannot be disturbed for a long time."

Mark could hear the concern in her voice and knew it was his strange behavior that caused it. He had no time to offer an explanation.

"The wall will open for me." He ran up the few stairs that led to the alcove and onto the chamber of the minister. He could flex his left hand now and, as he rolled his shoulder a little, he could tell, though it was sore, it was not badly damaged. He stopped before the wall and put his right hand on the green nodule. There was a brief moment when nothing happened. There had never been a time before when the Dome had not responded immediately to his family's commands. Barely had the thought come into his mind when he saw the seam appear and the wall begin to open.

When the opening was complete, he stepped into the room. In the center, Man-Den turned to greet him.

"Well, well. The boy king in the body of a man. Do not stand on ceremony. Please, come in."

Mark could hear the footsteps of Len-Wei as she came to a stop just outside the door.

"Husband, I..." Her voice drifted into silence. The room was still. Mark could not speak either. In front of him, Man-Den stood behind a long table, which held the entire contents of the royal chamber. The bracelets, the gold box, the book of the ancients. It was all there. All but the knife. The holder lay empty directly in front of the minister.

"Do not worry, Ja-Lil, it will be returned soon. Although I must say I am a little surprised to see you here."

Mark's eyes rose from the empty case to Man-Den. The minister's face in no way resembled the person he had known for all those years. He was smiling, and he held his arms over the table. But his eyes weren't smiling. In them, Mark saw only the pure glare of hate.

"You are resilient, boy, or is it just luck?"

Whatever the answers were to what he saw before him, Mark only needed one thing now.

"Why did you not take the life-thought of my father?" His own voice sounded strange in his ears.

"Oh, but you are wrong. I did take it." The minister walked along the table, his hand trailing lightly over the articles on it. He laughed, nothing more than a small giggle. "In fact, you are doubly wrong!" The laugh again.

"Then why did you not deliver him to the Nari-Tanta?" Something inside of Mark started to sound a warning, and he turned slightly to face Man-Den squarely. "Where is he?"

"He is here, my royal liege." Man-Den touched his head and chest. "Very safe and right here."

"I do not understand."

"That's right, you do not understand. And you certainly are the son of your father because he did not understand either." His voice gained strength and all humor left it. "Nothing stays the same, Ja-Lil. It is not supposed to. We, our people, this city. None of it is meant to stay the same. We cannot live forever ruled by this old book of recipes." He reached the end of the table and slammed his fist down on the book of ancients.

"What do you intend to do?"

"I do not intend anything. I have done it. I am leading. Only the king can control the Dome and activate these treasures."

A look of disgust came over Man-Den as Mark spoke.

"Is that so? Then how do you explain them being here? How did the royal chamber open?"

The sound of hate grew each time Man-Den spoke. "Anyone can control this city who has the talent. Why do you assume that the coincidence of birth gives someone the right to rule? My father had more talent than anyone in your great royal line." He almost spat out the last three words before continuing. "And it disgusted me to see him bow and scrape to your grandfather. I would sit with him night after night while he droned on about our family's privilege of serving the king. As a child, I would play with your father. We took our first tour together. There was no difference between us. Do you understand that?" The minister was yelling now and pacing the room. "There was not one thing that made him different than me, except his blood!"

Mark knew he had to reason with Man-Den and pull him back from whatever ledge he was approaching.

"You are the Minister of the Right and Left. It has been the honor of your line since the beginning."

"Right and Left mean nothing!" The explosion of his voice told Mark there would be no controlling this mad man. "There is only a Minister of the Right and Left because it says there must be in this." Once again his fist pounded the ancient book.

Both Mark and Len-Wei were silent. Neither of them moved. Mark, because each instant he was preparing what he might do next. His aunt, because she was stunned to immobility. Man-Den seemed to be responding to questions and statements that neither of them had asked.

"Everything could just as well have come to me rather than your father. That is why, after you left on your final tour and failed to return, I knew fate had given me the opportunity to take the action I did."

Mark could feel the blood hitting the side of his head with every beat of his heart. He didn't want to hear any of what was being said, while at the same time he felt like breaking open Man-Den's body and exposing everything he knew.

"Oh, my darling, what have you done?" Len-Wei asked.

Mark could just see her as she held on to the door opening to keep from sinking to her knees.

"I have started to take what is mine." He poked a finger to the ball that floated above its stand. With each of his touches, it moved a few inches and then, as if held by a rubber string, it returned to its original position. "First the king had to die."

"I saw everything when I was in the Kiv. I saw my father sleeping and I saw him dead and you were not there," Mark said in a steady, measured tone. He had thought over every instant in the Kiv as Man-Den was talking and was sure of what he had seen.

"Is that so? Then tell me, One Who Knows, what else did you see or not see. Think carefully and show me why I should drop to my knees."

Of course, at that moment, Mark knew what he not seen.

"You." He recalled it all at once. The history of the city, his family, Man-Den's family, all the citizens, and it was clear there was also no killer. "You," he repeated.

"Bravo! That was not so hard now, was it?" His face was contorted with a half smile and half sneer. He stretched upward and rose to his full height. "You did not see me, because I did not want you to see me. So I stopped the Dome from transferring any part of my existence to you. You did not see anything I did not want you to see. Oh, I was there in your father's bedroom and not just when the queen summoned me." Man-Den seemed to be watching some invisible play being acted out in front of him. He spoke softly now like he was afraid his players would hear him and stop their mime. "He lay there so close to her I could feel the warmth of her body myself. Every breath of hers washed my face instead of his. It should have been my skin she felt under her arm and leg. My hair her fingers were holding." His voice dropped to a whisper. "It would be so easy. There are so many ways to stop a life."

As if a curtain had come down, the minister remained motionless where he sat at the table. He looked over at Mark before continuing.

"I went back many times. I almost felt like I was truly invisible, and it would not have mattered if they had wakened...for they could not have seen me. I could even touch them, you know. He would move a little and I could rest my hand on her. I knew it comforted her even in her sleep." Man-Den stopped moving except for touching the tips of his fingers together over and over very softly. "So many times at night, in her chamber, I would caress her as she slept. I could drop my garment and lay quietly next to her without them being aware. Somewhere...somewhere deep in her heart, when she would reach out in her sleep, she knew it was me that she touched. She knew."

Mark used every power in himself not to kill this man. Revulsion surged from his stomach and through his body as he thought of the disgusting betrayal of his family.

"You see, Ja-Lil, I should have been the one she chose instead of your father. He knew I loved Myo-O, from the time I was four or five years old. He knew it!" Man-Den leapt from the table and covered the distance between himself and Mark in two strides. Mark braced his legs and was about to raise his hand to defend himself, but the older man stopped quickly. His eyes narrowed and he hissed the words.

"But he had the blood."

Mark could hear the soft crying of his aunt and wanted to find a way to stop her from hearing any more of Man-Den's painful story. He remained quiet though, afraid to disrupt the flow of Man-Den's mad confession.

"So he courted her. He did and said the things I would have said and done and she became his queen. The nearest I could get was to marry this," Man-Den tossed a disdainful hand gesture to Len-Wei, "pale imitation!"

Everything but her life was torn from her and, with no strength in her body, Len-Wei slid down the doorway to the floor. She sat there with one leg trapped under her and the other bent out in an awkward position, her arms limp at her sides. The crying was silent now and from her eyes, that never left her ranting husband, ran an unending flow of tears.

Completely ignoring his effect on her, Man-Den continued.

"It was the simplest plan, really. I chose my night and entered their chamber. From the knowledge I have of the sea and its powers, I placed a small drop of poison in his open mouth, deep in the back of his throat. It was almost instant. No pain. No panic. His breathing stopped and he was dead."

Mark was somewhere else now, looking down at this scene. He could see Man-Den as he walked around the room playing with the treasures like they were toys in a playground. He could see his mother's sister melting father down into the floor as if she were trying to will her own life to end and thereby stop the pain. He could even see himself standing without moving. He was screaming at that self: "Do something!" "Stop him!" "Kill him." But nothing changed. The tinny sounds of Man-Den's voice rose to where he was perched and he continued to observe.

"That kiss she speaks of? That last one from the king that touched her heart, even in her sleep? Mine! That was the moment I knew. When time had passed and we had all mourned, then she would be my queen. And I know she would have. This one," he didn't look at his wife this time, merely nodded his head in her direction, "would, unfortunately, die before her time, too. Then two grieving souls, who were meant to be together, would be. Everything was perfect! Except for you!"

When the minister turned to him with his last words, Mark returned to the scene and to his body. Now he looked into the eyes of a man who must be stopped. He couldn't act until he knew he could save his father if it was at all possible. Then he had to stop this mad man. If the only way was to kill him, he would.

"You sent the two men?"

"Perfection means nothing happening that you do not expect, Ja-Lil. You were gone and most, except your father of course, thought you were dead. I was merely verifying that fact. But you seem to have the most annoying habit of being in the wrong place at the wrong time...for me."

"Everything you have done is useless, Man-Den. No matter if you succeed in killing me and ruling the city, the line will have ended. Your line, you and your son...my friend, can never be the royal line. You will become like Those Who Walk on the Land. You will have only the ceremony, and the true knowledge will be lost forever."

Man-Den reacted as if he had been slapped across the face with an insult.

"Nothing is lost! I can lose nothing!"

Mark could see that this was his chance. If there was a way to find his father...if transference was still possible, Man-Den's ego was the key.

"No matter how brilliant your plan or how much more suited you think you are to rule than me or my father, you do not have the bloodline, and you are not a king!"

"I am every bit a king!" The growl was evenly mixed with his rage and increased another decibel. "Because I have the king! And I have his blood!"

This was not at all what Mark had expected. He was ready to take Man-Den the moment he exposed the whereabouts of the king, but the confession of having his father's blood turned him to stone. He stood granite-like staring in disbelief at the murderer before him

"Oh! Please do not worry, Ja-Lil; I am not of your blood. I am only your uncle by the unfortunate relationship I have with her." Again, no more compassion for Len-Wei than a nod of his head. "I mean I have some of his blood."

Man-Den almost danced with arrogance to a bench-like outcropping on the far wall. Placing his hand on the top, a seam appeared just down from the flat surface of its three extended sides. The top receded into the wall. Inside was flowing water, obviously diverted from the channel that ran along the outside of the building. It entered one end, gurgled along the five-foot length of the bench, and exited the other. Mark welcomed the sound of the stream, which placed a calming hand of reality to the macabre situation.

"You see, boy. It is all possible without being related." He ceremoniously rolled the left sleeve of his gown up and slowly submerged his hand into the water. Finding what he was after, he straightened saying, "Behold, the power."

Resting in his dripping palm was a pear-shaped glass vial. The water heightened the swirling colors of the glass and it gave the appearance of having a light inside.

"Here is what is left of your father. He gave it to me just as he died and before the poison could taint it."

The spot on the robe! It was, as Mark suspected, a drop of blood. What he could not understand before was how it had stained the garment. His father's body would have closed any wound before blood could have escaped. That one small drop fell from the vial after being extracted from his father.

"It is wonderful, I must admit, to see how quickly the Dome reacts to the smallest amount of this on the palm of my hand. Doors open. Secrets are revealed. Weapons activate. And now I am going to show you how these little toys are about to respond to their new king."

"Father! Ja-Lil."

The echo of Roi-Den's call from somewhere in the house stopped everything in the room. For a moment, Man-Den lost all the swaggering confidence he had been building up since Mark had come in. His eyes darted around at everything from the treasure chamber, and Mark thought, for a moment, he would drop the vial and run. That moment passed and Man-Den once again steadied his glare on Mark and called out.

"I am in my rooms, son."

Mark could tell by the clamor that his friend was not alone. That Roi-Den was here in the city meant he had won the battle with the killer. It was strange how two opposite emotions could manifest together as they did now in Mark's mind. He was happy to hear Roi-Den's voice and know he was victorious. While at the same moment his heart ached to think how his friend would react when he learned everything his father had done. Mark had no idea what would happen next.

"My lady, are you all right?"

The Elder, Nign-Ta was the first one Mark saw as she rushed to Len-Wei, knelt beside her, and placed her hand on her wrist. Immediately behind her, came three others and Roi-Den who held one of the bound arms of the man who had been sent to kill Mark.

"She is not hurt." Nign-Ta turned her kind face to Roi-Den before he could ask the question.

"He was not one to give up easily, Ja-Lil. He has not said anything except to tell me this," in his hand, Roi-Den held the sheathed knife, "belonged to the king."

"Ja-Lil, why have these been removed from the royal chamber?" The Elder standing behind Roi-Den and his captive was the first to notice the treasures arranged on the table. Not sure of why they were there, but knowing something was wrong, she stepped around Man-Den's son and up to the table. When Mark failed to speak and everyone else was silent, the newly arrived became aware of the tension that flooded the room. They looked back and forth between Mark and Man-Den while the two men never took their eyes off each other. Confusion and fear began to congeal in everyone. Danger had a substance. It was pulling against its restraints. No one wanted to be the first to trigger it into action. Time expanded in all directions and the moment kept on and on.

The sudden clatter sent a current to every nerve in Mark's body. Everyone in the room gave a start at the noise, but Mark's instinct was not to look at the source. Had Man-Den not held the vial, Mark would have reached him before the echo of the falling knife faded, but he held himself in check. Only when he knew the minister was not going to be the first to attack, did Mark look to the noise. Roi-Den's face was turned to no one, and his eyes shook as they randomly swept the ceiling. He glanced at Mark briefly and, with a look of confusion, he dropped his focus to where the knife lay on the floor.

Mark followed his gaze and also saw the knife by the hem of his friend's robe. It was then that he was aware of the dark moving shadow as it crept out from under the garment. As the light from the ceiling touched the blackness, it lost its darkness and began to brighten to a deep crimson color. It was then that he saw all the ruby-like marks that led from where his friend stood, out the door and down the hall. Roi-Den looked with wonder as the pool got larger and, with a drunk-like rolling of his head, he whispered, "I have never seen my blood before." The strength in his legs vanished and, had he not held onto the arm of the man he had fought, he would have collapsed. One Elder held onto the captive as the other took Roi-Den under the arm and helped him to the floor.

The perfect world Mark woke up to this morning had changed now to the tragic picture before him. The life of his best friend was draining from his body as he sat next to his devastated mother, and still no one moved.

"Now!" Man-Den's roar called everyone's attention except his son's, who was too close to death to be aware of much, and his wife, whose sole focus was her only son.

"Now, another sign that the time has arrived for a new king!" His madness was frightening. The tension that gripped his body had flushed his face bright pink and caused the veins of his neck to stand out from his skin like bluish strings.

"Only I! Only one who truly should be king can save my son." Leaving the lid open on the sea bench, Man-Den lurched to the far side of the table and pulled the top from the glass vial. The stopper for the vial had a finely tapered glass tube underneath. From the three-inch long needle, several drops of blood fell to the tabletop and struck many of the treasures where they lay. One bead struck the hovering round ball like a crimson teardrop. The instant it was touched by the brownish red drop, the pulsing color glow intensified. It began to revolve in small concentric circles above its base. All this went unnoticed by the minister.

"The blood of the king shall now dwell with the mind and body of the new king and my son will be reborn!" Snapping the small glass bead from the top of the stopper, he fit it snugly back into the vial, upside down. Not hesitating, he looked down at his exposed left arm. Clenching a fist until his entire arm was shaking, he placed the point of the needle against the bulging vein at the bend of his elbow and slid the glass into his skin.

"This city and my people will change the entire world!" Pacing like a tiger in a small enclosure, he held the vial to his arm and opened and closed his hand, pulling the liquid into his body.

"We will no longer observe and hide and be afraid to be known. I have been to the surface. Many times, I have walked with them and they want us to lead them. We can be like go..." His voice broke off and he looked around the room as if he had never seen it before.

"We must not let..."Another broken sentence. He lost his grip on the vial, the needle slipped from his vein, and the entire thing splintered to pieces on the floor. The opening in his arm sealed immediately, and Man-Den's body convulsed and his mouth moved, but there was no sound. Reaching out to try and regain a sure balance, his hands missed the edge of the table and he fell backwards into a small podium, which also crashed to the ground. Thrusting himself forward once again, he came to the table and, using it to help him walk, he staggered around to the front.

The Elders and Mark could do no more than stand between Man-Den and the door and watch.

"My son." The sound of a small child or young man had replaced his bellow. "I will heal you. I will take your pain. Please d..."

They all saw it. Later they would agree that it should remain a secret between the king and Elders; Roi-Den and his mother were not watching the transformation.

The wail accompanied the change in his features. It was not a sound made by vibrating vocal chords, but centered in the minister's chest and resonating up through his torso. He tried to continue to form the words he had started to say to his son, but his mouth widened and his lips became thicker. His eyes, which had always been a steel-colored gray and darker when he was excited or angry, started to reflect greenish overtones. Even the man's hair, which like Roi-Den's was a golden-straw color, darkened in front of them and became streaked with blackish lines. As soon as one change happened, another one would begin, and the first would revert to its original state.

Mark stood there staring as the minister's body pressed against his skin as if trying to escape. Man-Den pushed his head toward his son and worked his mouth, but then suddenly spun around and locked eyes with Mark.

"Ja-Lil." It was quick. It was so small and weak that he was not sure he even heard his name, but then he was sure he had. It had only been said once, and then the large head flopped back to look at his son and the blood on the floor. It was all Mark needed to uproot him from his place. His name being spoken yanked him to the side of the minister, and he wrapped his arms around him.

"Man-Den, stop! We will help you!" The moment he gripped his hands together around the raging man, he knew the strength in his bruised left arm had not fully returned.

Man-Den turned his head. There was no trace of green in those eyes now. Only a deep dark-gray, which turned even blacker

"Do not touch me." The sound was not a voice but merely air shooting forward by the force of hate. The large man's body went completely slack for a second, and then, with incredible power, he felt surging from some deep reservoir, he shrugged his arms and shoulders and threw Mark to the other side of the room.

"Do not touch me!" The action focused him once again and, straightening himself to his full height, Man-Den, operating like a man who was trying to hide the fact he was drunk with precise steps, rounded the table. Standing behind it now, he reached for the pair of bracelets at the very end.

"I can heal you, my son. You can come back to me." His words had an inebriated slur. The silver bracelet with the reddish stone clipped around his wrist with ease. Grabbing the other produced a completely different result. The object seemed most uncomfortable to touch and, with a confused expression and groaning with the extra effort needed, the minister forced the second golden bracelet with the white stone onto his right wrist.

The moment the metal touched his skin, Man-Den stopped moving and looked with bewilderment at both hands.

"I now...I..." His eyes closed slowly until they were clenched into thin lines, and his brow was ceased with pain. He tried one more time.

"I will not..." The skin under and around the metal of both bracelets reddened as the heat intensified. A brownish color followed a faint hissing sound.

The smell reached Mark as he leapt forward to grab the band that was searing the flesh. In his right hand, Mark didn't feel the heat from the burning skin, but only the natural coolness of the metal and stone. The hate, surviving even through the pain, inspired a physical outburst from Man-Den that shook Mark from his grasp.

Mark hit the floor again, but this time with the bracelet in his hand.

Man-Den reached for anything as a weapon to further his attack. His fingers found one of the handles of the floating ceramic-like ball that still hovered above its stand. From the moment he touched it, the two crystals emitted a pulsing greenish light. The ball started to pull on Man-Den and, as he attempted to throw it at Mark, it would at one moment rise in the air to where the large man would be almost on his toes and the next drop to just above the floor as if it weighed hundreds of pounds. In his last effort, Man-Den grabbed the other handle and raised the treasure above his head. When lifting it that high, Mark could see the small black smudges of skin on his wrist emitting tiny rivulets of smoke. He also saw the single crystal on the side of the orb facing him start to glow. Before he could say anything, the glow became an intense white, and from the crystal, a ray of light hit the pillar that stood in the far corner of the chamber. It floated into the air, and the movement startled Man-Den as he spun in its direction. That shift in position changed the angle of the ball, and it took the pillar through the air in a wide arc. It knocked several pieces of marble sculptures from their stands along the wall and sent them crashing to the floor.

Shocked at the destruction created by the airborne stone, Man-Den lost the grip he had with his right hand, and the pillar dropped from where it hovered and broke into three large pieces. Re-securing both hands around the handles, Man-Den whirled again towards Mark. The white ray shot again from the crystal and found the Elder Nign-Ta. When the light touched her garment, it jerked her from her feet and into the air in a wide sweeping circle. Again, distracted by the mayhem he was creating, the minister released the handles and the ray disappeared.

Mark had but an instant to brace himself before he caught the descending older woman. The impact of her weight dropping from that height slammed into his chest and shoulders. The electric shock in his left shoulder was followed shortly by the returning numbness that had been almost completely gone. He managed to hold onto her and get her to the ground, using mainly his right arm. The ceramic ball rotated in a small circle as it floated in the air directly in front of Man-Den's chest.

"Man-Den!" The new voice from a source he recognized stopped the minister completely. Simultaneously with the shout, the bound man kicked the royal knife, which still lay where it had dropped close to his feet, across the floor. It rattled in front of Mark, slid under the table, and came to rest behind the enraged and confused madman. Now Mark had no choice; he had to subdue Man-Den. The items he had been wielding were dangerous, but other than creating bedlam and chaos, they could be avoided.

Now, this man—with no control over his twisted mental state—was inches from a weapon that could destroy everyone.

Man-Den swayed back and forth as he scanned the room. Looking from person to person, it was impossible to tell whether he recognized the individuals or not. There was no care in his gaze—the look was cold and deliberate, whether it fell on an Elder, his wife, or his son. He did hesitate briefly when he looked at the bound man who had yelled his name and given him access to the knife. A little smile appeared on his lips, and he started to mouth a word, but the raging conflict of blood and mental processes in his body caused him to convulse and then he caught sight of Mark once again. The smile became a sneer, and he pushed away the now motionless ball that hung in the air in front of him. It sailed several yards and slowly halted, almost touching the wall closest to where they stood.

"Con-Or!" Hate and fear combined in his voice and eyes as he stood there pointing his finger at Mark. Everyone watched the man in disbelief. Man-Den dropped his gaze, saw the knife where it had stopped, and bent to retrieve it.

Taking the opportunity, Mark launched himself over the table and dragged several of the items with him in his flight. Mark hit the crouching man as he came up holding the knife by the sheath. The force of the collision sent both men to the floor and the weapon banging into the corner.

With the breath partially knocked out of him, Man-Den flailed at Mark, struggling to get to his own feet and to the knife. The blows were poorly aimed, and Mark could easily deflect most before they did any real harm. Two times, however, the minister was able to connect solidly on Mark's bruised shoulder, sending jabs of current tingling to his fingers and neck. Realizing it would be impossible to stand, Man-Den rolled to his stomach and started pulling his way to the corner. Several times he was able to break Mark's still-weakened grip and was making progress towards the blade. With one last swing of his elbow, which hit squarely on the battered arm, Man-Den rolled his restrainer off his back and lunged the remaining few feet.

Spinning to confront Mark once again, heaving with exhaustion, he held the knife in his open hands.

"This time, a few drops on the palm of a glove will not be necessary." With that, he put his right hand in the opening and held out the weapon. Mark froze as the sheath immediately began to withdraw, the gleaming point aimed at his throat. He knew, even if it resulted in his death, that he had to try, right now, to stop Man-Den.

Pulling his legs under him, Mark was about to reach out and take hold of the knife blade. He stopped when the sheath stopped. Instead of completely folding into the handle, it began once again to cover the razor-sharp double edges.

Man-Den stared in disbelief, and Mark could see he was straining to will the knife to obey him. Once more the covering began to withdraw.

Mark lunged.

He had no choice but to grab the wrist that held the knife with his damaged left hand. His only plan was to derail Man-Den's killing spree long enough to take possession of his father's life-thought. If, after that, he was killed, it would still be possible for someone to then transfer him and the king to the Nari-Tanta.

He felt the roughness of the charred skin, and he heard Man-Den cry out from the renewed pain. His forward motion knocked the minister against the wall, and Mark used his own weight to compensate for his weak arm. Touching his right thumb to his lips, he jabbed it to Man-Den's forehead and he continued driving with his legs, keeping his victim trapped in the corner. He then jammed his palm to where his thumb had been and locked his fingers to the skull that held his father.

Without the freedom to use his right arm or hand to protect him, Mark felt the continuous blows to his face and ribcage. Man-Den's energy doubled with the knowledge of what Mark was trying to do. He put every ounce of strength into each punch, and with every blow Mark could feel himself weakening. He could barely get a full breath of air and his head was spinning. He felt himself being pushed backwards, and then the minister and he were on their knees. Mark could see the two eyes, black with hate, burning into him from under his wrist. He knew Man-Den could see the advantage he gained with every punch.

"You will fail, Ja-Lil, just your father failed."

Fail? No! Failure was to give up, and that he would never do. He was not sure he could stop the madman from killing him, but he would never stop fighting. If he were to die this day, the Elders witnessing this fight would find a way to end the reign of this crazed man. What he could not fail at was retrieving his father. Man-Den would not release him freely. All Mark could do was concentrate on the Nahum spot and rely on the blood that flowed through both their bodies.

Man-Den now had him turned and backed against the wall. Not being able to use the full swing of his arm, he grabbed Mark by the throat.

"The line of Con-Or is over." As he spoke, Man-Den began to push the weight of his body against the two hands that fought for control of the knife. The sheath was still not fully retracted and oscillated up and down the blade several inches both ways.

Grayness hovered around the entire circle of Mark's vision and crept slowly toward the center. In his periphery he caught the reflection from the light on the blade, and then noticed the indecisive action of the cover. If it meant what he hoped, it was his only chance left because he was losing both his strength and his battle to remain conscious.

The knife was responding to both minds in the minister's body. The king's life-thought, because of the foreign blood in Man-Den was no longer in a purely latent state and had somehow, to some degree, activated. It could be the only explanation! His mother's words at his coronation came back to him. Their blood was the same, which meant they were two but not two.

The still exposed point of the knife pressed closer to Mark's chest.

Darkness tightened his vision, eliminating all but the knifepoint and the crazed face behind it. He must not fail. They must not fail! He tried to speak once, but his voice would not come. He must not fail!

The blade touched the fabric of his tunic and still Man-Den pushed.

"Father." The whisper barely escaped. "Father, please...please help me."

Almost all was gray now, and the two dark spots of hate were all Mark could see. Somewhere, inside that, was his survival. Mark couldn't tell whether he was getting stronger or whether the strength was leaving Man-Den, but he began to turn his hand and the blade point a little to the side. Feeling the wall behind his head, he pushed against it. He was able to catch a small bit of air, and he sucked it in. He pushed with his right arm and moved Man-Den's head away from his face. His mind called to his father. It was not a sound or a name. It was barely a thought, but it was pure desire. He turned the blade a little more.

He focused on the man before him and wanted him to know he would not accept failure.

The hoarse sound gained strength and he spoke.

"I am Ja-Lil, son of Con-Or. I am king of this city. I am of the royal blood from the time of the ancients."

The dark eyes blinked and stared out at him. Mark lunged with a final, desperate effort, turning his left hand as he did. Their bodies came together and he could feel the hard metal handle of the knife against his chest. Mark felt the hand drop from his throat as Man-Den gasped. The eyes were not full of hate now, but filled with confusion as they blinked again and looked down to see the blade imbedded to the hilt. The fabric of Man-Den's garment gathered around the weapon's handle. The area just beneath the cone-shaped hilt began to darken, and the stain worked its way rapidly down the cloth.

He felt it first in the palm of his right hand, warmth that was charged with a growing, intense energy. It traveled into his arm and simultaneously into every cell of his body. Man-Den's hand fell away from the knife handle and hung limply at his side like the other. His eyes once again opened and stared into Mark's face. Mark held the man's weight as if it almost did not exist. He knew when the transfer was complete and he took his palm from the man's head.

The minister slumped to the floor and rolled to his back. The knife handle stuck from his tunic like a large chainless pendant. The red life of the dying man now soaked the entire front of his garment. It continued to spread until it colored the edge of the floor where he lay. Everyone felt it in milliseconds. A rolling wave of energy left the dead body and coursed in all directions through the room and into the very walls. The light from the ceiling changed for a minute, and Mark knew the Dome itself felt the life of the minister pass through it and on out to sea. Then it was over.

Silence. The darkness was gone now, and only a slight numbness in his left hand remained.

The Elder rose from where she sat since being thrown through the air. She came to Mark. "I am all right."

Before he got to his feet, Mark pulled the remaining bracelet from Man-Den's wrist. He noted how cold Man-Den's skin had already become even though his life had barely ended. The bracelet was very warm to the touch, and as he held it he could hear a sound in his mind. He knew it was not audible to others or even in his own ears, but more of a sense. He had a brief image of a syncopated rhythm of half notes. Slipping the bracelet onto his left wrist, he hurried to the side of his friend, stooping to retrieve the second bracelet on his way. Kneeling beside Roi-Den, he looked into the lost eyes of his aunt. She held the lifeless head of her son in her lap.

Not thinking of what he was doing, Mark slipped the second bracelet onto his wrist, and then tore open the top of the now blood-soaked tunic. The sound had changed. A second, a third, and then an infinite variation of notes saturated his brain. The panic that tore the fabric was gone. Swept away like water over the edge of an overflowing pool. He was looking down now at a four-inch open wound, just to the left on his friend's chest. The knife had been thrust upward but must have been deflected by the ribcage as it then slid neatly in a forty-five degree angle, two inches upward towards the young man's right shoulder. From the wound down, his chest was covered with browning blood, but only a small patch of moist red was seeping from the bottom of the opening. The interior flesh was pressing out from the straight clean edge of the slit and looked like pursed lips contorted in an evil frown.

Mark placed his hands on both sides of Roi-Den's neck. There was no heartbeat though the skin was still warm to the touch.

"He's dead." The whispered words were barely sounds as Len-Wei's own hands kept brushing back the hair from her son's forehead. "He saw the disgrace and death of his father, and then he just stopped breathing."

"Yes, Len-Wei. His heart has stopped, but he is not gone. Yet." Mark was now pulling the bloody tunic off his shoulders. "Lie him down flat." He had no idea why he was doing this, but he felt sure of each move. When the boy's body was no longer across his mother's lap, death's mouth no longer smirked, and the lips parted slightly. Mark's hands descended to his friend's bloody chest. From the moment of contact, the stones in both bracelets erupted in a staggering blast of colored lights. Everyone but Mark briefly closed their eyes until they could adjust to the intense flashes of color that spun and darted, filling the entire chamber. With each move orchestrated by the music, Mark slowly pressed his fingers into the open area of the chest. Still moving upwards, he felt the rough edge of the chest bone where the knife blade had hit and bounced up to the left. Just past this point, he stopped. Mark felt that the blood in his hands was no longer circulating. It was still being pumped in but was not leaving. The pressure increased, his fingers felt fatter, and it was as though the temperature had doubled.

He didn't go to the end of the open wound. He knew death could be stopped where he was now. He pushed his fingers deeper into the chest cavity. He touched the heart.

Seeing nothing now except what his mind was showing his hands, he was not aware of his aunt and the Elders.

They, however, could not believe what they were witnessing. Some, still holding their hands to their eyes and peering between their fingers, watched in awe. In the history of the city, no one was ever permitted to observe a healing of this kind. The knowledge was passed from father to son and, when rarely needed, this action was done in the king's chamber or in an area cleared of all citizens. They also knew Mark had left the city before the king had been able to pass the knowledge to him and train him in the procedure. They stood quietly except for Nign-Ta, who sat attentively watching while she recovered from her flight across the room. Even Len-Wei stopped stroking Roi-Den's hair and looked from her son to Mark and back. Her eyes had lost their defeated look. She saw the gems of color darting across Roi-Den's face and streaking across the walls. She was no longer afraid, and she observed the healer of her city with calm anticipation.

Soon Mark felt the small nick in the aorta of the heart where the knifepoint had diverted Roi-Den's life. His eyes now closed as they were no longer needed, and the tip of his right finger paused at the lower edge of the small opening. The left finger found its own spot—not a quarter inch away on the other side of the cut. Like building blocks, like stones being stacked up to make a fence, or like stringing beads together in a long line. All these images and many more, Mark would later use to try and describe what he was feeling as the opening along both sides of the vessel joined once again in perfect order, closing the wound and healing the artery like it had never been damaged.

Tens of thousands of cells healed and Mark was aware of each one as it became whole again. The time it took, however, was less than a minute. With the blood vessel complete again, his fingers quickly moved to the top of the cut and he knew there was no more damage inside the body. Drawing out of the cut at the top, Mark placed his thumbs to the middle knuckle of his index fingers and then, joining the middle finger to the index fingers, he traced the edges of the cut along its angled course. The pressure of his hands pushed the skin together, and as the line passed between the tips of his fingers it disappeared and the wound closed. There was no scar. No lines where the opening had been. Just a small path unstained by the congealed blood where the healing had occurred.

"He is healed, Ja-Lil. You have given me back my son." Her voice was so faint that only Mark and the Elder who had knelt down beside him heard Len-Wei speak.

"Yes, Ja-Lil. Your father's blood flows deep in your life." The Elder dipped his head as a show of respect as he spoke to his king.

Mark was already rising to his feet. "Roi-Den's wound is healed and his body is whole again, but his life has stopped." As he spoke, he bent and put his arms under his friend's back and legs, lifted him, and turned from the room. "All Elders come with me to the Kivs." He was already in the corridor leading to the vestibule before the others could get to their feet and follow. They walked quickly to catch up. No one spoke. Some were still stunned by what had just happened in Man-Den's chamber. They had not seen violence like that among their own people in their lifetime. Others were in awe of Mark's inherent knowledge of the ways of the king's line and followed, confident in whatever he was going to do next.

As they left Man-Den's house, Mark turned down the road that led the short way to the main hall and the Kivs. Len-Wei was the last to leave the chamber and made her way through the Elders until she was at Mark's side. She put her hand on her son's forehead.

"His heart has stopped Len-Wei, and we have not much time before his life-thought will leave him."

"But..." she didn't know what to say. The small piece of light that had begun to glow in her life a minute before darkened just as quickly. She could only follow like a child. The touch of her hand on the chilling skin of her son was the only thing that connected her to the world. If she no longer felt him, she knew she would melt away into the blackness that surrounded her. "What will you do?"

Mark had just spotted Tei-La in the crowd that was beginning to gather and follow them to the Kivs. "I must take him to the Kivs."

As his eyes reached Tei-La's, he could see her bewilderment as to what was going on and his mind spoke to her. "Find To-Bay and quickly bring him to the Kivs."

The startled look on her face, as her mind heard his words, was just as quickly replaced with an expression that told him that she would do as he asked. He also saw the connections that would keep them together forever as his father and mother were. In a flash, she melted into the crowd and Mark turned the corner and walked towards the steps to the hall. The crowd parted for him and the procession as they approached the entrance.

At the top of the stairs, a wall between the top-most columns parted as Mark stepped to it. He entered and hesitated as the Elders and Len-Wei gathered near him.

"Ja-Lil!"

He turned to see Tei-La and To-Bay make their way through the last group of people then to the front of the crowd to start up the stairs.

"Both of you come with us." Mark was walking again as he spoke. He made his way into the open courtyard where only a short time ago he had sat with his mother before becoming the city's king. Now he carried the lifeless body of his best friend across the same floor, with no conscious idea of what he was going to do. He only knew that he knew. But what he knew was somewhere in the depths of his life and leading him on.

He crossed the floor and behind him the Elders, Roi-Den's mother, Tei-La, and To-Bay trailed up the steps. They strode up the second set of stairs and on to the Kivs. This time the Dome opened the wall long before Mark and the group approached. They all stepped into the royal chamber and stood in front of the transparent wall of the Kivs. Mark only hesitated for a moment and then moved to the steps that led to the king's Kiv above the others. "All of you must go to your Kivs." With a nod of his head, Mark indicated the Kivs at the farthest end of the line. "To-Bay, you will enter there."

This last statement stopped the Elders in mid-stride as they stepped to the slightly glowing wall. Before the first could speak and without looking back at them, Mark said, "To-Bay will replace Man-Den. Not just here, this one time, but all through the city as well."

There was no response necessary and, in fact, they all knew their king had spoken and what he said was right. They immediately turned back to their Kivs and raised their hands and placed them on the wall. Only To-Bay continued to stare at Mark. "Ja-Lil, forgive me, but I don't know what..."

"It is all right, To-Bay. Just stand in front and do as the others. Trust me in what I do." Mark was now directly in front of the king's Kiv. He turned slightly so he could look down at Tei-La and his aunt. Words were not needed. Tei-La looked up at him, and he saw in her everything he knew his father had seen in his mother. She was part of him. She knew his every thought and need and was there to support him in every way. They both smiled slightly at each other, and Tei-La drew Len-Wei to her side and placed an arm over her shoulder.

Mark turned the palms of his hands toward the wall as he held the lifeless form in his arms.

To-Bay had, by then, followed the example of the Elders and was still before the wall with his hands resting on the warm surface. As Mark touched the soft texture of the wall, it immediately softened and began to close around his hands and arms as he stepped forward. A split second later the Dome admitted the others to their Kivs, and in two steps all had entered the fluid-filled chambers.

Tei-La and Len-Wei stood staring at what no one, other than the king and the Elders, had ever witnessed before. All the Elders slowly turned, floating inside the Dome's compartments. The women could see them clearly through the transparent skin of the Kivs. The Elders did not return their gaze but seemed to be looking far into the distance. It looked as though they were seeing beyond the outer walls of the Dome itself.

The women then looked to the topmost Kiv, which held Mark and his burden. They hung there, suspended in their chamber like a living Pieta.

To-Bay had moved into the Kiv in one smooth motion. From the time his hand's penetrated the soft wall, it felt to him as if the Dome had drawn him in as much as he had stepped forward. The liquid inside was not seawater but also not like it. The sensation was one of supreme comfort. To-Bay felt completely secure. Not really knowing he was moving, he slowly turned and faced the direction he had entered. The liquid held him in suspension. It was warm. It felt exactly the same as his body temperature. He was thinking all these thoughts and, at the same time, he could feel himself drifting into a half-sleep, half-awake condition. He could no longer feel where his skin ended and the fluid began. In fact, trying to make logical sense of it, he realized he could not tell the difference between himself and the whole Kiv. This awareness broadened as the focus of his mind narrowed, and he soon *was* the entire city. The Dome. The people. Everything.

The myriad of every-day things that had made up his life had softened into an indefinable grayness, and he felt himself relax as he had never done before. Ja-Lil was in his mind. He could not hear the king's voice as he had in the city when Mark's father spoke to him. He could not see him, neither through the Kiv's walls nor in his mental vision. But Ja-Lil was there. It was so easy to let himself go to where he was being called. He now felt the others and knew the Elders, too, were directing their lives to the king's Kiv.

CHAPTER THIRTEEN

M ark felt the weight of Roi-Den lift from his arms as he entered
the Kiv. The body remained in its somewhat horizontal
position as Mark's hand drifted down to his sides. His father! He
felt him everywhere. And he felt his father's father. He knew they
were not actually here, but it was their history. For thousands of
years only the direct line of the kings had been in the Kiv. The
history was alive and now Mark was living it.

He could tell the others were all in the Kivs and in a state
of readiness. The Elders he had only known in his youth as
mysterious friends of his father were now a part of him. He knew
their lives and their histories. To-Bay was comfortable and with
the others and now part of the whole.

Mark felt a power he had never experienced before. The
Dome itself was a part of him and it was clear that his mind and
life-thought were guiding that power. His hands came slowly up
again to the lifeless form in front of him, and he gently turned
the body until it was parallel and slightly above him. Mark moved
now without thought, guided by information and instinct that
was coded in his very blood. Roi-Den must live.

With Mark and Roi-Den the last to enter the Kiv, Tei-La
and Len-Wei stood watching as all the Elders slowly turned and

became motionless. Everything was still. Their gaze roamed from Kiv to Kiv. Soon even the robes of the Elders settled. From the moment they had entered, Tei-La noticed an increase in the greenish glow of the walls. Now the entire floor pulsated with the changing color. The walls and ceiling began to join in the same regular rhythm. Tei-La recognized it immediately as a heartbeat. It was the life of the city itself.

Both women's heads tilted back slightly and their eyes came to the king's Kiv. The outer walls were transparent enough that they could clearly see everything inside. They watched as Mark moved Roi-Den into an upright position. They could see Mark place his hands on each side of his friend's chest. The light in the room around them grew brighter and the rate of pulsation picked up. Mark's head tipped back a little, and Tei-La became aware of nothing else but Roi-Den. She sensed her mind focusing not on the person in the chamber whom she knew so well, but on his very life. Beside her, Roi-Den's mother was going through the very same process.

In an instant, Tei-La knew everyone in the city was doing the same thing. Mark was directing the entire living entity that was the city towards the life of Roi-Den. Tei-La and Len-Wei walked forward and placed their hands on the portion of wall that separated two of the Kivs and concentrated.

Mark was not aware of the light or the increasing rate of its pulses. He only had a feeling like something was about to happen. It was approaching like a sound from a distance or the feeling in your feet when a train is coming. He was gathering everything and making it happen. The Dome was connecting all and it was being directed to Mark.

All through the city there was not a sound and nothing moved. Everyone, in a matter of moments, had ceased whatever they were doing. Wherever they were, they went to the nearest portion of the living Dome and gently placed their hands on the surface. Everyone could sense the focus of their efforts and willed their support toward their king and his mission.

In the Kiv, Mark's hand pressed tighter against the sides of Roi-Den's chest. He could feel the rib bones through his skin. He was aware now of how sensitive his hands and fingers were. From there, he knew that his entire body was now one with the elements of the Kiv—its fluids, its walls, and beyond. He was, in fact, becoming the Dome and its environs. Even the sea life around the exterior of the Dome wall began to slow their activities. The fish and sea life on the ocean floor were drawn to the Dome's outer walls. Mark could see all of this as if it were being played out before him on a screen. It was as though he had turned himself inside out and all that was outside of him had become an integral part of his life, his being.

The energy in all the things that were now Mark began to gather. To focus. It was the sound he thought he heard and the train he could feel coming. This energy, given by all the lives in the city, was traveling to him now through the living tissue of the Dome. It raced toward him in a gentle inexorable torrent.

Tei-La opened her eyes and lifted her head. The light in the chamber of the Kivs was brilliant now—almost constant rather than pulsating. From where she stood, she looked up at Mark and at Len-Wei's son. Under her feet and through her body, she felt the energy intensify. One moment there was almost nothing; the next moment practically knocked both women off their feet. The floor and the walls in the chamber seemed to flex and bend with the force traveling through them. The glow that was reflected on her face from the Elder's Kiv grew to a brilliant blue-green. The walls carried that energy up the floor to the second level and it gathered under the king's Kiv.

Inside, Tei-La could still see Mark holding Roi-Den at arm's length. There was a pause when the light under Mark stopped moving but continued to get brighter. Just when she thought she could no longer stare into the sun that was forming in front of her, she saw Mark's head drop slightly back. At that moment, the light entered his Kiv. Mark's body seemed to absorb everything as it entered the chamber. His arms, legs, and torso radiated with the energy he was gathering. In the next instant, there was a sound. She couldn't tell if it came from the energy, the Dome, or herself. But with the sound, the brilliant glow in Mark's body raced from his legs and torso, down his arms, and to his hands. Every muscle and sinew contracted to where it looked like they would snap and tear with the force being exerted upon them. Mark raised the body of Roi-Den when the force shot down his arms. It stayed in his hands for a long moment and filled the space between them. She watched as the eye-aching glow faded into Roi-Den's torso. Then, with a near explosion, light and energy erupted from his body. It pushed through the chamber and into the walls and floor. Suddenly, with a shudder from the Dome, it was gone. All was still. Tei-La blinked and looked around. Len-Wei's hands had dropped from the wall, and she stood there motionless with her head hanging as if she were about to fall asleep. Slowly, looking back at the king's Kiv, they could see Mark lowering Roi-Den's body. Tei-La left Len-Wei's side and raced up the steps, stopping in front of the entrance wall. Through the membrane, she watched Mark release his hold on his friend and place the palm of his hand on the young man's forehead.

Mark's mouth was moving slightly, but there was no way for her to know what he was saying. When he took his hand away, she stared in wonder as Roi-Den's eyes flickered open and a small smile formed on his lips. Mark placed his hand on his friend's shoulder for a moment, and then turned to leave.

Tei-La stepped back a little as Mark exited the Kiv—his hands first and then his body came through.

He looked at Tei-La and wanted so much to be able to explain what he had just experienced, but no words came. He could tell her what he knew. "He will be well." He put his arms around her and held her tightly before pulling away and looking deep into her eyes again.

She turned and they walked down the steps.

Len-Wei had seen her son open his eyes, but she understood nothing of what had just happened. When the couple appeared before her, she looked immediately to the Kiv above. There was her son with his eyes open and one hand rubbing his left shoulder. It was not a dream. She had not imagined it. "Ja-Lil, will he be..." Words failed her.

"He will need more time in the Kiv." Mark helped his aunt to the bench near the wall and she sat. "His body has much to repair, and the Dome will help him. You may return to your home. The Elders will know when he emerges."

"May I stay here for awhile, please?"

"Of course. I must leave the city for awhile, but when I return we will all meet." Mark could see the pain in her eyes because of all that had happened. "Everything will be all right."

"Ja-Lil, I will stay with her awhile here." Tei-La looked at him as she sat next to Len-Wei. "I will be at your house when you come back."

CHAPTER FOURTEEN

Many conflicting thoughts alternated in Mark's mind as he traveled northward from the city to meet with the Nari-Tanta. The biggest questions were about Man-Den. Why had he harbored such hatred for Mark's father for so long? How could the king have never suspected Man-Den's true desires? His other thoughts gave him great joy. Within him, he carried the life-thought of his father and soon it would be united with his mother's in the Nari-Tanta. The knowledge of the line of kings would now continue unbroken. It was important to Mark (or Ja-Lil as he now thought himself), but somewhere deep in his life he knew it was important for much greater reasons.

As always, the sea gave him the limitless space to think. Everything that had happened since he was attacked on his dock so long ago had been a roadmap to some great event in the future. Mark felt that only he could move circumstances from day to day now in the direction of the event. His family. The treasures, the city itself and the other Ones Who Know of the Air and Land. Somehow, all of what he had learned of that history would act itself out within his lifetime. These were the true questions, and their answers would come with the transfer he was about to do.

As he drew in the seawater, felt the shifting nuances of the tides and pull of the earth, he kept adjusting his direction, a direction that he knew would lead to the same large area where he had sat before. As soon as he had left the city, he began to send out his song and was confident that many creatures of the ocean had caught it and were relaying it to the Tanta. Small brown squids, with their large eyes, calmly tacked out of his path as he approached. Their brownish skin color reddened a little, which Mark knew was a sign that they were happy to see him. He passed over thousands of starfish of various colors. Surface names appeared in his mind. Sunstar. Feather star. Blood Henry. As the ocean floor rose and the water depth became shallow, sea life became more abundant. Breadcrumb sponges clung to the rock in big blobs of green and orange and brown. Urchins of all sizes and colors dotted the sea floor and coral ridges where countless small fish and crustaceans darted in and out in their endless search for food.

The terrain was familiar, and he swam with his vision as his guide. He had not come upon any sea mammal yet, as he had the first time, that could inform the Nari-Tanta of his presence, but he knew the message had been delivered. He soon dropped over the gentle ledge that surrounded the large open area with small circles of stones. Swimming slowly to the center, he saw a large manta ray boil out of his resting place, just under the sand, and glide out and away from the field, with the small feeder fish catching up to hitch a ride with him. Two beautiful nautiluses, a large female and the smaller male, also pulsed away as he approached. The rays of sunlight that pierced down through the water touched their brown and white shells and seemed to turn their surfaces to soft fabric.

By the time Mark settled into a sitting position in the center of the stone circle, the creatures that had been in the area had made a respectful exit from the field. Some continued over the ledge and out into the sea while others came to rest outside the field on the upslope and settled into a waiting position as Mark had done.

Mark continued to sing the calling song of his family, the string of notes and sounds easing him into a deepening meditative state. Knowing what to expect this time, it was easy for him to let his mind expand out into the ocean. The song had many voices for him now. He wanted the Nari-Tanta to hear his father singing and calling for Myo-O. They had always been united in love and now needed to be one in being. In the depths of his life, as conscious thought started to evaporate and he became one with the sea, he was aware that he was calling to his destiny.

The arrival was as before, but this time Mark could welcome it as a friend. Just after he had begun to hear the deep hum of the whale's song, two young beaked whales darted up over the ridge directly in front of him and paused just over the edge. Their brown skin and white heads, with their mouths in that permanent smile, was the first announcement for the Nari-Tanta. They swam smoothly to the right as the large, dark mass of the great Tanta rose like a giant blue-gray planet from behind the crest of the ridge. It filled his field of vision, and he could feel the water push around him like around a rock in the stream as the whales came over the ridge and eased into the saucer-like open area.

Mark waited. The Tanta had slowed and stopped. Resting at a three-quarter angle to Mark, he could see all along its side. The markings and scars stood out like a visual history of the animal that seemed almost without beginning. Mark knew the time was right and he eased up from the sandy floor and followed the ancient customs and manners that only the cells of his blood knew. For the second time, he swam to the same welcoming gaze of the great whale.

The large animal had come to a stop, with its broad U-shaped snout, just above where Mark had sat in the circle. As he rose from the sand and swam along the curve of the whale's mouth, he could see that its tail was not quite inside the large circle of the open area. Coming to the end of its gentle smile, Mark dropped his feet from the swimming position and came to an upright stance in the water opposite the eye. He paused and slightly bowed his head. He was not sure why, but the feeling of respect seemed natural and he wanted to wait until the Tanta bid him to continue.

Looking past the surface of the eye and its active mucus covering, he felt himself peering into the soul of the great animal. He felt a kindness that he knew he had been too awed before to be aware of. He was welcomed and, as the feeling grew in his heart, the old whale spoke in his mind, "Son of Con-Or and Myo-O, you have brought the king to reside with his mate. It is right and welcome." As before, the words were simply inside his mind.

"The life-thought of my father is here with me. I wish to join him with his wife." Mark wanted nothing more than to do what his words just said, but he also knew it would be difficult. Since winning the battle with Man-Den and taking his father's life-thought, he had sensed himself fulfilling a mission. In that action, he was taking care of his father, as he now knew his father had taken care of him. He knew, whether close to him or separated by time and oceans, he had always been in his father's care. As he did now, his father had held him in his heart and thoughts and had tried to protect him with the action of his very life. It was this closeness he now felt that made it difficult to release his father and thereby end his most cherished job.

"It is natural. And it has always been so." With that response, Mark saw that it was not only that he was looking through the large eye and into a life; the Tanta was reading every thought and emotion that was reverberating through him also. "When you release him, you will not be lacking." It was a simple statement, but instantly Mark trusted it and desired to continue.

He rose slightly so he could place his hands in the same place as last time. As before, once set in that position, he could feel the growing of his father's physical being inside him as it was being called to the whale. The increased sensitivity in his hands and arms were recording an intense energy. Much more than when he had released his mother. All through his body, Mark felt the life gather and become one again. And as before it reached almost painful extremes and then began to quickly push along his torso and out into his arms and hands.

It was leaving him now, and it had become the former king completely. Taking its place, even for only the shortest of moments, was a deep feeling of sadness. Of loss. There was that moment when the life-thoughts passed from his fingertips and away. Mark was about to focus his thoughts and drop back from the whale when a very different feeling glued his hands tightly to where they were.

Something was coming back to him. What had left him was a life. It was the second time it had happened and even with the remarkable difference between the two times, he knew it was the same action. The same process. But this was entirely different. This was not life or being of some kind. This had no substance or concept that words could define. It merely was. It filled him entirely and yet he could not feel it. Mark actually stopped trying to see or feel or know what it was. He simply let it in. He let whatever the Nari-Tanta was giving him become him.

Every atom of his being was evenly placed throughout the universe. Each atom a sending and receiving living being. He saw it all, everything. He was, at the same time, everything he saw. The past was now this very instant and he experienced it as the present. It was all there at the same time. Because of that, it was so obvious what would lead where. This progression was not just for him but for all things. Time was no longer this dark place, this expanding sightless void that was illuminated second by second, on and on as he lived. It was clear and bright in all directions and knowable. That was it!

His heart rate almost doubled and he could not help but smile. He had never felt this complete, this free or happy. It was all so simple. He knew!

"Ja-Lil."

"My son."

The voices of his parents did not startle him. Somewhere out there or in there, they were part of the Mark that now, somehow, knew. His hands separated from the skin of the Tanta. Still he gazed into that dark orb. "Father, mother. You are together now."

"Yes, son." His father's voice carried the comfort of his childhood as he now remembered and heard it at the same time "My queen is here with me, and you have completed the continuance."

Mark now settled back a little from the whale and let the conversation flow throughout his mind.

"Ja-Lil, I am proud that you have come to this time and place by yourself, through your own actions, and by using your own wisdom. Without the guidance of a father, like I had, you have proven the purity of your line."

Time was once again fluid, and Mark was sitting on the small stool by his father's chair. He could almost feel the large warm hand on his shoulder.

"The great Tanta has released to you the complete life of our line and the knowledge of our people. You are aware that it is you who will complete the task of the city."

Mark knew all these things. In that moment of transfer, he saw the Three Peoples. The Land, Sea, and Air. He saw their placement and beyond the city's history that he had witnessed while in the king's Kiv. He had seen the history of both Those of the Air and Those of the Land. The royal blood of Those of the Air, he knew as well as his own. Their placement, at first was close to his city. And then as his people traveled farther out into the oceans, he followed their history of interaction with the ordinary People of the Land. He saw completely how they worked with the people at first then slowly drew away from them and, after a while, stopped almost completely taking physical form. He also knew that soon he must find the great king Nordhus' people for the convergence.

More troubling to him was the story of Those of the Land. Their history stopped in its purity and was now fragmented throughout the world. There seemed to be none left with a true line of the blood. They had not been able to keep their traditions true. There had been a break in the bloodline a long time ago when the second king died without an heir. As rulers, not of the line, they had tried to duplicate the rites and healings and ceremonies, but the civilization was no longer in possession of its power. He was painfully aware of how close his people had come to the same fate.

"Father, why did Man-Den behave as he did?" Mark, with everything he had experienced, could not understand. "He was a respected citizen of the city with a pure family history."

"All the knowledge you have now received will not answer all questions, my son. His actions came as a result of thoughts and deeds and, at some point, his smaller self gained the advantage."

Mark once again saw the evil look in Man-Den's eyes as they struggled with the knife.

"Had you not been able to stay his hand, Father, our city would have followed the history of Those of the Land."

"It was not me, Ja-Lil." There was added warmth in his father's voice when he heard it now. "No matter how strong the evil side of a life becomes, it can never eliminate, completely, the good. It was Man-Den who hesitated. It was my dear friend from long ago who, for a moment, was strong enough to do the right thing."

"I will tell Roi-Den and his mother. They only saw the very worst of his last moments. Though his life-thought was lost in the sea, they will welcome his last act into the line."

Mark knew, though a small thing, it would be something they both could hold as a good memory of the husband and father. Even with what he had just learned about Roi-Den and his purpose in the city he knew his friend would need so much more, and now that Mark was in the Dome to stay he would help.

He was not sure there was anything he, or anyone, could do to ease the pain that Len-Wei felt in those last moments during her husband's betrayal. She had been shown that the life she had led for so many years had not really existed. The dignity of her husband's love and care that she had worn as a badge all that time was stripped from her. The sense of her worth had vanished. Mark had felt it in her touch when they were walking to the Kiv, and he had heard it in her words.

"Father, Roi-Den will recover in body and mind and will find encouragement in what I can tell him, but I fear the damage to his mother will never heal."

"What you have learned must only live with you until the time of convergence. Roi-Den must arrive at that moment free from any sense of obligation."

The moment his father spoke, Mark knew he was right and the secret would remain one until the time was right.

"Ja-Lil, my son." His mother's voice again. It carried the soft strength that could calm his fears. "However great the pain she feels at this time, it will subside. My sister has the same quality of love as I for your father. The result of their union is her foundation now, and in Roi-Den she will see all the good and kindness that was in her husband. As you were my future, Len-Wei will find her strength in her son."

"Tell them," his father's voice now, "the life-thought of Man-Den has not dispersed. It is here with me. I took it as he died and held it until you brought me here to the Nari-Tanta."

"But, father," Mark was now completely confused by what he heard and what he knew, "I felt the energy of his life leave him and pass through the Dome."

"You and everyone else felt the energy, but not the life-thought. Since I possessed it before you took me, Man-Den willed his remains to the sea."

Mark looked again into the large eye opposite him.

"The great Tanta could have refused to accept him, but instead will hold him until the convergence. Tell them both they will be as they first were. Together, in love and family."

The large whale began to turn slowly in the basin and Mark drew back some distance. He saw the two small whales quickly swim to the crest of the ridge, some two hundred yards apart as if on cue. Knowing they were there to ensure the safety of the great Tanta, Mark heard the high pitch of their signal that all was well.

"I will return and tell you all that happens, father."

"The Tanta will not return for some time, son. You must act on your own wisdom. Let your will be the happiness and wellbeing of others. The pride we have in you is of your own making. Trust yourself." The voices of his parents blended into a chorus that carried to him on the deep rumbled note of the Nari-Tanta. "We must leave now, but I will always be with you."

There was no goodbye, nor did he wish for one. The feeling of loss that had briefly been there when he deposited his father was now replaced with fullness. He had never felt so close or so completely one with the lives of his parents.

As the current of sea water pushed against him from the powerful downward thrust of the whale's fluke and the giant beast rose to the top of the circled hill, Mark was his father and his father's father. All the way to the beginning. Backing up, as he watched the last view of the great shadow drop behind the crest, he turned and started back to the city. He was different. He knew it, and he could feel it. It was beyond an image in his mind or a memory or anything from the tangible world. He was... the One Who Knows.

CHAPTER FIFTEEN

L eaving the entrance chamber and entering the city was, this time, as if he were a completely different person. His memory and feelings and experiences were all still there, but a whole new person contained them. Walking down the corridor to the entrance to the city, he passed several people. They nodded with a smile and walked by. In response, Mark slightly raised his hand and smiled back. Was this really the first time he felt like an adult? No, or course not, but somehow the feeling of responsibility for the city and all it contained added some indefinable weight to his life and it was something he had never experienced before.

All this he was sorting and filing in his mind. He knew, however, this present he was living was only a very small part of what his life was about from here on. The knowledge from the Nari-Tanta would guide his every move and every decision from now on. The present was not his only responsibility now, but the future as well. All of this, as immense as the potential was, was not daunting, nor did it worry him in the least. What was it? Why was it so important for him now? With everything he knew he must do from now on, why did it feel so enjoyable?

Turning onto the avenue that would lead to his home, he continued toward a small group of people at the center fountain. As he approached, an older couple followed the gaze of others and turned to see him coming. They stepped from the crowd and met him a few feet from the onlookers. The man he could remember seeing several times since he first returned to the city. He was quite old and very dignified in the way he carried himself. Mark now also knew the man's history. Through the Dome, he had seen the old man's parents, his birth, and entire line. He saw, even now, in the wrinkled face of his wife, the beautiful dark-haired girl that became his bride so many years ago.

The man stood quite erect, just behind the old woman as she took Mark's hands in hers. They both looked into Mark's face for a long moment with a kind of pride.

"Ja-Lil." Her voice was small and very soft. "Son of Con-Or. We welcome our new king to guide and care for us and the city."

Whether it was what she said or the way she said it, Mark had no way of knowing, but at that moment it was clear to him exactly what he had been feeling since he entered the city. It was parental. The love he felt for them and the knowledge that he would do anything for their wellbeing and happiness echoed in this heart. It was the echo of his father and mother. How safe and cared for he had felt all his life was how he wanted to care for this city. His pride in their lives was that of a parent. He felt great satisfaction in seeing their confidence and trust in him and his line. With that satisfaction, there was also the determination to serve their trust completely. His life was now to be lived for them.

"Live well, Na-Leen, and both of you continue in happiness." Mark rested a hand briefly on her shoulder and, after returning the old man's smile, continued on to his home.

He entered the large atrium and knew that Tei-La was somewhere in the house. He stopped in the center of the room between the stairs and the door leading to the healing room. How close he felt to her. He didn't know where she was. He stood there feeling everywhere around him. "Your mother is the heartbeat of everywhere she is." His father had told him that several times when he'd been young. He remembered standing very still and trying to hear it and picking up nothing and feeling disappointed. "I cannot hear it either, son. It is the life you can feel. Someday you will know exactly what I mean and be joined with such a life yourself."

His house was now alive, and he could feel that life and he could hear the heartbeat. "Tei-La." Going up the stairs, he met her on the landing that led to his bedroom.

"Ja-Lil, Roi-Den has gone." Her voice was strong and steady.

"He has left the Kiv already?" Mark knew that the strength-giving powers of the Kiv could not have worked completely in so short a time.

"Len-Wei and I left the chamber, and I had taken her to her home to rest." Tei-La took Mark's arm and continued as she led him to the sitting area of his room. "She started to sleep so I was returning to the Kivs. I met Roi-Den as he was coming down the stairs into the Elder's chamber."

Now Mark could hear fear and worry take the place of the strength that had been there a moment earlier.

"Oh, Ja-Lil, he was not well yet at all. He could barely make it down the stairs without stumbling. He would not stop so I could only walk with him and support him the best I could."

"Where did he go?" Fearing he already knew the answer, Mark let her continue.

"He left the city. He would not even stop to see his mother. He said that only disgrace and dishonor lived in his line. He said the citizens would forgive his mother as she was pure in her blood and deed. It was he and the line of Man-Den that must end." Tei-La stepped back to where she could put her arms around Mark.

He looked in wonder at the beautiful face. Before him was the heart—not just of his house or life—of the city. The house his father referred to was limitless in size and the heart of his queen was pure compassion. This was what he saw in the face of the woman he loved. It was not fear or even the worry that came from weakness. It was care and compassion that sprang freely from the strength of her heart.

"Ja-Lil, he said his father's betrayal was his now to cleanse." She cupped his face in her hands. "It was because of you he felt he could not stay. He could not expect you to trust him if he could not trust his own line himself."

Was this happening just minutes after he had felt so wonderful? Could so short a time change his entire world completely? He had entered the city this last time as its leader. He knew his future and what his mission was for the convergence. And he had felt great joy in anticipation of what was to come. He never dreamed so much could change so quickly.

Taking her by the hand, he and Tei-La quickly left the room and went downstairs. All the way, Mark was recounting what he had learned at his father's transfer about Man-Den and his last great act of loyalty to the king. He knew she would have the right words to explain everything to Len-Wei. He also knew, with Tei-La's help, his aunt would find the quality in life once again to make her happy.

What was harder to put into words was the responsibility he had to act upon. If he was responsible to the entire city, that meant each person by themselves. He could not sacrifice one, or all would be diminished.

"When I was away from the city for so long, I learned many things." Mark wanted to tell her so much more than he was going to be able to at this time. "Life on the surface can be very dangerous. I fear he wants to shorten his life and never return here."

They had reached the bottom of the stairs and were standing in the exact spot where he had felt her great life force only minutes before. Mark bent his head and kissed her lightly on the lips. "I must go to the treasure chamber before I leave. I will be back to say goodbye." He needed the few extra minutes the visit to his chamber would give him to find the right way to explain to her what he must do and why. The look in her eyes before he turned away came close to making him change his mind, and he knew he could not do that.

Mark placed his hand on the spot next to the chamber entrance and the line appeared and the Dome made the opening for him. After he had left Roi-Den in the Kiv, he had stopped at Man-Den's house and had gone to the room where they had fought. People had removed Man-Den's body and had carried it away to be prepared for deposit in the sea. Nothing else had been touched. Stepping around the browning pool of his friend's blood, he had quickly gathered the treasures and carried them back here to the chamber. They were where he had put them, here on the long table. He paused to look at them there together. The light from the Dome was not shining on the empty pedestals but was concentrated on the table only in one large spotlight.

He took a moment to place them all on their proper stand or table. As he did, the light shifted in intensity from the table to each treasure. He felt apprehension for this great being that affected and reacted so quickly and so correctly. The two bracelets were the last to be returned to their spots. Everything was back to normal. In fact, the entire city was now in balance and he knew it would function accordingly. With that reassuring him, he lifted the lid of the small box that contained the sand. Taking a small vial from his tunic, he carefully twisted off the cap. The cord that ran through the two small loops on each side of the container caught the light from the ceiling in its fine golden threads.

The box in front of him—the pure white sand it contained and the golden lid with the circle—was so familiar now. "The primary start!' It had made some kind of disjoined sense when To-Bay had first explained the box to him. Primary start and its purpose, of all the treasures, was the city's lifeline to the future, and Mark felt it would be the key to his and Ro-Den's survival. To-Bay had related everything that his father had told him about it. But, as with the other treasures and their care and function, To-Bay's explanation was merely a blueprint. Now Mark knew all that every king in the history of the city had known about them. They were connected to his life like the closest of family heirlooms.

Looking down into the box, he put his hand into the sand. At the first touch, the fine grains began to move. They swirled and eddied around and through his fingers as if they were fluid rather than solid granules. The coolness was apparent, and he noticed a definite increase in the energy he felt in his body. Cupping his right hand, he lifted a vial out and much of the sand flowed through his fingers, back into the box. This left a small pool in his palm. Very carefully, he tipped his hand and let the sand trickle into the vial. Screwing the lid back on, he put the cord around his neck and placed the vial inside his tunic.

He paused at the door and looked back at the room. Here he felt close to his father. In that room, his father lived again as the king of the city. If he could, he wanted to reach inside his body and pull out some *thing* that he felt was his parents and leave it here where it belonged. "What I cannot do in action, must be done in determination." With that as his silent oath to the city, he nodded his head in reverence, backed from the room, and watched as the opening closed off his view.

In the small sitting room of his mother's, he found Tie-La where he knew she would be.

"She sat on this bench, didn't she?" she said. Tei-La knew Mark had entered, although she had not looked over to the door and he had come in without making a sound. "I can feel her watching and protecting me. Us. And I think the entire city." Now she lifted her head and looked at him and their smiles met. "Ja-Lil, I want so much to be for you what she was for your father."

"Tei-La, you are the strength I will rely on for the rest of my life." Mark went to her and sat down. Her body was warm and he could feel her softness beside him. This he must remember, he told himself. This was what he would return to.

He quickly outlined what she must do here in the city. The Elders would treat her as they did his mother. They would look to her for guidance and she must have confidence in her instincts. She must tell them that To-Bay was to be accepted as minister in Mark's absence.

"I will find Roi-Den and bring him back. He does not know it, but he has a mission for the city that only he can do. Without him, our very reason for being here will fail. That is for only you to know, my love. It is important that little time is wasted before I leave." He kissed her once again.

"I will walk with you to the exit chamber. Every second until you leave the Dome will be ours together." She looped her arm around his as they left their home and preceded down the streets, through the center of town, and past the fountain. They didn't speak and looked straight ahead as they walked.

Mark knew her fear and concern, and he loved her all the more for not saying anything to stop him from going. Every once in a while, he caught the faint perfume of her hair and made a conscious thought to memorize it as a beacon for his return.

The people they passed seemed to know what he was about to do, If not in detail, they were all aware of what had happened with Man-Den and of Roi-Den's departure. They quietly stepped aside without comment but silently wished Mark well and too have safe travels and a quick return. A few streets before the entrance to the hallway leading to the chamber, Mark set his mind to speak to To-Bay.

"To-Bay, it is Ja-Lil. Where are you?" He made no movement that would indicate to Tei-La that he was communicating to his friend.

"Yes, Ja-Lil, I am at the Elder's hall. Should I come to you?"

"No, my friend." Mark and Tei-La left the open city and entered the long corridor to the exit chamber. "To-Bay, I must ask you once again to serve your city in secret. As you kept the knowledge of my father and taught it to me, I ask you now to be ready for my queen if the need should come. If I do not return, you must be her right hand and her second heart. You will know the time. I can only hope that your dedication, her purity, and the protection of the Dome will allow our people to accomplish the task of convergence." There was nothing left to say, and they tuned into the open door as he heard the last words from his friend.

"It is done."

The chamber was empty, as he knew it would be, and they stood there in front of the row of garments. She still held him tightly, and he felt the deep rise and fall of her breathing. He turned completely to her and held her in his arms. "There are not certainties in this world, and though my heart will always be here," he placed on hand on her breast, "I have no idea how long I will be gone."

She smiled. "You have been gone before, and here you are with me now. You will come back to me again." There was no wishing in her tone. No uncertainty. Her confidence was her faith in the future. What she said, would be. She would leave no room for failure.

How wonderful and strange, Mark thought, that she would be so much in spirit like his mother. The infatuation of his youth had tuned to love, and he knew it had been fated. They were together, had always been together, and would always be together. Her strength grew from truth and knowledge and, therefore, truth was all he could tell her.

"There are so many lands beyond the sea, Tei-La, and in them great evil and great good. I have learned much in my time on the surface and Roi-Den knows little. It will take time to find him and more time for him to want to come home. Nothing is certain."

"Do I have to say what I have said before?" She put her own hand where his had been. "I will keep you right here until I see your face again." She would say nothing that would influence him from doing what he knew he must do.

Mark stepped to the exit wall and turned to her. She was drawn into his arms one last time, and the force of their kiss pressed the very air from their bodies. Their parted lips left almost no room for speech

"Guide the city in my place."

She made a motion to speak, but Mark stopped her with a small kiss.

"You can trust To-Bay in all things."

The next was the hardest to say.

"If I cannot return then the line of kings will be broken. The convergence will go forward, and you must complete the task."

Together they let their arms fall to their sides. It was done. He must go and she would stay. Looking deep into her eyes, as he placed his palms on the wall, he felt he would live forever if she would only...

"Remember me," he said. Then he passed through the wall and was gone.

Tei-La stared at the place where he had stood. She stepped up to the wall, put one hand on the spot he had disappeared through, the spot that was now the start of her memories.

"I will remember you, my love." Her other hand was gently over her heart, touching the pendant of the former queen. "And you will forever live with me here." In a moment that was forever, she slid both hands down to her stomach. "Your line will never be broken. I will see to it that your child remembers you...always."

ABOUT THE AUTHOR

Patrick Duffy starred in *The Man from Atlantis* in 1976-77. Although raised in Montana, he was trained with SCUBA by his sister, a professional diver. He then went on to pursue his theatrical career. After *The Man from Atlantis* he spent 13 years on TV's *Dallas* and then 7 years on *Step by Step*.

But Duffy never forgot his desire to fill in the missing pieces of Mark Harris's life. After moving to his Oregon ranch in 2001 he used his down time to write the first of his *Man from Atlantis* books. Not needing to confine his imagination to the special effects limitations of the 1970's he has fleshed out an incredible life history of not just Mark Harris but of his entire Atlantean race.

You can connect with Patrick Duffy at www.Patrick Duffy.com